PENGUIN CLASSICS

THE GAMBLER/BOBOK/A NASTY STORY

FYODOR MIKHAILOVICH DOSTOYEVSKY was born in Moscow in 1821, the second of a doctor's seven children. His mother died in 1837 and his father was murdered a little over two years later. When he left his private boarding school in Moscow he studied from 1838 to 1843 at the Military Engineering College in St Petersburg, graduating with officer's rank. His first story to be published, 'Poor Folk' (1846), had a great success. In 1849 he was arrested and sentenced to death for participating in the 'Petrashevsky circle'; he was reprieved at the last moment but sentenced to penal servitude, and until 1854 he lived in a convict prison at Omsk, Siberia. Out of this experience he wrote *Memoirs from the House of the Dead* (1860). In 1861 he began the review *Vremya* with his brother; in 1862 and 1863 he went abroad where he strengthened his anti-European outlook, met Mlle Suslova who was the model for many of his heroines, and gave way to his passion for gambling. In the following years he fell deeply into debt, but from 1867, when he married Anna Grigoryevna Snitkina, his second wife helped to rescue him from his financial morass. They lived abroad for four years, then in 1873 he was invited to edit *Grazhdanin*, to which he contributed his *Author's Diary*. From 1876 the latter was issued separately and had a large circulation. In 1880 he delivered his famous address at the unveiling of Pushkin's memorial in Moscow; he died six months later in 1881. Most of his important works were written after 1864: *Notes from Underground* (1864), *Crime and Punishment* (1865–66), *The Gambler* (1866), *The Idiot* (1869), *The Devils* (1871), and *The Brothers Karamazov* (1880).

FYODOR DOSTOYEVSKY

The Gambler
Bobok
A Nasty Story

TRANSLATED
WITH AN INTRODUCTION BY
JESSIE COULSON

PENGUIN BOOKS

PENGUIN BOOKS

Published by the Penguin Group
Penguin Books Ltd, 27 Wrights Lane, London W8 5TZ, England
Penguin Books USA Inc., 375 Hudson Street, New York, New York 10014, USA
Penguin Books Australia Ltd, Ringwood, Victoria, Australia
Penguin Books Canada Ltd, 10 Alcorn Avenue, Toronto, Ontario, Canada M4V 3B2
Penguin Books (NZ) Ltd, 182–190 Wairau Road, Auckland 10, New Zealand

Penguin Books Ltd, Registered Offices: Harmondsworth, Middlesex, England

This translation first published 1966
19 20

This translation copyright © Jessie Coulson, 1966
All rights reserved

Printed in England by Clays Ltd, St Ives plc
Set in Linotype Juliana

CONTENTS

INTRODUCTION

IN September of 1866, Fyodor Mikhailovich Dostoyevsky was faced with what seemed an impossibly difficult task: he had to write a complete new novel for delivery to the publisher Stellovsky by 1 November, or lose his only profitable source of livelihood. The payments he received from the proprietors of the magazines in which his writings were first published had never been very great, but once a writer was established, much more could be hoped for from subsequent editions in book form. In the previous year Dostoyevsky had been forced by pressure from his creditors to sell Stellovsky the right to produce a collected edition, in three volumes, of all his previous works. The price of 3,000 roubles Stellovsky paid for the privilege was to include a new book 'of not less than ten printed sheets' (160 pages); in the event of failure to fulfil this part of the contract he was to be given the right to reprint all Dostoyevsky's past and future work at any time without further payment. Dostoyevsky always maintained that Stellovsky forced him to accept these terms by buying up his promissory notes from creditors who had expressed their willingness to wait for their money, and then making those creditors insist on immediate payment. Thus he was merely transferring the greater part of the 3,000 roubles to his own pocket.

Dostoyevsky had never learned to handle money wisely or successfully, but he was not really to blame for the desperate situation in which he found himself in 1865. It resulted largely from his unquestioning acceptance of a responsibility he was by no means obliged to take on himself, the responsibility for his beloved brother Michael's widow and young family. Michael's sudden death in July 1864 came at a time when the brothers were struggling to put their new literary and political magazine, the *Epoch*, on its feet, but the magazine was practically still-born and they had only the remotest chance of success. Their first monthly journal, *Time*, started by Michael in January 1861, had been both successful and prosperous. Dostoyevsky had thrown himself with enthusiasm into the (unofficial) running of the editorial side, dealing with the contributors and himself writing articles and publishing *Memoirs from the House of the Dead* and other novels there, while Michael, nominally responsible for the whole magazine, confined most of his attention to the business management of the enterprise. But an article on the Polish rising which appeared in the number for April 1863 was so displeasing to the censors that the magazine was immediately suppressed. What made the disaster overwhelming was that despite all their efforts the brothers could not get permission to resume publication even after several months; instead, too late to advertise for subscribers or bring out the first issue before March, Michael was allowed to start an entirely new magazine in January 1864. He worked like a slave to get the first (double) number out, borrowing to the utmost limits of his credit to pay the contributors, arranging for printing and . for supplies of paper on credit, and struggling with the editorial work as well. Fyodor contributed the first part of *Memoirs from Underground* to this January–February number, but was unable to help in any other way: from November 1863 onwards he was in Moscow, unable to leave the bedside of his sick wife Masha, who died of consumption on 15 April 1864. At the end of the month he returned to St Petersburg and tried to take some of the burden from Michael, whose health, never very robust, had suffered severely from all the strains and anxieties of the past year. Michael, however, continued to drive himself as hard as ever, and when he too died less than three months later his family was convinced that it was the *Epoch* that had killed him.

In view of the enormous debt the magazine had now accumulated, and of the fact that as a former political prisoner he was not permitted by the censors to use his own name as either editor or publisher, Dostoyevsky, with his brother's widow and children and his own stepson Pasha all dependent on him, would have been wiser, as he later realized himself, to

assign the magazine to the creditors . . . together with the furniture and household bits and pieces, and take the family to live with me. After that to work, produce journalism, write novels, and keep my brother's widow and orphans. . . . The creditors of course would not have received even twenty per cent. But the family, having renounced its inheritance, would not legally have been bound to pay anything. During these five years [after his return from exile in Siberia], working for my brother and the magazines, I have been earning from eight to ten thousand a year. Consequently I could have kept both them and myself – working, of course, from morning till night all my life. But I preferred ... to continue to issue the magazine. ... I went to Moscow, succeeded in obtaining from my elderly aunt the ten thousand she intended to leave me in her will and ... began to publish the magazine. ... I spared neither money nor my health and strength. I was the only editor, I dealt with the authors and the censorship, I amended the articles, procured the money, sat up till six in the morning and slept five hours out of the twenty-four, but although I got the magazine into good order it was too late. ... But the main thing was that ... I was not able to write or publish in the magazine a single line of my own. The public never came across my name and did not know, even in St Petersburg, not to mention the provinces, that I was editing the magazine. ... Now for want of money we can no longer publish the magazine and have to announce our temporary bankruptcy; and besides this I have debts of some ten thousand secured by promissory notes, and five thousand on my word of honour.

The letter quoted above was written in April 1865, when Dostoyevsky had already made his bargain with Stellovsky. Nearly eighteen months later the new novel was still not begun, and it looked decidedly as though the publisher had acquired a valuable property for a very small sum: he, at any rate, thought so. In the early summer Fyodor Mikhailovich wrote to a friend:

1 November is in four months; I thought I would buy myself off by paying a forfeit; but Stellovsky will not have it. I have asked him for an extension for three months – he refuses and tells me *straight out,* that since he is convinced I now *haven't time* to write a novel of 160 pages, especially as I have written scarcely half [of *Crime and Punishment*] for the *Russian Messenger* yet, it will pay him better not to agree to an extension or a forfeit, because then everything I write afterwards will be his. ... I intend to do an extraordinary and unheard-of thing: to write in four months thirty printed sheets of two different novels, of which I shall write one in the mornings and the other in the evenings, and finish on time.

The intention was not fulfilled, however; the editors of the *Russian Messenger* thought some parts of *Crime and Punishment* morally dangerous, and they had to be revised and even rewritten. By the end of the summer the writing of the novel intended for

Stellovsky, *The Gambler*, seemed to have become a physical impossibility.

An old friend in St Petersburg had a suggestion to make: he knew the director of the first Russian shorthand school, and on the director's recommendation his star pupil, a young woman of twenty, Anna Grigoryevna Snitkina, was engaged. Dostoyevsky asked for and was granted a month's grace in the preparation of the sixth part of *Crime and Punishment*, and began working with her on 4 October, dictating every day from twelve noon until 4.30; every evening Anna Grigoryevna transcribed her shorthand notes, and on the 31st *The Gambler* was finished, copied out, and ready for delivery the next day to Stellovsky. Dostoyevsky himself took it to the publisher's, but Stellovsky being away and his clerk unwilling to accept delivery of the MS., ingeniously left it at the local police station and obtained a dated receipt. Three days later he called on Anna Grigoryevna and asked her to continue to act as his stenographer until *Crime and Punishment* was finished; on 8 November he asked her to marry him and was accepted.

Dostoyevsky hated writing to order or with a fixed time-limit: working 'under the lash', he called it, 'forced labour', 'penal servitude', and he complained that it corrupted his talent and ruined the 'idea' of any novel. His natural tendency was to rewrite again and again, he often discarded long sections and began again, and it was quite usual for gaps of a month or more to occur in the serial publication of a book because he had not been able to complete an instalment in time. *The Gambler*, however, does not seem to have suffered unduly from the haste with which it was written and may even have gained in clarity and simplicity; it has always rightly been considered one of Dostoyevsky's best short novels. The dramatic or theatrical form of construction which is nearly always clearly evident in his novels is particularly conspicuous in it; it seems to fall naturally and easily into four acts. The plan had of course been carefully thought out some time before the writing was begun, and the theme had occupied Fyodor Mikhailovich's mind for a considerable time.

It is first mentioned in a letter written from Rome in 1863, when it was already substantially the same as the central idea of *The Gambler*.

The subject of the story is ... one type of Russian abroad. ... I take a straightforward character, a man of many-sided development though, but still immature in every way, one who has lost all faith but dare not disbelieve, rebelling against authority but afraid of it. ... But the main thing is that all his vitality, his strength, his impetus, his courage, have gone into *roulette*. He is a gambler, but no more a mere gambler than Pushkin's *Avaricious Knight* is a mere miser. He is a poet in his own way, but ashamed of this poetry because he is profoundly conscious that it is unworthy, although the necessity of *risk* redeems him in his own eyes. ... If the *House of the Dead* was a picture of convicts, who had never been drawn *from the life* before, this story will certainly attract attention as a very detailed first-hand account of the game of roulette.

Unfortunately for Dostoyevsky, 'first-hand' is exactly what his account of a desperate gambler was: like his hero, he must have realized from the beginning that he was one himself. In August of 1863, when he had every reason to hurry towards Paris, he nevertheless stopped in Wiesbaden (the 'Roulettenburg' of *The Gambler*) and made his first acquaintance with roulette. He won 5,000 francs, 'that is, I won 10,400 francs at first, took them home and shut them up in a bag, and intended to leave Wiesbaden the next day without going back to the tables; but I got carried away and dropped half my winnings.'

From Paris Fyodor Mikhailovich wrote to his sister-in-law, asking her to send on to his wife some of the money he had won, and telling her of his experiences in Wiesbaden.

During those four days ... I watched the players closely. There were a few hundred people playing and on my honour I did not find any who knew how to play, except two. There were a Frenchwoman and an English lord playing there and these two knew how to play and did not lose heavily; on the contrary, they almost broke the bank. Please don't think I am so pleased with myself for not losing that I am showing off when I say that I know the secret of how not to lose but win. I really do know the secret; it is terribly silly and simple and consists of keeping one's head the whole time, whatever the state of the game, and not getting excited. That is all, and it makes losing simply impossible and winning a certainty. But that is not the point; the point is whether, having grasped the secret, a man knows how to make use of it and is fit to do so. A man can be as wise as Solomon and have an iron character and still be carried away. . . . Therefore blessed are they who do not play, and regard the roulette-wheel with loathing as the greatest of stupidities.

Alas, Dostoyevsky must have known that he did not belong to them; he had already caught the fever that was to torment him for so long.

Only a week later he wrote from Baden-Baden to ask for some of the money back again : he had stopped there on the way to Rome and now had only 250 francs in his pocket. To his brother Michael, who knew more than his sister-in-law of the other circumstances of this journey, he tried to explain what had happened :

You ask how anybody who was travelling with the one he loved could gamble away everything. My dear Misha, in Wiesbaden I invented a system, used it in actual play, and immediately won 10,000 francs. The next morning I got excited, abandoned the system and immediately lost. In the evening I returned to the system, observed it strictly, and quickly and without difficulty won back 3,000 francs. Tell me, after that how could I help being tempted, how could I fail to believe that I had only to follow my system strictly and luck would be with me? And I need the money, for myself, for you, for my wife, for writing my novel. Here tens of thousands are won in jest. Yes, I went with the idea of helping all of you and extricating myself from disaster. I believed in my system, too. Besides, when I arrived in Baden I went to the tables and in *a quarter of an hour* won 600 francs. This goaded me on. Suddenly I began to lose, could no longer keep my head and lost every farthing. After I had sent you my letter from Baden I took my last money and went to play; with four napoléons I won thirty-five in half an hour. This extraordinary luck tempted me, I risked the thirty-five and lost them all. After paying the land-lady we were left with six napoléons d'or for the journey. In Geneva I pawned my watch. . . .

Once more, on the way back to St Petersburg after parting from Polina Suslova, with whom he had spent most of his few weeks abroad, Dostoyevsky found an opportunity to go to the gaming tables, this time in Baden-Baden. In Suslova's diary there is an entry : '27 October. Yesterday I had a letter from Fyodor Mikhailovich. He has lost everything gambling and begs me to send him some money. I had no money. . . . I decided to pawn my watch and chain.' It was not until after he had sold the collected edition of his works to Stellovsky that Dostoyevsky was able to afford to go abroad again, and then he made straight for Wiesbaden. A few days later he was writing to Turgenyev:

Out of the whole 3,000 I left myself with only 175 silver roubles to come abroad with; I could not do more. Two years ago in Wiesbaden I won upwards of 12,000 francs in one hour. This time, although I had no thought of restoring my fortunes by gambling, I really did want to win about 1,000 francs, so as to get through at any rate the next three months. I have been five days in Wiesbaden and already I have lost everything, the whole lot, even my watch, and I owe my hotel bill.

Here, then, in Dostoyevsky's personal experience, were the main outlines and much of the detail of the parts of *The Gambler* directly concerned with roulette. His later experiences in the casinos of Homburg, Wiesbaden, Baden-Baden and Saxon-les-Bains, during the years he spent abroad with his wife after his second marriage, clearly show that when he wrote the book he already knew the whole truth about one kind of compulsive gambler. The incidents of these casino visits varied in detail, but the underlying pattern of his repeated attempts to force his fortunes into a happier mould was always the same: Dostoyevsky went alone to the resort, taking with him all the money they could spare, and a day or two later wrote to his wife for more – a small sum to rescue him from his terrible position. He would have lost every farthing, pawned his watch, left his hotel bill unpaid and quite often suffered a humiliating refusal to supply him with meals as a consequence. Anna Grigoryevna would have managed to keep a few francs back, or she would find something she could pawn, and send him the money without so much as a murmur of reproach; then as often as not she would have another abject letter explaining that after settling his bills and redeeming his watch her husband had stopped at the roulette tables on his way to the train, and now was again destitute and unable even to pay for his ticket home. The last time the pattern was repeated was some two months before the Dostoyevskys returned to St Petersburg in 1871; after that, although he had plenty of opportunity, Fyodor Mikhailovich never played roulette again. Many years later, in her *Reminiscences*, Anna Grigoryevna expressed the idea that her husband's bouts of gambling were both essential and beneficial to him, harassed as he was by all the tensions of his work, the poverty and personal griefs of his life in exile, the anxieties of his still-unpaid debts, the worries about his dependent relatives. 'The change of scene, the journey, the repeated experience of tempestuous emotions, radically changed his mood.' She adds that the whole total of his losses at roulette could not have added up to more than about five hundred roubles, but of course the important point was not the amount of the loss but the fact that every time it was all they had, and reduced them from poverty to destitution.

The greatest attraction of *The Gambler* lies in its gallery of portraits, especially those of the General, Mademoiselle Blanche, Polina, the narrator Alexis, and 'Grandmamma'. The original of this formidable and fascinating old woman appears to have been the second wife of Dostoyevsky's grandfather, the lively, strong-willed, generous, extravagant Olga Yakovlevna Nechayeva, whom all the Dostoyevskys called *babushka* ('granny'). Alexis Ivanovich, the narrator of the novel, is undoubtedly a self-portrait, or rather a reflection of two sides of Fyodor Mikhailovich's temperament and personal history, one that of the gambler, the other embodied in the hero's relations with and feelings for Polina. *The Gambler* is only the first of Dostoyevsky's monuments to the woman who established the strongest hold on his passions and imagination of all those who really influenced his life, Apollinaria Suslova. She was nearly twenty years younger than he, and they first met in about 1862, when she was a student at the University of St Petersburg and attended a lecture given by the great and popular author, who had so recently returned from the exile and imprisonment he had suffered in a cause that was still dear, especially to the young. It was when he was hastening to meet her in Paris (she had been too impatient to wait for him in St Petersburg through all the delays caused by the suppression of *Time*) that he broke his journey in Wiesbaden and succumbed to the temptations of roulette for the first time. The few weeks of his journey abroad that summer were the only prolonged time they spent together; their last meeting, as far as we know, was in 1865 (although, to Anna Grigoryevna's chagrin, their correspondence continued for some time after his second marriage); and their association was hardly ever a source of happiness, yet it obsessed him for several years and left traces on his work for the rest of his life. Polina was the original of all the proud, 'demonic', passionate, exacting women of his later novels, but it was in *The Gambler* that he painted his most complete portrait of her, a portrait detailed, intimate, affectionate and indeed tender, and plainly labelled with her name.

There is a strain of humour running through all Dostoyevsky's work, even the blackest. In *The Gambler* it is of the kind that simply recognizes that most people are naturally ridiculous, even, or perhaps especially, when they feel most serious. But his humour is frequently of another type, which seems to many critics more characteristic, an unkinder type based on caricature and the grotesque: the other stories in this volume, *Bobok* and *A Nasty Story*, offer two contrasting examples of this other humour.

Bobok is a sharply satirical little piece belonging to a highly creative and productive period of Dostoyevsky's life. It first appeared in 1873 in *A Writer's Diary*, the new and brilliantly successful form of periodical publication he had invented for himself, which enabled him to air his views on political questions, criticize past and current literature in Russia and abroad, discuss the cases in the criminal courts that had always attracted his passionate interest, revive memories of long-past events and old friends and enemies, and express his boundless and generous enthusiasm and admiration for all sorts of men, movements, and ideas. He found room in it also for a number of more imaginative writings, which include some of the best of his short stories, like *Bobok*.

Perhaps because of its macabre setting in – or rather under the surface of – a public cemetery, many critics fail to see even a spark of humour in *Bobok*; at most they find it 'grimly ironical'. *A Nasty Story* is one of the works that give readers essentially out of sympathy with him an opportunity to condemn Dostoyevsky's 'cruelty'. When he began to write again after his years in prison, the influence of his first literary model, Gogol, showed very clearly in all Dostoyevsky's work except *Memoirs from the House of the Dead*. *Uncle's Dream* and especially *The Village of Stepanchikovo* (1859) inevitably make one think of *The Inspector General* and *Dead Souls*; and *A Nasty Story*, which was written for *Time* in 1862, belongs to the same group. Its theme is the terrible gulf between a man's idea of himself, his ideals, and his motives, and what they prove to be in the harsh light of reality. Its cruelty lies in the recognition that the tragedy of failure to come up to one's own expectations, the incongruity between 'man as he is' and 'man as he ought to be', is essentially comic, and in the relentless pursuit of the farcical in the most shameful depths of wounded and humiliated vanity and self-esteem. Perhaps a generation hardened by greater displays of cruelty will find Dostoyevsky's sense of humour less shocking and more convincing than some of his contemporaries and more immediate successors.

J. C.

The Gambler

CHAPTER ONE

I AM back at last after my absence of two weeks. Our party has been in Roulettenburg since the day before yesterday. I thought they would have been expecting me with inexpressible impatience, but I was mistaken. The General looked at me with the coolest detachment, uttered a few condescending words and sent me to his sister. It was evident that they had borrowed some money somewhere. I even thought the General was a little ashamed to see me. Maria Philippovna was extremely busy and held only a short conversation with me; she took the money, however, counted it, and listened to everything I had to report. Mezentsov, the little Frenchman, and some Englishman or other were expected to dinner; as usual, as soon as there is some money there is a dinner-party; the same as in Moscow. Polina Alexandrovna, when she saw me, asked why I had taken so long, and then walked away without waiting for an answer. Of course she did it on purpose. All the same, we shall have to have a talk. A lot of things have accumulated.

I have been allotted a little room on the third floor of the hotel. I am known to belong to *the General's suite*. Everything goes to show that they have somehow managed to make an impression. Everybody here takes the General for somebody very rich and very grand. Even before dinner he found time to give me, among other commissions, two thousand-franc notes to change for him. I changed them in the hotel. Now they will look on us as millionaires for at least a week. I was intending to fetch Misha and Nadya and take them for a walk; but as we came downstairs I was summoned to the General; he deemed it necessary to inquire where I was taking them. The man is definitely incapable of looking me in the face; he would very much like to, but I reply every time with a look so intent, that is to say so disrespectful, that it seems to disconcert him. He gave me to understand in a highly pompous speech, piling one sentence on top of another and finally getting into a complete muddle, that I must take the children for their walk somewhere in the park as far as possible from the railway station. In the end he quite lost his temper and added abruptly, 'Otherwise, perhaps, you will be taking them into the station, to the roulette tables. You must excuse me,' he added, 'but I know you are still rather irresponsible and perhaps capable of gambling. In any case, although I am not your mentor and have no desire to play the part, I have at least the right to desire you not, so to speak, to compromise me. . . . '

'But after all, I haven't even any money,' I answered quietly, 'and one must have some before one can lose it.'

'You shall have it immediately,' the General answered, reddening slightly. He rummaged in his desk and consulted a notebook, and it turned out that he owed me about a hundred and twenty roubles.

'But how are we going to work it out?' he began; 'we shall have to convert it into thalers. Here, take a hundred thalers – it's a round figure and the rest won't be lost, of course.'

I took the money without speaking.

'Please don't take offence at what I said, you are so touchy. . . . If I passed a remark I was only, so to speak, putting you on your guard, and of course I really have some right to do so. . . .'

As I was returning home with the children before dinner I met a positive cavalcade. Our party were on their way to see some ruins or other. Two splendid carriages, magnificent horses ! Mademoiselle Blanche in one carriage with Maria Philippovna and Polina; the Frenchman, the Englishman, and our General all on horseback. The passers-by stopped to watch; it made a sensation, but it won't do the General any good. I calculated that with the 4,000 francs I had brought, added to what they had evidently contrived to borrow, they now had seven or eight thousand francs; that is not enough for Mademoiselle Blanche.

Mademoiselle Blanche is also staying in our hotel with her mother; our Frenchman is here somewhere as well. The servants call him *Monsieur le comte*, and Mademoiselle Blanche's mother is *Madame la comtesse*; well, perhaps they really are a *comte* and a *comtesse*.

I knew that *Monsieur le comte* would ignore me when we assembled for dinner. The General, of course, would never think of introducing us, or even of presenting me to him; and *Monsieur le comte* has been to Russia and knows that what they call an *outchitel* is very small fry there. He knows me very well all the same. But I must admit that I appeared at dinner unbidden; I think the

General had forgotten to make the arrangements, otherwise he would have sent me to dine at the *table d'hôte*. I appeared of my own accord, and the General looked at me disapprovingly. Good Maria Philippovna at once told me where to sit; but it was the meeting with Mr Astley that saved me, and I proved to belong to the party willy-nilly.

I met this strange Englishman for the first time in Prussia, in a railway-carriage where we were sitting opposite each other, when I was on the way to join our party; afterwards I ran into him going to France, and finally in Switzerland; that was twice during the past fortnight – and now I suddenly encountered him in Roulettenburg. I have never met so shy a man in my whole life; he is so shy as to seem stupid, and of course he is himself well aware of this, because he is in fact not stupid at all. He is very nice and gentle, though. I managed to get him into conversation at our first meeting in Prussia. He told me he had been at the North Cape this summer and that he would very much like to visit the fair at Nizhny Novgorod. I don't know how he made the General's acquaintance, but he appears to be head over ears in love with Polina. When she came in, he went as red as fire. He was very pleased that I was sitting next to him at the table and already seems to regard me as a bosom friend.

At dinner the Frenchman put on extraordinary airs; his manner to everybody was haughty and negligent. In Moscow, I remember, he used to talk a lot of bombast. He talked a great deal about finance and Russian politics. The General sometimes ventured to disagree with him, but modestly, only as far as he could without damaging his own consequence.

I was in a strange mood; of course, even before half-way through dinner I had managed to ask myself my usual invariable question, 'Why do I hang about round this General, why haven't I left them long ago?' Occasionally I glanced at Polina Alexandrovna; she took absolutely no notice of me. I ended by getting annoyed and making up my mind to behave badly.

I began by loudly joining in other people's conversation, suddenly, unasked and without any excuse. What I chiefly wanted was to quarrel with the Frenchman. I turned to the General and remarked very loudly and clearly, interrupting him, I think, that it was almost completely impossible for Russians to dine at a *table d'hôte* this summer. The General gazed at me with astonishment.

'If you are a person of any self-respect,' I went on, 'you are sure to expose yourself to abuse and will have to put up with extraordinary slights. In Paris, on the Rhine, and even in Switzerland, there are so many wretched little Poles and their French sympathizers that it is impossible to utter a word if you happen to be Russian.'

I had said this in French. The General looked at me, in two minds whether to be angry or merely surprised that I had so far forgotten myself.

'So somebody somewhere has been teaching you a lesson,' said the Frenchman, carelessly and contemptuously.

'In Paris I quarrelled first with a Pole,' I answered, 'and then with a French officer who backed him up. But afterwards even some of the French came over to my side when I told them about how I felt like spitting in Monsignore's coffee.'

'Spitting?' asked the General in pompous perplexity, even looking round for sympathy. The Frenchman was watching me mistrustfully.

'Exactly,' I answered. 'As I had been certain for the past two days that I might have to go to Rome for a short time on our business, I went to the secretariat of His Holiness's Embassy in Paris to have my passport viséd. There I was met by an abbé, a shrivelled-up little man of about fifty, with a frosty face; he heard me out politely, though extremely coldly, and asked me to wait. I was in a hurry, but of course I sat down to wait, took out my *Opinion Nationale* and began reading a dreadful attack on Russia. Meanwhile, I heard somebody going through the next room into Monsignore's; I could see my abbé bowing to him. I repeated my former request; even more coldly than before he again asked me to wait. A little later a stranger – some Austrian – came in on business; he was listened to and immediately taken upstairs. Then I got very annoyed; I got up, went over to the abbé and told him firmly that as Monsignore was seeing people he could deal with me as well. The abbé positively recoiled in utter amazement. He simply couldn't understand how an insignificant Russian dared put himself on the same level as Monsignore's guests like that! With the greatest insolence he looked me up and down from head to foot, as though delighted to be able to insult me, and shouted, "Do you really imagine Monsignore is going to leave his coffee for you?" Then I shouted as well, but louder, "In that case, let me tell you I don't give a damn for your Monsignore's coffee! If you don't finish with my passport this instant, I shall go to him myself!"

' "What, when the cardinal is with him?" cried the abbé, recoiling from me in horror, and he rushed to the doors and barred them with outstretched arms, looking as if he would die rather than let me through.

'Then I retorted that I was a heretic and a barbarian (*que je suis hérétique et barbare*) and didn't care a straw for his Archbishops and Cardinals and Monsignores, et cetera, et cetera. In short, I didn't look like giving up. The abbé looked at me with unutterable hatred, snatched away my passport and took it upstairs. In one minute it had been viséd.

'Here it is, would you like to see it?' I took out my passport and displayed the Roman visa.

'But you . . .' the General began.

'What saved you was calling yourself a barbarian and a heretic,' smiled the Frenchman. '*Cela n'était pas si bête!*'

'Is that the way to look on us Russians? We sit here without daring to utter a squeak, and are even perhaps ready to deny that we are Russians. At least I began to be treated with much more consideration in my hotel in Paris after I had told everybody about my fight with the abbé. The fat Polish gentleman who was my most determined enemy at the *table d'hôte* faded into the background. The French even suffered me to tell them that two years ago I saw a man who had been shot by a French *chasseur* in 1812 simply because he wanted to unload his gun. The man was a twelve-year-old child at the time, and his family had not managed to get out of Moscow.'

'That's impossible!' the Frenchman flared up. 'A French soldier wouldn't shoot a child!'

'All the same, it happened,' I answered. 'It was a respectable retired Captain who told me, and I saw the bullet-scar in his cheek for myself.'

The Frenchman began talking very fast and at great length. The General tried to support him, but I advised him to read, for example, at any rate extracts from the *Memoirs* of General Perovsky, who was a prisoner of the French in 1812. Finally Maria Philippovna began talking in order to change the subject. The General was very displeased with me because the Frenchman and I had been almost shouting at each other. But Mr Astley seemed delighted with my argument with the Frenchman; he rose from his place and invited me to drink a glass of wine with him. In the evening I duly succeeded in having about a quarter of an hour's conversation with Polina Alexandrovna. Our talk took place during a walk. Everybody had gone into the park on the way to the station. Polina sat down on a bench facing a fountain and allowed Nadenka to go and play with some children close at hand. I had already let Misha go off to the fountain and we were alone at last.

We began, of course, with business. Polina was really angry when I gave her only 700 gulden. She had been certain that I would bring her back at least two thousand gulden from Paris after pawning her diamonds.

'I need some money,' she said, 'and it must be got at all costs; otherwise, I shall simply be done for.'

I began to ask about what had happened in my absence.

'Nothing, except that we've had two items of news from St Petersburg: first that Grandmamma was very ill, and two days later, I think, that she had died. The news came from Timothy Petrovich,' added Polina, 'and he's a reliable man. We are waiting for a last letter confirming it.'

'So everybody here is in a state of expectation?' I asked.

'Of course: everybody and everything; this has been all we had to hope for in the last six months.'

'Are you hoping, too?' I asked.

'Well, I'm not related to her at all, you know, I'm only the General's stepdaughter. But I know for certain that she has remembered me in her will.'

'I should think you'll get a great deal of money,' I said positively.

'Yes, she was fond of me; but why should *you* think so?'

'Tell me,' I answered with another question, 'is our marquis also privy to all the family secrets?'

'And why are you interested in all this?' asked Polina, looking at me with cold severity.

'Why not? If I'm not mistaken, the General has already contrived to borrow money from him.'

'You are very good at guessing.'

'Well, then, would he have given him the money if he had not known about Grandmamma? Did you notice at dinner, when he was saying something about her, he called her Grandmamma, "la grand'maman", three times? What familiar and even intimate terms to be on!'

'Yes, you're right. As soon as he knows I get something by the will, he will begin making advances to me at once. Is that what you wanted to know?'

'Only begin advances? I thought he had been making them for a long time.'

'You know very well he hasn't,' snapped Polina. 'Where did you meet that Englishman?' she went on after a moment's silence.

'I just knew you would ask me about him straight away.'

I told her about my previous meetings with Mr Astley on the way here.

'He's shy and susceptible, and of course he's in love with you, isn't he?'

'Yes, he's in love with me,' answered Polina.

'And, of course, he's ten times as rich as the Frenchman. Has the Frenchman really got anything? Isn't there some doubt about it?'

'No, there isn't. He owns a château. The General told me so quite definitely only yesterday. Well, is that enough for you?'

'In your place I would certainly marry the Englishman.'

'Why?' asked Polina.

'The Frenchman is handsome, but he's more of a scoundrel; and the Englishman, besides being honourable, is ten times richer,' I said shortly.

'Yes, but on the other hand the Frenchman is a marquis – and cleverer,' she answered with the utmost coolness.

'But are you sure of that?' I went on in the same manner.

'Absolutely.'

Polina very much disliked my questions, and I could see she

wanted to annoy me by the tone and wildness of her answer; I spoke of this at once.

'Well, the way you fly into a temper really amuses me. You ought to be made to pay for the mere fact that I allow you to ask such questions and make such suppositions.'

'I do really consider I have the right to ask you any kind of question,' I answered calmly, 'just because I am ready to pay for them any way you want, and don't think my life of any value now.'

Polina laughed.

'Last time, on the Schlangenberg, you said you were ready to throw yourself over the edge at a word from me, and it must be a drop of almost a thousand feet. I will say that word one day solely in order to see you pay up, and you may be quite sure I shall not relent. I hate you – precisely because I have allowed you so much, and even more because I need you so much. But for the time being I need you – I must cherish you.'

She started to get up. She had been speaking with irritation. Recently she has always finished a conversation with me full of ill-nature and irritation, and the ill-nature is real.

'Allow me to ask you what Mademoiselle Blanche is,' I asked, unwilling to let her go without having things out.

'You know yourself what Mademoiselle Blanche is. There is nothing to add since those days. Mademoiselle Blanche will certainly become the General's wife – if, of course, the rumour about Grandmamma's death is confirmed, because Mademoiselle Blanche and her mamma and her third cousin the marquis all know quite well that we are ruined.'

'And is the General utterly in love?'

'That's not the point now. Listen and remember: take this seven hundred florins, go and play roulette, and win me as much as ever you can; I must have money at all costs now.'

Saying this, she called to Nadenka and went off to the station, where she joined the rest of our party. I turned left into the first path I came across, thoughtful and wondering. After that order to 'go and play roulette', I felt as though I had been struck on the head. It was strange: I had plenty to think about, and yet I was absorbed in analysing my feelings for Polina. Really, it had been

easier for me during my two weeks' absence than now, on the day
of my return, although during my journey I had been as melancholy as a madman, rushing about like one possessed and seeing
her constantly before me, even in my sleep. Once (this was in Switzerland), falling asleep in a railway-carriage, I apparently began
talking out loud to her, to the amusement of all my fellow-passen-
gers. And now once more I asked myself the question, 'Am I in love
with her?' And once more I did not know how to answer it, or
rather I answered once more, for the hundredth time, that I hated
her. Yes, I hated her. There were moments (to wit, at the end of
every one of our conversations) when I would have given half my
life to strangle her! I swear if it had been possible to bury a sharp
knife slowly in her breast, I think I would have seized it with
pleasure. And yet I swear by all that's holy that if on the fashionable peak of the Schlangenberg she had indeed said to me, 'Cast
yourself down', I would have done so immediately and even enjoyed doing it. I knew that. One way or another the matter must be
settled. She understands all this very well indeed, and the idea that
I recognize with full certainty and clarity all her inaccessibility
to me, all the impossibility of realizing my fantastic dreams – that
idea, I am convinced, gives her extraordinary pleasure; otherwise
could she, cautious and clever as she is, be on terms of such intimacy and frankness with me? I think that up to now her attitude
to me has been like that of the empress of antiquity who would
undress in front of her slave, not considering him a man. . . .

However, I had a commission from her – to win at roulette at all
costs. I had no time to wonder why or how soon it was necessary
to win, and what new plans had sprung to life in that perpetually
scheming head. Besides, during these two weeks a thousand and
one new facts, of which as yet I knew nothing, had evidently
accrued. All these things must be divined, everything must be
gone into, and as soon as possible. But meanwhile I had no time to
lose: I must go to the roulette tables.

CHAPTER TWO

I ADMIT I found it distasteful; although I had made up my mind to play, I was not at all disposed to begin doing so for somebody else's benefit. It even threw me out of my reckoning, and I entered the gaming rooms with a feeling of great annoyance. There, at first glance, nothing pleased me. I have no patience with the flunkeyish attitude of the gossip-writers of the whole world, and especially of our Russian newspapers, where almost every spring our journalists produce stories about two things: first, the extraordinary magnificence and luxury of the gaming rooms in the casinos of the towns on the Rhine, and secondly, the heaps of gold that are supposed to lie on the tables. They don't get paid for it; they do it out of disinterested obsequiousness. There is nothing magnificent about those squalid rooms, and gold, far from lying in heaps on the tables, is hardly to be seen there at all. Naturally, in the course of the season, some odd fish will suddenly turn up somewhere or other, some Englishman or Asiatic, perhaps a Turk, as it was this year, and will proceed to win or lose very large amounts; but the others all play for petty sums and, on the average, very little money is seen on the tables. When I entered the gaming rooms (for the first time in my life), it was some time before I could make up my mind to begin to play. Besides, there was too much of a crowd. But even if I had been alone, I think I should soon have left without playing. I confess that my heart was beating heavily and I was not at all cool and collected; I was certain and indeed determined, as I have been for a long time, that I would not leave Roulettenburg the same man as I arrived there; some radical and decisive change in my destiny will inevitably take place. It must and will. However comical it may be that I should expect to get so much out of roulette, the routine opinion, accepted by everybody, that it is absurd and silly to expect anything at all from gambling seems to me even funnier. And why is gambling worse than any other means of acquiring money, trade, for example? It is true that only one person in a hundred wins. But what do I care about that?

In any case I had decided to watch at first, and not to start in earnest this evening. This evening, if anything did happen, it

would be slight and accidental – and that I assumed. Besides, I had
to study the actual play; because in spite of the hundreds of des-
criptions of roulette I had read with so much eagerness, I understood absolutely nothing of how it worked until I had seen it for
myself.

  For one thing, everything seemed to me so dirty – somehow
morally bad and unsavoury. I am not talking at all of those greedy
and anxious faces which surround the tables in their scores and
even hundreds. I see absolutely nothing dirty in the desire to win
as much as possible as quickly as possible; the idea of the secure
and well-fed moralist who answered somebody's excuse that 'After
all, they play for small stakes' by saying 'So much the worse, because the greed is petty' has always seemed to me very stupid. As
though petty greed and massive greed were not the same thing!
It is a question of proportion. What is a trifling sum to a Rothschild is riches to me, and as for profits and winnings, people everywhere, not only at roulette, are always winning or taking away
something from one another. Whether profits and winnings are
always bad is another question. But I am not trying to settle it
here. Since I was myself completely mastered by the desire to win,
all the greed and the greedy corruption, if you like to call it that,
were somehow natural and familiar to me from the moment I
entered. It is a very good thing when people do not stand on ceremony with one another but act openly and informally. And what
is the use of deceiving oneself? It is an empty-headed and impru-
dent occupation! What was ugliest, at first sight, in all that
gambling riff-raff was their respect for what they were doing, the
earnest and even deferential way in which they all clustered round
the tables. That is why there is a sharp distinction here between
the kind of play that is called *mauvais genre* and the kind a respectable person can allow himself. There are two kinds of gambling, one that is gentlemanly and another that is vulgar and
mercenary, the gambling of the disreputable. The distinction is
strictly drawn – and yet how essentially base the distinction is! A
gentleman, for example, may stake five or ten louis d'or, rarely
more; he may, however, stake as much as a thousand francs if he
is very rich, but only for the sake of gambling itself, for nothing
more than amusement, strictly in order to watch the process of

winning or losing; he must not by any means be interested in the winnings themselves. When he wins he may, for example, laugh aloud, or pass a remark to one of those standing nearest to him, and he may play again, and then double his stake once more, but solely out of curiosity, to observe and calculate chances, not out of any plebeian desire to win. In short, he must regard all these roulette or trente-et-quarante tables as an amusement arranged solely for his pleasure. He ought not even to suspect the greed and trickery on which the bank is founded and constructed. It would even be highly gratifying if, for example, all the rest of the players, all that wretched trash trembling over a gulden, were quite as rich and gentlemanly as himself, and were gambling simply and solely for amusement and entertainment. Such complete ignorance of reality and such an innocent view of humanity would of course be extremely aristocratic. I saw many fond mothers bringing forward innocent and refined young misses of fifteen or sixteen, their daughters, giving them a few gold coins and teaching them how to play. The young ladies won or lost, never failed to smile, and went away very well satisfied. Our General approached the table with a sedate and consequential air; a flunkey rushed forward to give him a chair, but he took no notice of him; very slowly he drew out his purse, very deliberately he took from the purse three hundred francs in gold, staked them on black and won. He did not pick up his winnings but left them on the table. Black came up again; he did not take his winnings that time either, and when red came up on the third spin he lost twelve hundred francs at one blow. He walked away with a smile, keeping a stiff upper lip. I am convinced that he was sick at heart and if the stake had been two or three times as big he would have given way and displayed emotion. A real gentleman, though, even if he loses everything he owns, must show no emotion. Money must be so far beneath a gentleman that it is hardly worth troubling about. It is of course highly aristocratic not to notice at all the squalor of all the rabble and the whole surroundings. Sometimes, however, the opposite procedure, of noticing the rabble, by which I mean gazing at them and even inspecting them closely, perhaps through a lorgnette, for example, is not less aristocratic; but it must be done as though one took the crowd and all the filth for a form of entertainment, as if it were a performance put on for the amusement of the upper classes. It is possible to rub shoulders with the crowd and yet look round you with the complete conviction that you are only a spectator and in no way a part of it. But then again, one should not watch too closely, this would again be unbecoming to a gentleman, because in any case the scene does not deserve prolonged or too detailed inspection. There are, indeed, few spectacles worth a gentleman's close attention. I personally thought the present one well worth watching very intently, all the same, especially since I had not come merely to watch, and sincerely and honestly reckoned myself a part of the riff-raff. As for my innermost moral convictions, there is of course no place for them in my present reasoning. Be that as it may; I am making a clean breast of things. But I must make one remark: recently it has somehow always been terribly repugnant to me to measure my actions and thoughts by any moral standards. I have been governed by different considerations. . . .

The rabble really do play a very dirty game. I am even willing to believe that a great deal of ordinary thieving goes on at the tables. The croupiers, who sit at the ends of the table, look after the stakes, and do the paying out, have an enormous amount of work. They are riff-raff too! Most of them are Frenchmen. However, I was not watching and noting everything in order to describe the game of roulette; I was trying to get used to it so as to know how to conduct myself in the future. I have noticed, for example, that nothing is commoner than for somebody's hand to stretch out suddenly (from the other side of the table) and take your winnings. This starts an argument, and not seldom shouting and – you would have a job to find witnesses to prove that it was your stake!

To begin with, the whole business was Greek to me; I could only guess, and somehow I made out that money was staked on numbers, *pair* and *impair*, and colours. I made up my mind to try my luck with a hundred gulden of Polina Alexandrovna's money that evening. The idea of beginning to play for somebody else somehow threw me out. The sensation was extremely unpleasant and I wanted to be free of it as quickly as possible. It seemed to me that by beginning to play for Polina I was spoiling my own luck. Is it really impossible to touch gambling without immediately becoming infected with superstition? I began by taking out five friedrichs d'or, that is fifty gulden, and placed them on evens. The wheel spun, and the number thirteen came up – I had lost. With a sick feeling, and solely to be done with it and get away, I put five more friedrichs d'or on red. Red came up. I staked all ten friedrichs d'or – red came up again. Again I staked the whole lot and red came up once more. Receiving forty friedrichs d'or I staked twenty on the twelve middle numbers, not knowing what the result would be. I was paid three times the amount. Thus my ten friedrichs d'or had suddenly become eighty. My sensations were so intolerably strange and unusual that I decided to leave. It appeared to me that I should not have played at all like that if I had been playing for myself. However, I put one more stake on *pair*, the whole eighty friedrichs d'or. This time four came up; I was counted out another eighty, picked up the whole pile of 160 friedrichs d'or, and went to look for Polina Alexandrovna.

They were still somewhere in the park, and I did not manage to see her until supper. This time the Frenchman was not there and the General let himself go; among other things, he thought it necessary to remark once more that he would not care to see me at the roulette table. In his opinion he would be compromised if at any time I lost too much; 'But even if you were to win a very large amount, even then I should still be compromised,' he added significantly. 'Of course I have no right to dictate your conduct, but you will agree. . . .' Then, as usual, he left his sentence unfinished. I answered coldly that I had very little money and that consequently I could not lose too conspicuously even if I began to play. Going upstairs, I managed to hand Polina her winnings and told her that another time I would not play for her.

'Why not?' she asked, disturbed.

'Because I want to play for myself,' I answered, looking at her with surprise, 'and this prevents me.'

'So you definitely continue to be convinced that roulette is your only hope and salvation?' she asked derisively. I told her, again very seriously, yes; as for my certainty of winning, it might be comical, I agreed, 'but please leave me alone.'

Polina Alexandrovna tried to insist that I must share today's winnings equally with her, attempted to give me back eighty friedrichs d'or and proposed that we should go on playing on that basis. I absolutely and finally refused the half share and declared that I could not play for anybody else, not because I didn't want to, but because I should certainly lose.

'All the same, however silly it may be, I have almost no other hope than roulette either,' she said thoughtfully. 'So you really must go on playing in partnership with me and – of course – you will.' With that she left me, not staying to listen to any further objections.

CHAPTER THREE

YESTERDAY, however, she did not say a word to me about gambling all day. Indeed, she avoided talking to me at all yesterday. Her earlier manner to me has not changed. The same casual treatment when we meet, and even a shade of contempt and hostility. She has not the least wish to conceal her dislike of me; I can see that. In spite of that, she does not conceal either that for some reason I am necessary to her or that she is sparing me for some reason. The relationship that has been established between us is strange and to me largely incomprehensible, considering her pride and arrogance towards everybody. She knows, for example, that I am insanely in love with her, and even allows me to talk about my passion – and, of course, nothing could more completely express her contempt than this permission to speak freely and without censorship of my love. It is as good as saying 'I think so little of your feelings that as far as I am concerned it makes absolutely no difference what you say to me or what your feelings are towards me.' She used to talk to me about her own affairs even before this, but she has never been entirely open with me. What is more, her disregard of me has had refinements like, for example, this: suppose she knows that I am aware of some circumstance in her life or something that worries her extremely; she will even tell me something of her circumstances, if she must use me in some way for her purposes, like a slave or an errand-boy; but she will tell me exactly as much as it is necessary for somebody employed to run errands to know and, if I still don't know all the ins and outs, even if she can see for herself that I am tormented with worry over her anxieties, still she will never condescend to set my mind completely at rest by friendly openness although, employing me as she often does on commissions that are not merely troublesome but even dangerous, she is in my opinion morally bound to be open with me. But is it worth while to trouble about my feelings or the fact that I too am worried and perhaps three times as anxious and unhappy over her cares and misfortunes as she is herself?

I have known for three weeks of her intention to play roulette. She even informed me beforehand that I must play instead of her, because it would be improper for her to do so. I noticed at the time, from the tone of her remarks, that she had some serious worry, not merely a desire to win money. What is money in itself to her? There is some purpose here, some situation I may guess at but don't as yet know. Of course, the humiliating subjection in which she keeps me might give me (and extremely often does give me) the possibility of crudely and directly questioning her. Since I am her slave and altogether insignificant in her eyes, she feels no reason to be offended by my boorish curiosity. But the trouble is that while she allows me to ask questions, she does not answer them. Sometimes she does not even notice them. That is how things are between us!

There was a great deal of talking all day yesterday about a telegram dispatched to St Petersburg four days before, to which there has been no reply. The General is obviously disturbed and preoccupied. It is, of course, a question of Grandmamma. The Frenchman is worried too. Yesterday, for example, the two had a long and serious conversation after dinner. The Frenchman's tone with all the rest of us was unusually arrogant and off-hand. As the saying is: invite a pig to dinner and he'll put his feet on the table. He was casual to the point of rudeness even with Polina; he took part with enjoyment, however, in the general saunters in the station and the excursions into the country on horseback or by carriage. I have been familiar for a long time with some of the circumstances binding the Frenchman and the General together: in Russia they were setting up a factory in partnership; I don't know whether the plan has failed or whether they are still talking about it. Besides that, I happen to know part of a family secret;

last year the Frenchman really did come to the General's rescue and gave him thirty thousand roubles to make up a deficit in public funds when he retired. And now, of course, the General is in his clutches; but at this moment it is Mademoiselle Blanche who is playing the principal part in the whole thing, for all that, and I am sure I am not mistaken in this.

Who is Mademoiselle Blanche? Here she is said to be a French noblewoman, possessing a mother, who is here with her, and a colossal fortune. She is also known to be related to our Marquis, only rather distantly, some sort of second or third cousin. It is said that before my trip to Paris the Frenchman and Mademoiselle Blanche behaved with much greater ceremony towards one another, were on a somewhat more subtle and delicate footing; but now their acquaintanceship, or their friendship and kinship, emerge as somehow cruder and more intimate. Perhaps our affairs seem to them in such a bad way already that they do not even think it necessary to stand on ceremony or try to conceal their feelings with us. The day before yesterday I noticed Mr Astley watching Mademoiselle Blanche and her mother. It seemed to me that he knew them. It even seemed to me that our Frenchman, too, had met Mr Astley before. Mr Astley, however, is so shy, diffident and reticent that it is almost possible to rely on him not to wash dirty linen in public. At any rate the Frenchman barely exchanges greetings with him and almost never looks at him, which means he's not afraid of him. That is understandable enough; but why doesn't Mademoiselle Blanche look at him either? Especially as yesterday the Marquis let something slip: in the course of general conversation he suddenly said, in what connexion I don't remember, that he knows for a fact that Mr Astley is immensely rich and that he, the Marquis, knows what he is talking about: at this point Mademoiselle Blanche might have been expected to look at Mr Astley! Altogether, the General is in an anxious position. It is easy to understand what a telegram about his aunt's death could mean to him now!

Although I felt certain that Polina was purposely avoiding conversation with me, I too adopted a cold and indifferent manner; but I kept thinking she might come up to me at any moment. On the other hand, yesterday and today I paid attention mostly to

Mademoiselle Blanche. The poor General is absolutely done for! To fall so passionately in love at fifty-five is of course a misfortune. Add to that his widowerhood, his children, the utter ruin of his estate, his debts and, finally, the woman he had to fall in love with. Mademoiselle Blanche is beautiful to look at. But I don't know whether I shall be understood if I say that she has one of those faces that can be terrifying. At any rate, I have always been afraid of such women. She is probably about twenty-five. She is tall and broad, with sloping shoulders; her neck and bosom are magnificent; her skin is rather swarthy and her hair as black as jet, and she has an enormous lot of it, enough for two women. Her eyes are black, with yellowish whites, her glance is bold, her teeth extremely white, and her lips always painted; her perfume is musky. She dresses effectively, richly, fashionably, but with great taste. Her hands and feet are admirable. Her voice is a husky contralto. She sometimes laughs aloud, showing all her teeth, but usually sits silent, with an insolent stare – at least in the presence of Polina and Maria Philippovna. (There is a strange rumour that Maria Philippovna is going back to Russia.) Mademoiselle Blanche seems to me completely uneducated, and perhaps she is not even intelligent, but on the other hand she is suspicious and cunning. I think her life has not been without adventures. To tell the truth, it may be that the Marquis is not related to her in any way, and that her mother is not really her mother at all. But there is evidence that in Berlin, where we met them, she and her mother had some respectable acquaintances. As for the Marquis himself, although I still remain doubtful whether he is really a marquis, it does not seem open to doubt that he does belong to respectable social circles, among us in Moscow, for example, and in some places in Germany. I don't know what his standing is in France. He is said to have a château. I thought a lot of water would have flowed under the bridges during these two weeks, and yet I still don't know for certain whether anything definite has been said between Mademoiselle Blanche and the General. Everything now is completely dependent on the state of our fortunes, that is on whether the General can produce some money. If, for example, news were to come that Grandmamma has not died I am certain Mademoiselle Blanche would immediately disappear. I am sur-

prised and amused to find I have become such a gossip. Oh, how
I loathe all this! With what delight I would abandon everybody
and everything! But can I leave Polina, can I drop my espionage
round her? Spying, of course, is a low occupation, but – what does
that matter to me?

Mr Astley has also interested me greatly in the last two days.
Yes, I am sure he is in love with Polina! It is odd and amusing to
see how much the glance of a shy and painfully chaste man can
sometimes convey when he has felt the touch of love, especially
at times when the man would of course much rather sink through
the floor than say or imply anything at all, either by word or by
look. Mr Astley often meets us on our walks. He takes off his hat
and walks past, although of course he is dying to join us. If, however, he is invited to do so, he refuses at once. Wherever we sit
down, in the station or near the band or the fountain, he is certain
to take up his position somewhere not far from our seat, and where-
ever we are, in the park or the woods or on the Schlangenberg, we
have only to raise our eyes and look round and there, on the
nearest path or behind a bush, is Mr Astley's lurking-place. He
seems to me to be looking for a chance of talking to me by myself.
This morning we met and exchanged a word or two. Sometimes
his conversation is extremely abrupt. Without even saying good
morning he began by blurting out:

'Ah, Mademoiselle Blanche. . . . I have seen plenty of women like
Mademoiselle Blanche!'

He stopped and looked meaningfully at me. What he meant by
it, I don't know, because when I asked him he nodded his head
with a sly smile and added, 'Quite right. . . . Is Mademoiselle
Pauline very fond of flowers?'

'I don't know,' I answered. 'I've no idea.'

'What? You don't even know that?' he exclaimed with the
utmost amazement.

'I don't know, I've never noticed,' I repeated, laughing.

'Hm, that gives me a special idea.' He inclined his head and
walked on. He looked pleased, however. Our conversation had been
conducted in atrocious French.

CHAPTER FOUR

TODAY has been funny, outrageous and absurd. It is now eleven o'clock at night. I am sitting in my little room and remembering it all. To begin with, I was forced to go to the roulette rooms in the morning to play for Polina Alexandrovna. I took her sixty friedrichs d'or on two conditions: first, that we should not go halves, that is, I refused to take anything for myself if I won, and secondly, that this evening Polina should explain to me precisely why it was so essential for her to win and precisely how much money she needed. All the same, I simply cannot suppose that it was merely for money. Obviously, money is essential, and as soon as possible, for some special purpose. She promised to explain and I set off. There was a terrible crowd in the rooms. How impudent and greedy they all are! I elbowed my way into the thick of them and stood close to the croupier; then I began playing modestly and tentatively, staking two or three coins at a time. Meanwhile I watched and took note; it appeared to me that pure calculation means fairly little and has none of the importance many gamblers attach to it. They sit over bits of paper ruled into columns, note down the coups, count up, compute probabilities, do sums, finally put down their stakes and – lose exactly the same as we poor mortals playing without calculation. But on the other hand I drew one conclusion, which I think is correct: in a series of pure chances there really does exist, if not a system, at any rate a sort of sequence – which is, of course, very odd. For example, it may happen that after the twelve middle numbers, the last twelve turn up; the ball lodges in the last twelve numbers twice, say, and then passes to the first twelve. Having fallen into the first twelve it passes again to the middle twelve, falls there three or four times running, and again passes to the last twelve, and from there, again after two coups, falls once more into the first twelve, lodges there once and then again falls three times on the middle numbers, and this goes on for an hour and a half or two hours: one, three, two; one, three, two. This is very entertaining. One day, or one morning, it will happen, for example, that red and black alternate, changing every minute almost without any order, so that neither red nor black ever turns up more than two or three times in suc-

cession. The next day, or the next evening, red only will come
up many times running, twenty or more, for example, and go on
doing so unfailingly for a certain time, perhaps during a whole
day. A great deal of all this was explained to me by Mr Astley,
who remained standing by the tables all the morning but did not
once play himself. As for me, I was cleaned right out, and very
speedily. I staked twenty friedrichs d'or on *pair* straight away,
and won, staked again and again won, and so on two or three more
times. I think about four hundred friedrichs d'or came into my
possession in some five minutes. I ought to have left at that point,
but a strange sort of feeling came over me, a kind of desire to
challenge fate, a longing to give it a fillip on the nose or stick out
my tongue at it. I staked the permitted maximum – 4,000 gulden
– and lost. Then, getting excited, I pulled out all I had left, staked
it in the same way, lost again, and after that left the table as if I
had been stunned. I could not even grasp what had happened to
me, and I did not tell Polina Alexandrovna about losing until just
before dinner. I had spent the time until then wandering un-
steadily about in the park.

At dinner, I was again in an excited mood, exactly as I had
been two days earlier. The Frenchman and Mademoiselle Blanche
were again dining with us. It appeared that Mademoiselle Blanche
had been in the gaming saloon in the morning and seen my exploits. This time she talked to me somewhat more kindly. The
Frenchman was blunter and simply asked me whether it was
my own money I had lost. I think he is suspicious of Polina.
In short, there is something there. I lied and said at once that it
was mine.

The General was extremely surprised : where had I got so much
money? I explained that I had begun with ten friedrichs d'or, that
six or seven wins in succession, at even money, had brought me
up to five or six thousand gulden, and that I had then lost the lot
in two coups.

All this, of course, was plausible. As I explained it, I looked at
Polina, but I could make out nothing from her face. She had
allowed me, however, to lie, and had not corrected me; I concluded
from this that I had done right to lie and hide the fact that I was
playing for her. In any case, I thought to myself, she owes me an

explanation, and a short time ago she promised to give me a partial one.

I thought the General would make some comment, but he said nothing; on the other hand, I noticed that his face showed he was disturbed and anxious. Perhaps in his ticklish position he simply found it painful to hear of such a respectable sum of money coming into and slipping out of the grasp of such an improvident fool in one quarter of an hour.

I suspect that he and the Frenchman had a sharp disagreement yesterday evening. They were talking with some heat behind closed doors for a long time. When the Frenchman left he seemed angry about something, and early this morning he came to see the General again – probably to continue yesterday's conversation.

When he heard of my losses, the Frenchman remarked caustically and with some ill-will that I ought to have had more sense. I don't know why he added that although Russians play a great deal of roulette, they have not in his opinion the capacity for it.

'And in my opinion, roulette might have been created expressly for Russians,' I said, and when the Frenchman grinned scornfully at my reply, I remarked that the truth was of course on my side, because when I spoke of the Russians as gamblers I was criticizing rather than praising them and might therefore be believed.

'What is your opinion based on?' asked the Frenchman.

'On the fact that in the catalogue of the merits and virtues of civilized western man the faculty of acquiring wealth historically occupies all but the most important place. And the Russian is not only incapable of acquiring wealth, he even squanders it outrageously and for nothing. All the same,' I added, 'Russians also need money, and so we are very glad to have, and very addicted to, ways, like for example roulette, of getting rich quickly, in a couple of hours, without working. It's a great temptation to us; and as we play without purpose or effort, we lose everything we possess!'

'That is partly true,' the Frenchman commented smugly.

'No, it's not true, and you ought to be ashamed of talking about your country like that,' remarked the General sternly and impressively.

'Oh come!' I answered. 'After all, nobody really knows which is worse; the scandalous Russian goings-on or the German capacity for making a pile by honest toil.'

'What a shocking idea!' exclaimed the General.

'What a Russian idea!' exclaimed the Frenchman.

I laughed; I desperately wanted to provoke them.

'I'd rather fritter away my whole life in a Kirghiz tent,' I cried, 'than worship the German idol.'

'What idol?' cried the General, who was beginning to get really angry.

'The German capacity for amassing wealth. I haven't been here long, but all the same, everything I have had time to notice and study rouses my Tartar blood. I swear I've no use for such virtues! Yesterday I had time to cover about ten versts of country round about. Well, it's all exactly like one of those moralizing little German picture-books; everywhere among these people every house has its Vater, dreadfully virtuous and exceedingly honest. So honest, in fact, that it's terrible to go near him. I can't stand people who are so honest it's terrible to go near them. Every one of those Vaters has a family, and in the evening they all read improving books aloud to one another. The elms and chestnut trees rustle above the little cottage. There is the sunset, and a stork on the roof, and everything is extremely touching and poetic.

'Don't be angry, General, let me tell it as touchingly as I can. I remember my own poor dead father used to read similar little books to me and my mother under the linden trees in the garden in the evenings. . . . I can form a sound judgement about it. Well, every family of that sort here belongs to the Vater in complete servitude and subjection. They all work like slaves and they all scrape up money like Jews. Suppose the Vater has already got together a few gulden, and is counting on handing over his trade or his bit of land to the eldest son; to this end the daughter is not given a dowry and remains an old maid. To this end also the younger son is sold into bondage or the army, and the money is added to the capital of the household. This really does happen here; I have been making inquiries. It is all done out of nothing but honesty, honesty carried to the point where even the younger son who has been sold believes that he was sold out of pure honesty – and it is an ideal state of affairs when the victim himself rejoices at being led to the slaughter. And what next? Next, things are no easier even for the elder son; he has his Amalchen, with whom his heart is united – but they can't get married because not enough money has been scraped together yet. They wait virtuously, and, smiling in all sincerity, they too go like lambs to the slaughter. Amalchen's cheeks are sunken, she is growing withered. At last, after about twenty years, the fortune has increased; the gulden have been honestly and virtuously amassed. The *Vater* gives his blessing to the forty-year-old son and the thirty-five-year-old Amalchen, with her withered breasts and her red nose. . . . Thereupon he weeps, moralizes, and dies. The elder son is now transformed into a *Vater* and the whole story begins all over again. So after fifty years, or seventy years, the first *Vater's* grandson really has acquired a substantial fortune, which he hands on to his son, and he to his, and he again to his, and after some five or six more generations there emerges Baron Rothschild himself, or Hoppe and Co., or the devil knows who. Well, sir, what a majestic spectacle! a century or two's continuous labour, patience, intelligence, honesty, strength of character, steadfastness, foresight, and storks on the roof! What more can you want? There is after all no higher ideal than this, and from this elevation they begin judging the whole world, and instantly punishing the guilty, anybody, that is, who is different from them in the smallest particular. Well, so here's the point: I would rather be a Russian rake or make my pile at roulette. I don't want to be Hoppe and Co. after five generations. I need money for myself, and I don't look on myself as merely an indispensable factor in the acquisition of wealth. I know I've talked an awful lot of nonsense, but I don't care. That's what I think!'

'I don't know whether there's much truth in what you were saying,' remarked the General, thoughtfully, 'but I do know one thing; as soon as you're allowed the slightest chance of forgetting yourself, you begin to show off insufferably and . . .'

In his usual way, he neglected to finish what he was saying. If our General ever began to say something with even the tiniest bit more significance than the commonplaces of everyday conversation, he never finished it. The Frenchman had listened carelessly, goggling a little. He had understood almost nothing of what I was saying. Polina had looked on with a certain supercilious indifference. She seemed not to have heard anything that was said at table this time, not only by me, but by anybody else either.

CHAPTER FIVE

SHE was unusually thoughtful, but immediately we left the table she bade me accompany her on a walk. We took the children and went towards the fountain in the park.

Since I was in a particularly excited mood, I rudely and bluntly blurted out the question why our Frenchman, the Marquis de Grieux, not only did not escort her when she went out, but sometimes did not even speak to her all day.

'Because he's a scoundrel,' she answered strangely. I had never before heard her express such an opinion of de Grieux, and suddenly fearful of understanding her petulance, said no more.

'Did you notice that he's not very friendly with the General today?'

'You want to know what it's all about,' she answered shortly and irritably. 'You know the General has mortgaged everything to him, the whole estate is his, and if Grandmamma doesn't die, the Frenchman will take possession at once of everything that has been mortgaged to him.'

'Ah, so it is really true that everything is mortgaged? I had heard so, but I did not know it was absolutely everything.'

'Of course it is.'

'In that case, good-bye Mademoiselle Blanche,' I remarked. 'She wouldn't be the General's wife then! Do you know, I think it possible that the General is so much in love that he'll shoot himself if Mademoiselle Blanche gives him up. At his age it's dangerous to fall so deeply in love.'

'I think myself that something will happen to him,' said Polina Alexandrovna thoughtfully.

'And how splendid that is!' I cried; 'it couldn't be more crudely demonstrated that she consented to be married only for the sake of money. The conventions were not even observed, it was all done quite without ceremony. Marvellous! As for Grandmamma, what could be funnier and nastier than sending telegram after telegram inquiring: "Is she dead yet? Is she dead yet?" Eh? How do you like that, Polina Alexandrovna?'

'That's all rubbish,' she said disgustedly, interrupting me. 'On the contrary, I'm surprised you are in such a cheerful mood. What are you pleased about? Is it really because you have lost my money?'

'Why did you give it to me to lose? I told you I couldn't play for anybody else, much less for you. Whatever order you give me, I obey you; but the result doesn't depend on me. After all, I warned you that nothing would come of it. Tell me, are you very distressed to have lost so much money? What do you need so much for?'

'Why do you ask?'

'But you promised to explain, you know. . . . Listen, I am absolutely sure that when I begin to play for myself (and I have twelve friedrichs d'or) I shall win. Then borrow as much as you need from me.'

She pulled a scornful face.

'Don't be angry with me for making such a suggestion,' I went on. 'I am so thoroughly conscious that I don't count beside you, at least in your eyes, that you can even take money from me. You can't take offence at a gift from me. Besides, I lost your money.'

She threw a swift glance at me and, seeing that I was speaking angrily and sarcastically, again interrupted the conversation.

'There is nothing of interest to you in my position. If you want to know, I'm simply in debt. I borrowed some money and I should like to return it. I had a strange, mad idea that I should be certain to win at roulette here. Why I had this idea, I don't know, but I believed it. Who knows, perhaps I believed it because I had no choice – there was nothing else left.'

'Or because it was so very *necessary* for you to win. It's exactly like a drowning man clutching at a straw. You must admit that if he wasn't drowning he wouldn't take a straw for a tree-trunk.'

Polina was astonished.

'Then how is it,' she asked, 'that you yourself hope for exactly the same thing? You talked to me for a long time once, two weeks ago, about how you were completely convinced you would win here at roulette, and tried to persuade me not to think you were mad; or were you joking? – but I remember you were so serious about it that nobody could have taken it for a joke.'

'That's true,' I answered thoughtfully, 'and I'm still completely convinced I shall win. I own you have now brought me to the question of exactly why my stupid and shocking losses today haven't left any doubts in my mind. I am utterly sure, for all that, that as soon as I begin to play for myself I can't fail to win.'

'Why are you so absolutely sure?'

'If you like – I don't know. I only know I *have to* win, that for me too it's the only solution. Well, perhaps that's why it seems to me that I absolutely must win.'

'So it's very *necessary* for you to win, too, if you are so fanatically convinced?'

'I'm willing to bet that you doubt whether I'm capable of feeling a serious need.'

'It's all the same to me,' answered Polina with calm indifference. '*Yes*, if you like, I am doubtful whether anything can seriously worry you. You can worry, but not seriously. You are an unsettled and unstable person. What do you want with money? I found nothing serious in any of the reasons you advanced then.'

'By the way,' I interrupted, 'you said you must repay a debt. So it's a good debt! Is it to the Frenchman?'

'What sort of questions are these? Your tone is very sharp today. You're not drunk, are you?'

'You know I allow myself to say anything, and sometimes ask very frank questions. I am your slave, I repeat; people are not ashamed with slaves, and a slave can't give offence.'

'That's all rubbish. I can't endure that "slave" theory of yours.'

'Please note that I don't speak of my slavery because I want to be your slave, but simply mention it as a fact that doesn't depend on me at all.'

'Give me a straight answer: what do you want money for?'

'What do you want to know for?'

'As you please,' she replied, with a proud movement of her head.

'You can't endure the "slave" theory, but you insist on the slavery: "Answer and don't argue!" All right, then. You were asking what I want money for? How can you ask what for? – money is everything!'

'I understand that, but one mustn't let wanting it make one mad! You know you let yourself be driven to absolute frenzy and fatalism yourself. There is something here, some special purpose. Tell me without beating about the bush, I will know.'

She was apparently beginning to be angry, and I was terribly glad that she should question me so irritably.

'Of course there's a purpose,' I said, 'but I don't know how to explain it to you. It's nothing more than that with money I shall become a different person to you, not a slave.'

'What? How will you achieve that?'

'Achieve it? What, don't you even understand how I can manage to make you regard me as anything but a slave? Well, that's exactly what I don't want, that kind of surprise and perplexity!'

'You said you enjoyed the slavery. And I thought you did myself.'

'You thought so,' I exclaimed with a sort of strange enjoyment. 'Well, that unsophisticated tone is good, coming from you. Well, yes, yes, I do enjoy being enslaved by you. There is, there really is enjoyment in the utmost degree of humility and insignificance,' I rambled on. 'God knows there may even be enjoyment in the knout, when it falls on the back and cuts the flesh to fragments. . . . But perhaps I want to try other enjoyments as well. Not so long ago at table, the General read me a lecture in your presence on the seven hundred roubles a year which perhaps I shan't even receive from him. The Marquis de Grieux stares at me with his eyebrows raised, and at the same time doesn't even see me. But perhaps I, in my turn, long passionately to pull the Marquis de Grieux's nose in front of you!'

'Spoken like a milksop. One can behave with dignity in any situation. If there is conflict here, it ennobles, not humiliates.'

'Straight out of the copy-book! You simply assume that I don't know how to behave with dignity. That is, although I may in fact be dignified, I don't know how to behave as if I were. Do you understand that this is quite possible? All Russians are like that, and you know why: all Russians are too richly gifted and too many-sided to be able to find an acceptable form immediately. It's all a question of form. Most Russians are so richly gifted that finding our proper form needs genius. Well, but the genius usually doesn't exist, because it is rare anywhere. It is only the French and perhaps a few other Europeans who have such a well-defined form that they can look extremely worthy and yet be utterly unworthy. That is why formality means so much to them. A Frenchman can bear an insult, a genuine, deliberate insult, without a frown, but he won't bear a fillip on the nose on any account, because that is a violation of the accepted and time-honoured rules of propriety. The reason why our young ladies have such a weakness for Frenchmen is that their form is so good. In my opinion, though, they haven't any form at all, and le coq gaulois is nothing but a cock. However, I can't understand these things; I'm not a woman. Perhaps cocks are good too. Besides, I've been talking nonsense, and you don't stop me. You must stop me more often; when I talk to you I want to say everything, everything, everything. I lose all my form. I'm even prepared to agree that besides having no form, I haven't any good qualities at all. I make no bones about it. I don't even trouble about good qualities. Everything is at a standstill with me now. You know why. I haven't a single human idea in my head. It's a long time now since I knew what was going on in the world, either in Russia or here. Here I've been through Dresden and I don't even remember what it's like. You know what takes all my attention. As I haven't any hope, and as I'm a cipher in your eyes, I can tell you plainly I see nothing but you wherever I am, and nothing else matters to me. Why I love you, how I love you, I don't know. Do you know, perhaps you're not good at all? Imagine, I don't know whether you're good or not, even to look at! You probably have a bad heart and an ignoble mind; that's very likely.'

'Perhaps that's why you expect to buy me with money,' she said, 'because you think I'm ignoble.'

'When did I expect to buy you with money?' I cried.

'Your tongue ran away with you and you didn't realize what you were saying. You think you can buy my respect with money, if not me myself.'

'Well, no, that's not quite it. I told you it was difficult to explain what I meant. You have an overwhelming effect on me. Don't be angry with me for rambling on. You know why you can't be angry with me: I'm mad. It makes no difference to me, though; be angry if you like. Upstairs in my little cell I have only to remember and imagine the merest rustle of your dress and I am ready to gnaw my hands off. And why are you angry with me? Because I call myself a slave? Take advantage of my slavery, profit by it, make use of it! Do you know, one day I shall kill you! Not because I shall stop loving you, or out of jealousy, but – I'll simply kill you, just like that, because sometimes I long to devour you. You laugh. . . .'

'I'm not laughing,' she said angrily. 'I order you to be silent.'

She paused, panting with rage. I honestly don't know whether she is pretty, but I have always liked to look at her when she stops like that in front of me, and so I have often enjoyed making her angry. Perhaps she had noticed this and was angry on purpose. I said as much to her.

'What a nasty idea!' she exclaimed with disgust.

'It makes no difference to me,' I went on. 'Do you know something else? It is dangerous for you to walk alone with me: many times I have felt an irresistible longing to beat you with my fists, disfigure you, strangle you. And do you think it won't come to that? You will drive me crazy. I'm not likely to shrink from the scandal, am I? Or your anger? What's your anger to me? My love is hopeless, and I know that afterwards I should love you a thousand times more. If I ever kill you, you know, I shall have to kill myself as well; well, I shall try for as long as possible not to kill myself, so as to savour the unbearable pain of being without you. Do you know an incredible thing? Every day I love you *more*, and that's almost impossible, you know. After that, how can I help being a fatalist? You remember, on the Schlangenberg the day before yesterday, I whispered to you when you provoked me, "Say the word and I will leap into that abyss!" If you had said a word, I would have jumped. You do believe, don't you, that I would have jumped?'

'What silly talk!' she cried.

'I simply don't care whether it's silly or clever,' I exclaimed. 'I know that when I'm with you I must talk and talk and talk – and I do talk. I lose all my self-respect with you, and I don't care.'

'Why should I want to make you jump from the Schlangenberg?' she said coldly and with a peculiarly insulting look. 'It would be no use to me.'

'Magnificent!' I cried. 'You said that magnificent "no use" on purpose to crush me. I can see through you. No use, you say? But after all, pleasure is always some use, and savage, boundless power, even though it's only over a fly, is after all a pleasure in its way. Man is a despot by nature and likes inflicting pain. You enjoy it terribly.'

I remember she looked at me with a particularly fixed kind of attention. My face must have reflected all my incoherent and absurd feelings. I recollect that our conversation was almost word for word as I have recorded it here. My eyes were suffused with blood. There was dried foam at the corners of my lips. As for the Schlangenberg, I swear on my honour, even now, that if she had ordered me to throw myself down, I would have done it! If she had said it simply as a joke, or with careless scorn – even then I would have flung myself over!

'No, why? I believe you,' she said, but she said it as only she can sometimes speak, with such contempt and malice, so arrogantly that I really could have killed her at that moment. She was running a risk. I had not been lying on that point either, when I talked to her.

'Are you a coward?' she asked me suddenly.

'I don't know, perhaps I am. I don't know . . . I haven't thought about it for a long time.'

'If I said to you, "Kill this man", would you kill him?'

'Who?'

'Anyone I wanted.'

'The Frenchman?'

'Don't ask questions, but answer me – anybody I told you. I want to know if you were speaking seriously just now.' She waited for my answer so earnestly and with such impatience that I felt somehow strange.

'Will you at least tell me what's going on?' I exclaimed. 'What's the matter, are you afraid of me? I can see all the mess here for myself. You are the stepdaughter of a ruined madman, stricken with passion for that she-devil Blanche; then here's that Frenchman with his mysterious influence on you, and – now you are seriously asking me – a question like that. Let me at least know; otherwise I shall go mad on the spot and do something desperate. Or are you ashamed to do me the honour of being frank? But can you be ashamed with me?'

'I am not talking about that at all. I asked you a question and I am waiting for the answer.'

'Of course,' I cried, 'I'll kill anybody you tell me to, but can you really . . . will you really order me to do it?'

'Why, do you think I shall spare you? I shall give the order, but I shall stay on one side myself. Can you endure that? But no, why should you? You may perhaps kill at my command, but then you will come and kill me too, for daring to send you.'

I felt somehow stunned by these words. Of course, even then I half took her question as a joke, a challenge; but all the same, she spoke very seriously. All the same I was startled that she had spoken so openly, that she maintained such rights over me, that she consented to exercise such power over me, and could say so directly, 'Go to your perdition, and I will remain on one side.' In those words there was something cynical and open that went much too far for my taste. How did that mean she looked on me? Things had already gone beyond slavery and insignificance. Such a view raises a man to one's own level. And however absurd and unlikely all our talk had been, my mind wavered.

Suddenly she laughed. We were sitting on a bench facing the playing children, right opposite the spot where the carriages stopped and set down their passengers in the avenue in front of the station.

'Do you see that fat baroness?' she cried. 'She is Baroness Wurmerhelm. She arrived here only the day before yesterday. You see her husband: the tall dried-up Prussian with a stick. Do you remember how he looked us over two days ago? Go at once and walk up to the Baroness, take off your hat and say something to her in French.'

'Why?'

'You swore you would jump off the Schlangenberg; you swear

you are ready to kill somebody if I tell you to. Instead of all these killings and tragedies I simply want to laugh. Go along and don't argue. I want to see the Baron strike you with his stick.'

'You are challenging me; do you think I won't do it?'

'Yes, I'm challenging you; go, I wish it!'

'I'll go if you like, although it's a crazy fancy. But there's one thing: how to avoid unpleasantness to the General, and through him to you. I'm really not worrying about myself, but about you and – well, about the General too. And what a thing to take into one's head, to go and insult a woman!'

'No, you're only a talker, I see,' she said scornfully. 'If your eyes were bloodshot just now, it was perhaps only because you drank a lot at dinner. And do you suppose I don't understand that it's a silly, vulgar trick and that the General will be angry? I simply want something to laugh at. Well, I want it, and that's all about it! And why should you insult a woman? You're more likely to get a thrashing with a stick.'

I turned on my heel and went without another word to do her bidding. Of course it was stupid, and of course I couldn't get out of it, but as I began to approach the Baroness, I remember that something, the sheer schoolboyish quality of it, seemed to egg me on. And I was feeling very irritable besides, as though I was drunk.

CHAPTER SIX

IT is now two days since that stupid day. And what a lot of clamour and uproar and talk and noise! And what a lot of confusion and disorder, stupidity and vulgarity it all comes to, and I am the cause of it all. Sometimes, however, it is funny – to me, at any rate. I can't realize what has happened to me, whether I am indeed in a state of frenzy or have simply left the road and am running wild until I am restrained. Sometimes I think my mind is disturbed. And sometimes I think I am still not far from childhood and the schoolroom bench, and am simply playing crude childish pranks.

It is Polina, it's all Polina! Perhaps if it were not for her, there wouldn't be any schoolboy tricks, either. Who knows, perhaps I did it all out of despair (however stupid it may be to reason in this way). And I don't know, I don't even know what there is attractive about her! And yet she is pretty, she is; I think she's pretty. After all, she drives other men mad as well. She is tall and shapely. Only very thin. I think you could tie her into a knot or fold her in two. Her footprint is long and very narrow – agonizing. Really agonizing. Her hair has a tinge of red. Her eyes are really feline, but how proudly and arrogantly she can use them. About four months ago, when I had only just joined them, she once had a long and heated conversation with de Grieux one evening in the drawing-room. And she looked at him in such a way ... that afterwards, when I retired to bed, I could imagine she had slapped his face – had just done so and stood looking at him. ... I was in love with her from that evening.

To my story, however.

I walked along the path to the avenue, stopped in the middle of it, and waited for the Baron and Baroness. At a distance of five paces I took off my hat and bowed.

The Baroness, I remember, was wearing a silk dress of enormous circumference, light grey in colour, with flounces and a crinoline and a train. She is short and immensely stout, with a terribly fat and overflowing chin, so that her neck is quite invisible. A crimson face. Little eyes, malicious and impudent. She walks as if she were conferring an honour on everybody. The Baron is tall and desiccated. The usual sort of German face, twisted and covered with a thousand tiny wrinkles; spectacles; forty-five years old. His legs begin practically at the waist: that means breeding. Proud as a peacock. A little clumsy. Something sheeplike in his expression, a substitute in its own way for profundity.

All this leapt to my eyes in three seconds.

My bow and the hat held in my hand at first barely arrested their attention. The Baron only knit his brows slightly. The Baroness simply sailed straight down on me.

'Madame la baronne,' I said with loud distinctness, emphasizing every word, 'j'ai l'honneur d'être votre esclave.'

Then I bowed, put on my hat, and walked past the Baron, turning my face towards him and smiling.

She had told me to take off my hat, but I bowed and made my

adolescent joke of my own accord. The devil alone knows what prompted me. I seemed to have lost control of myself.

'*Hein!*' cried, or rather croaked, the Baron, turning to me in startled indignation.

I turned round and stood politely waiting, continuing to look at him and smile. He was evidently puzzled and his eyebrows were raised as high as they would go. His face grew darker and darker. The Baroness had also turned towards me, and she too was looking at me in puzzled annoyance. One or two passers-by had begun to stare. Some even stopped. '*Hein!*' croaked the Baron again, twice as hoarsely and twice as angrily.

'*Jawohl!*' I drawled, continuing to look him straight in the eye.

'*Sind sie rasend?*' he cried, waving his stick and apparently beginning to falter. Perhaps my clothes confused him. I was very tastefully and even foppishly dressed, like a man completely at home in the most respectable society.

'*Jawo-o-ohl!*' I shouted suddenly at the top of my voice, lengthening the 'o' in the same way as the Berliners, who are always using the word *jawohl* in conversation and prolonging the vowel 'o' more or less, to express varying shades of thought and feeling.

The Baron and Baroness turned round swiftly and almost ran away from me in terror. Some of the spectators began to talk, others looked at me in perplexity. I don't remember very clearly, though.

I turned away and began walking back at my usual pace to Polina Alexandrovna. But before I had got within a hundred paces of her seat, I saw that she had risen and was walking towards the hotel with the children.

I overtook her at the door.

'I have performed . . . the farce,' I said as I came up with her.

'Well, what of it? Now get yourself out of it,' she answered without even looking at me, and went upstairs.

I spent all that evening walking in the park. I even walked across the park and then through the wood into the next principality. I ate an omelette and drank wine in a rustic cottage; they rooked me one and a half thalers for the idyll.

I did not return home until eleven o'clock. I was immediately summoned to the General.

Our party occupies two suites in the hotel; they have four rooms. The first – a large one – is a drawing-room, with a grand piano in it. Next door to it is another large room – the General's sitting-room. Here he was waiting for me, standing in the middle of the room in a sublimely majestic attitude. De Grieux was lolling on the sofa.

'Allow me to ask, sir, what folly you have committed !' began the General, turning to me.

'I should like you to come straight to the point, General,' I said. 'You probably want to talk about my encounter with a certain German today?'

'A certain German? That German is Baron Wurmerhelm, sir, and a person of consequence ! You were discourteous to him and the Baroness.'

'Not at all.'

'You alarmed them, sir,' cried the General.

'Nothing of the kind. While I was in Berlin my ears were endlessly assaulted by that *jawohl* they repeat at every other word and drawl so disgustingly. When I met them in the avenue, this *jawohl* suddenly sprang into my mind, I don't know why, and it had an irritating effect on me. . . . And besides, whenever the Baroness meets me, as she has already done three times, she makes a habit of bearing straight down on me as though I was a worm she could tread on. You must admit I can have my pride too. I took off my hat and politely (most politely, I assure you) said, "*Madame, j'ai l'honneur d'être votre esclave.*" When the Baron turned round and shouted, "*Hein!*" – something suddenly made me shout back "*Jawohl!*" And I shouted it twice: the first time in an ordinary way, and the second, drawling it as hard as I could. And that's all.'

I confess I was terribly pleased with this extremely childish explanation. I was terribly anxious to spin the story out as absurdly as possible.

And the further I went, the more I relished it.

'Are you making fun of me?' roared the General. He turned to the Frenchman and told him in French that I was definitely asking for trouble. De Grieux smiled disdainfully and shrugged his shoulders.

'Oh, don't get that idea; that wasn't it at all !' I exclaimed. 'I

behaved badly, of course, I confess it with the utmost frankness.
My action might even be called a stupid and disgraceful schoolboy
prank, but no more than that. And I must tell you, General, that
I regret it extremely. But there is one circumstance that in my
eyes almost absolves me even from regretting it. Recently, for
some two weeks, or even three, I have been feeling unwell: ill,
nervy, irritable, fanciful, and sometimes quite unable to control
myself. Indeed, sometimes I have wanted dreadfully to turn to the
Marquis de Grieux and . . . However, I won't finish; he might be
offended. In short, these are symptoms of illness. I don't know
whether Baroness Wurmerhelm will take this circumstance into
account when I ask her pardon (because I intend to ask her pardon). I suppose she won't, especially as I know that in the legal
sphere the circumstance has recently begun to be abused: lawyers
in criminal cases have begun trying to justify their guilty clients
very frequently with the excuse that they couldn't remember anything at the moment of the crime, and they allege that this is the
same kind of disease. "He remembers nothing about killing him,"
they say. And imagine, General, medicine agrees with them – it
really confirms that there is such a disease, a kind of temporary
insanity when a man remembers almost nothing, or only half remembers, or a quarter. But the Baron and Baroness belong to an
older generation; besides that, they are Prussian Junkers and land-
owners. This progress in the realm of forensic medicine must be
still unknown to them, and so they will not accept my explanations. What do you think, General?'

'That's enough, sir!' said the General shortly and with restrained indignation, 'that's enough! I will try, once and for all,
to spare myself the consequences of your adolescent humour. You
will not apologize to the Baron and Baroness. Any dealings with
you, even if they consisted solely of your apologies, would be too
degrading for them. The Baron, hearing that you belonged to my
household, spoke to me about it in the station, and, I tell you
plainly, it would have required only a little more for him to demand satisfaction from me. Do you understand what you have
exposed me – me, sir – to? I, sir, I have been obliged to apologize
to the Baron and give him my word that you would immediately,
this very day, cease to belong to my household.'

'Allow me, General, allow me, did he really demand uncondi-
tionally that I should cease to be a member of your household, as
you are pleased to express it?'

'No; but I considered myself obliged to give him that satisfaction and of course the Baron was pleased. We are parting, sir. I
owe you an additional four friedrichs d'or and three florins on the
current account. Here is the money and here is a written account;
you may verify it. Good-bye. From now on we are strangers. I have
had nothing from you but worry and unpleasantness. I will call
the waiter at once and tell him that from tomorrow I will no
longer be responsible for your expenses in the hotel. I have the
honour to remain your obedient servant.'

I took the money and the piece of paper on which the account
was written in pencil, bowed to the General, and said very
solemnly,

'General, matters cannot end there. I am very sorry that you
have been exposed to insults from the Baron, but – excuse me –
you are to blame for that. How did you come to take it on yourself
to answer to the Baron for me? What is the meaning of your
expression that I belong to your household? I am simply a tutor
in your house, and that's all. I am neither your son nor your ward,
and you cannot answer for my actions. I am myself legally competent to do so. I am twenty-two, I am a university graduate, and
I am a nobleman. I am a complete stranger to you. Nothing but
my unbounded respect for your merits prevents me from demand-
ing satisfaction on the spot and a further accounting from you for
having taken on yourself the right to answer for me.'

The General was so astounded that he flung out his hands, then
turned abruptly to the Frenchman and hurriedly told him that I
had all but challenged him to an immediate duel. The Frenchman
roared with laughter.

'But I have no intention of letting the Baron off,' I went on with
utter composure, not in the least disconcerted by Monsieur de
Grieux's laughter, 'and since you, General, by consenting to listen
to the Baron's complaint today and entering into his interests, have
made yourself a party to the whole affair, I have the honour to inform you that no later than tomorrow morning I shall on my own
behalf demand of the Baron a formal explanation of the reasons

for which, having business with me, he addressed himself over my head to another person, as though I was incapable or unworthy of answering for myself.'

What I had foreseen happened. The General was terribly scared when he heard this new folly.

'What, do you really intend to prolong this damned affair?' he yelled, 'but good Lord! what are you doing to me? Don't dare, don't you dare, sir! or I swear . . . there are authorities here too, and I . . . I . . . in short, with my rank . . . and the Baron as well . . . in short, you will be arrested and sent away from here with a police escort to prevent you from making trouble. Understand that, sir!' And although he was breathless with rage, all the same he was in a terrible funk.

'General,' I answered with a composure intolerable to him, 'nobody can be arrested for causing a disturbance before the disturbance has been caused. I haven't begun to have it out with the Baron yet, and you are completely ignorant of what my intentions are and on what basis I mean to proceed. I only wish to clear up the offensive suggestion that I am under the tutelage of a person who is supposed to have authority over my free will. You are alarming and distressing yourself to no purpose.'

'For God's sake, Alexis Ivanovich, for God's sake drop this senseless idea!' muttered the General, suddenly changing his wrathful tone for one of pleading, and even seizing my hands. 'Well, think, what will be the result of it? More unpleasantness! You must agree that I must behave in a special manner here, especially now! especially just now! . . . Oh, you don't know, you don't know all my circumstances! . . . When we leave here, I am ready to take you back. I am only doing this now . . . well, in short, you know the reasons, after all!' he cried desperately. 'Alexis Ivanovich, Alexis Ivanovich! . . .'

Retreating to the door, I once more earnestly begged him not to worry, promised that everything would go off decently and well, and hurried out.

Russians abroad are sometimes too faint-hearted and terribly afraid of what people will say, or what will be thought of them, and they worry about whether it will be proper to do this thing or that, and in short behave as though they were wearing stays, especially those with pretensions to importance. What they like best of all is some preconceived, established code, which they follow slavishly – in hotels, out walking, at assemblies, on journeys. . . . But the General had let out that over and above all that, there were special circumstances in his case, that he must 'behave in a special manner'. That was why he had so suddenly lost his spirit and his nerve and changed his tone with me. I had regarded that as informative and taken note of it. And of course, tomorrow he might be foolish enough to go to some authorities or other, so that I must really be careful.

I was not in the least desirous, however, of annoying the General; but now I wanted to make Polina angry. Polina had treated me with such cruelty and had urged me into such a stupid course, that I longed to reduce her to begging me to stop. My schoolboy tricks might finally compromise her as well. Besides, other sentiments and desires were developing within me; if, for example, I wilfully dwindle into nothing with her, that doesn't mean I'm a milksop with other people, and of course there's no question of the Baron 'striking me with his stick'. I've begun to want to have the laugh on the lot of them, and come out as the dashing young hero. Let them watch me! Never fear, she will take fright at the scandal and call me back to her. And even if she doesn't, she will see that I'm not a milksop. . . .

(Astonishing news: I have only this moment heard from the children's nurse, whom I met on the stairs, that Maria Philippovna went off all by herself today by the afternoon train to her cousin's in Carlsbad. What can that mean? Nurse says she's been meaning to go for a long time; but how is it nobody knew? However, perhaps it was only I that didn't know. Nurse told me that Maria Philippovna had words with the General the day before yesterday. That's probably Mademoiselle Blanche. Yes, something decisive is coming.)

CHAPTER SEVEN

NEXT morning I called the waiter and told him my bill must be made out separately. My room was not expensive enough for me to get alarmed and leave the hotel altogether. I had sixteen friedrichs d'or, and there . . . there, perhaps, is riches! It's a strange thing, I haven't won yet, but I feel and think like a rich man and can't imagine being anything else.

In spite of the early hour I was getting ready to go and see Mr Astley at the Hotel d'Angleterre, which is very near us, when de Grieux suddenly came into my room. This has never happened before, and besides, my relations with the gentleman have recently always been extremely strained and distant. He has plainly not been trying to hide his disdain for me, has indeed even tried to show it; and, as for me, I – I have had my own reasons for not feeling friendly towards him. In short, I hate him. His arrival greatly astonished me. I realized at once that something special was brewing.

He came in very amiably and said something pleasant about the room. Seeing that I had my hat in my hands, he inquired whether I was really going out for a walk so early. When he heard, however, that I was going to see Mr Astley on business, he turned it over in his mind for a while, and his face took on an extraordinarily worried expression.

De Grieux is like every other Frenchman, that is to say cheerful and obliging when it is necessary and convenient, and unbearably dull when being cheerful and obliging has ceased to be essential. A Frenchman is rarely amiable by nature; he always seems to be obliging calculatingly and to order, when it pays him. If, for example, he sees the necessity of being eccentric, not commonplace, original, out-of-the-ordinary, his eccentricity, of the silliest and most unnatural kind, will be made up of previously adopted and long-since vulgarized formulas. The natural Frenchman consists of the most bourgeois, petty, everyday stodginess – in short, he is the most boring creature in the world. In my view, only innocents, and especially Russian young ladies, are charmed by the French. Every decent person at once notices the conventionality of their long-established forms of drawing-room politeness, ease, and gaiety, and finds it intolerable.

'I have come to see you on business,' he began in an extremely independent tone, although courteously enough, 'and I won't conceal from you that I am an ambassador, or rather an intermediary, from the General. As I know very little Russian, I understood almost nothing yesterday; but the General has explained all the details, and I must admit ...'

'But listen, Monsieur de Grieux,' I interrupted, 'you have undertaken to be an intermediary in this affair. Of course, I am only an *outchitel*, and have never claimed to be a close friend of the family or to be on any kind of intimate footing, and therefore I don't know all the circumstances; but tell me, are you really a member of the family already? Because, after all, you are so involved in everything, and now you absolutely have to be the intermediary in everything. . . .'

He did not like my question. It was too transparent for him, and he did not want to give any secrets away.

'My connexion with the General is partly a matter of business affairs, and partly *certain special* circumstances,' he said coldly. 'The General has sent me to ask you to abandon your intention of yesterday. Everything you thought of was of course very witty; but he has asked me to put this precise point to you, that you cannot possibly succeed; moreover, the Baron won't see you; and finally, in any case he has, you know, the means of sparing himself any further unpleasantness from you. You must admit that. Then tell me, why go on with it? The General promises faithfully to take you back into his house as soon as ever circumstances are favourable, and until then to continue your salary, *vos appointements*. After all, that will be quite advantageous, won't it?'

I retorted very coolly that he was slightly mistaken; that perhaps I should not be turned away by the Baron, but listened to, and I asked him to admit that he had come precisely in order to try to get me to say how I intended to set about the business.

'Good heavens, since the General is so interested, of course he will like to know what you are going to do and how you are going to do it. It's very natural!'

I set about explaining, and he began to listen, lolling back with his head inclined slightly sideways towards me and a distinct and unconcealed shade of irony in his face. His attitude was altogether extremely condescending. I did my best to pretend that I was looking at the affair from the most serious point of view. I explained that since the Baron had addressed his complaint about me to the General, as though I were the General's servant, he had in the first place lost me my job and secondly treated me as a person who was not in a position to answer for himself and who was not worth speaking to. Of course, I felt justifiably offended; understanding, however, the difference in our ages, our positions in society, and so on and so forth (I could hardly keep a straight face at this point), I did not wish to commit a new folly by directly challenging the Baron, or even merely inviting him, to give me satisfaction. Nevertheless, I considered myself fully entitled to offer him, and especially the Baroness, my apologies, particularly as recently I really had been feeling unwell, unsettled and, so to speak, fanciful, and so on and so forth. The Baron, however, by yesterday's insulting application to the General and insistence that I should be dismissed, had put me in a position where I could no longer offer him and the Baroness my apologies, because both he and the Baroness, and everybody else as well, would probably think I had come to apologize out of fear and in order to get back my post. From all this it followed that I now found myself obliged to ask the Baron to apologize to me himself, in the most moderate terms – by saying, for example, that he had had no intention of insulting me. Then, when the Baron had said that, I should be free to offer him my own sincere and heartfelt apologies. In short, I concluded, all I asked was that the Baron should untie my hands.

'Pah, how punctilious and over-refined! And why should you apologize? Monsieur, monsieur, admit you are launching into all this on purpose to annoy the General . . . and perhaps you have some particular ends . . . *mon cher monsieur* . . . *pardon, j'ai oublié votre nom – Monsieur Alexis, n'est ce pas?*'

'But excuse me, *mon cher marquis*, what has it to do with you?'

'*Mais le général . . .*'

'Or with the General? He said something yesterday about having to be very careful in his conduct . . . and he was very worried . . . but I didn't know what he was talking about.'

'There is ... there definitely is a particular circumstance here,' de Grieux put in, in an imploring tone, through which his annoyance was more and more plainly audible. 'You know Mademoiselle de Cominges? ...'

'Do you mean Mademoiselle Blanche?'

'Well, yes, Mademoiselle Blanche de Cominges ... *et madame sa mère* ... you must agree that the General ... in short, the General is in love and even ... perhaps the marriage will take place here. And in that case, think of all the different scandals and rumours.'

'I don't see either scandals or rumours connected with the marriage.'

'But *le baron est si irascible, un caractère prussien, vous savez, enfin il fera une querelle d'Allemand.*'

'But that will be with me, not with you, because I no longer belong to the household. ...' (I was purposely trying to be as dull-witted as possible.) 'But excuse me, it is settled that Mademoiselle Blanche is to marry the General, then? But what are they waiting for? I mean, why conceal it, at any rate from us, the rest of the household?'

'I can't ... besides, it is not yet quite ... however ... you know they are waiting for news from Russia; the General has business matters to arrange.'

'Ah, ah! *la grand'maman!*'

De Grieux looked at me with hatred.

'In short,' he interrupted, 'I am completely confident of your innate amiability, your intelligence, your tact ... you will of course do this for the family in which you were received as one of themselves, liked, respected. ...'

'Excuse me, I have been turned out! You are now maintaining that it is only for form's sake; but you must admit, if someone said to you: "Of course, I don't want to pull your ears, but for form's sake be good enough to allow your ears to be pulled. ..." Surely it comes to almost the same thing.'

'If that's it, if no requests have any influence on you,' he began with haughty severity, 'allow me to assure you that steps will be taken. There are people in authority here, and you will be sent away this very day – *que diable! un blanc-bec comme vous* attempting to challenge a personage like the Baron to a duel! And do you think you will be left alone? Believe me, nobody here is afraid of you! If I made a request to you, it was more on my own responsibility because you were a nuisance to the General. And do you think, do you really think the Baron won't simply have you thrown out by the footmen?'

'But I shan't be going myself, you know,' I answered with the utmost composure; 'you are mistaken, Monsieur de Grieux, it will all be done with much greater propriety than you think. I shall go at once to Mr Astley and ask him to be my intermediary, in short to be my second. He likes me and is not likely to refuse. He will go to the Baron, and the Baron will receive him. If I am a mere *outchitel* and seem to be in some way *subalterne* and, well, unprotected, Mr Astley is the nephew of a lord, a real live lord, as everybody knows, Lord Pibroch, and that lord is here. Believe me, the Baron will be polite to Mr Astley and listen to him. And if he doesn't, Mr Astley will consider it an insult to himself and send one of his friends to the Baron, and his friends are people of importance. You must now make up your mind that the result may not be at all what you suppose.'

The Frenchman definitely turned tail; all this really was very plausible and consequently it appeared that I was indeed in a position to cause trouble.

'But I beg you,' he began in an extremely imploring voice, 'drop all this! You seem positively pleased that a scandal will result! You don't want satisfaction, you want a scandal! I said the result would be amusing and even witty – which is perhaps what you are trying to achieve, but – in short,' he concluded, seeing that I had stood up and was taking my hat, 'I came to give you these few lines from a certain person; read them – I was told to wait for an answer.'

Saying which, he took from his pocket and handed to me a little note, folded up and sealed with a wafer.

The contents, written in Polina's hand, were these:

It has occurred to me that you intend to prolong this affair. You are angry and beginning to behave like a schoolboy. But there are special circumstances involved, and I will perhaps explain them to you later; but please stop and calm down. How silly all this is! I need you, and you promised to obey me. Remember the Schlangenberg. I beg you, and if necessary I order you, to obey.

Your P.

PS. If you are angry with me about yesterday, please forgive me.

Everything seemed to swim before my eyes when I read these lines. My lips turned pale and I began to tremble. That damned Frenchman looked on with an air of exaggerated self-effacement, turning his eyes aside as though to avoid seeing my confusion. It would have been better if he had laughed aloud.

'Very well,' I answered, 'tell *mademoiselle* not to worry. But permit me to inquire', I added sharply, 'why you did not give me this note for so long. Instead of babbling on about nothing, I think you ought to have begun with that . . . if you came expressly on that errand.'

'Oh, I wanted . . . all this is altogether so odd that you must forgive my natural impatience. I wanted to find out for myself what your intentions were from your own lips, as soon as I could. Besides, I don't know what is in the note, and I thought I should always have time to give it to you.'

'I see; you were simply told to give it me only in the last resort, and not to hand it over at all if you could settle it by word of mouth. Isn't that so? Tell me straight, Monsieur de Grieux !'

'*Peut-être*,' he said, adopting a particularly discreet air and looking at me oddly.

I took up my hat; he bowed and went out. I thought there was a mocking smile on his lips. Indeed, what else was to be expected?

'You and I will have a reckoning yet, my little Frenchman; I'll cross swords with you,' I muttered as I went downstairs.

I was still unable to grasp anything clearly; I felt stunned. The fresh air revived me a little.

After about two minutes, as soon as I began to think coherently, two ideas occurred to me with great clarity : the *first*, that such trifles as a few callow, improbable, puerile threats, so lightly spoken yesterday, had aroused such *general* alarm ! and the *second* – what is that Frenchman's influence over Polina, though? One word from him, and she does everything he wants, writes me a letter, even *begs* me. Of course, the relations between them have always been enigmatic to me from the very beginning, from the time when I first knew them; recently, however, I have noticed a definite dislike and even contempt for him in her, and he has ignored her, has even been downright rude to her. Polina has spoken to me about her loathing for him; she has not been able to help making some extremely significant admissions. . . . So she is simply in his power, he has some kind of hold over her.

CHAPTER EIGHT

ON the promenade, as they call it here, that is in the chestnut avenue, I met my Englishman.

'Oh, oh!' he began as he caught sight of me, 'I was just coming to see you and you were coming to see me. So you have already parted from your friends?'

'Tell me, first of all, how do you come to know all that?' I asked in astonishment; 'does everybody know all about it?'

'Oh no, not everybody; besides, it's hardly worth knowing. Nobody is talking about it.'

'Then how do you know?'

'I know, I mean I happened to hear about it. Now where will you go from here? I like you, and that's why I was coming to see you.'

'You are a good fellow, Mr Astley,' I said (I was seized with immense curiosity, however, about where he could have heard it from), 'and since I haven't had my coffee yet, and yours was probably not very good, let's go into the café at the station, and we can sit down and have a smoke, and I'll tell you everything, and . . . you can tell me, as well.'

The café was not a hundred yards away. They brought us some coffee, we settled down, and I lit a cigarette. Mr Astley did not smoke but fixed his eyes on me and prepared to listen.

'I'm not going anywhere, I'm staying here,' I began.

'I was sure you would stay,' said Mr Astley approvingly.

On my way to see Mr Astley I had had no intention of telling him anything about my love for Polina, and had even deliberately decided not to do so. All this time I had hardly said a word to him about it. Besides, he was himself very shy. I had seen from the first that Polina had produced an immense impression on him, but he never mentioned her name. But now, oddly enough, as soon as he had taken his seat and fixed on me the intent gaze of his pewter-coloured eyes, I felt for some unknown reason a sudden desire to tell him everything, all about my love, I mean, in all its nuances. It took me quite half an hour, and I found it extremely pleasant to be telling somebody about it for the first time! When I noticed, moreover, that at certain particularly ardent passages he became embarrassed, I purposely intensified the ardour of my story. There is one thing I regret: I said too much about the Frenchman, perhaps. . . .

Mr Astley listened, sitting quite still opposite me, and looking straight into my eyes, without uttering a word or making a sound; but when I began to talk about the Frenchman he checked me suddenly and asked me sternly whether I had any right to mention this unconnected circumstance which was no business of mine. Mr Astley always expressed his questions very strangely.

'You are right: I am afraid not,' I answered.

'You can't produce anything more precise than mere conjecture about this Marquis and Miss Polina?'

I was again surprised at so categorical a question from a man as shy as Mr Astley.

'No, nothing precise,' I answered, 'of course not.'

'In that case, you have done wrong . . . not only to speak of it to me, but even to think of it yourself.'

'Very well, very well! I admit it; but that's not the point now,' I interrupted, wondering to myself. Then I told him the whole of yesterday's story in full detail, Polina's caprice, my adventure with the Baron, my dismissal, the General's extraordinary apprehensions; finally I gave him a detailed account of every aspect of my visit this morning from de Grieux; and in conclusion I showed him the note.

'What do you make of it?' I asked. 'I was coming expressly to find out what you thought. As for me, I could kill that nasty little Frenchman, and perhaps I will.'

'So could I,' said Mr Astley. 'As for Miss Polina, well . . . you know, we form connexions even with people we loathe, if necessity forces us. There may be relations here you know nothing about, which depend on extraneous circumstances. I think you may make your mind easy – to a certain extent, of course. As for her action yesterday, it was certainly strange – not because she wanted to get rid of you and sent you to face the Baron's ash-plant (which he did not use, I can't understand why, since he had it in his hand), but because a prank like that is unbecoming in such ... in such a charming miss. Of course, she could not foresee you would carry out her jesting wish literally ...'

'Do you know what!' I exclaimed suddenly, watching Mr Astley closely; '– it seems to me you have already heard all this from, do you know whom? – Miss Polina herself!'

Mr Astley stared at me in amazement.

'Your eyes are sparkling and I can read suspicion in them,' he said, returning immediately to his former calm, 'but you have not the least right to voice those suspicions. I cannot recognize any such right and I absolutely refuse to answer your question.'

'Well, say no more! There is no need!' I cried, strangely excited, and not knowing why it had come into my mind! When, where, and how could Mr Astley have been chosen by Polina as a confidant? Recently, however, I have almost lost sight of Mr Astley, and Polina has always been an enigma to me – so much so that now, for example, having embarked on telling Mr Astley the story of the whole course of my love, I had been struck by the fact that I could say hardly anything precise and positive about my relations with her. On the contrary, it was all fanciful, strange, insubstantial and not even remotely like anything else.

'Well, all right, all right; I'm in a muddle and there are a lot of things I can't grasp,' I answered, gasping as though I was out of breath. 'However, you are a good man. Now about another matter, and I want to ask – not your advice but your opinion.'

I paused and then began :

'Why do you think the General was so scared? Why have they all made such a to-do about my very stupid tomfoolery? Such a to-do that de Grieux himself found it necessary to take a hand (and he takes a hand only in the most important happenings), called on me (how do you like that?), begged and implored me – he, de Grieux, imploring me! Finally, note that he came at nine o'clock or a little before, and Miss Polina's note was already in his hands. The question then arises, when was it written? Perhaps Miss Polina was waked up to do it! Apart from the fact that from all this I can see that Miss Polina is his slave (because she begs even my pardon!) – apart from that, what is all this to her, to her personally? Why is she so interested? Why should they be frightened of any baron? And what does it mean that the General is marrying Mademoiselle Blanche de Cominges? They say that as a result of that circumstance they have to conduct themselves in a *special* fashion – but this after all is altogether too special, you must agree. What do you think? I am sure from the look in your eyes that here again you know more than I do.'

Mr Astley smiled and nodded.

'I think I really do know a great deal more about this than you,' he said. 'This whole business affects only Mademoiselle Blanche, and I am sure that is the absolute truth.'

'Well, what about Mademoiselle Blanche?' I cried impatiently (I had suddenly conceived the hope that something would be revealed about Mademoiselle Polina).

'I think Mademoiselle Blanche has at the present moment a special interest in avoiding any encounter with the Baron and Baroness – still more an unpleasant encounter and most of all a scandalous one.'

'Well! well!'

'Two years ago, during the season, Mademoiselle Blanche was here in Roulettenburg. I also happened to be here. Mademoiselle Blanche was not called Mademoiselle de Cominges at that time, and her mother, Madame *veuve* Cominges, was equally non-existent. At least, she was never even mentioned. De Grieux – de Grieux did not exist either. I feel the strongest possible conviction that not only are they not related to one another, but they have not even been acquainted for very long. De Grieux has also become a marquis only very recently – there is one circumstance that makes me sure of it. One may even suppose that he did not even begin to call himself de Grieux until recently. I know one person here who has met him under another name as well.'

'But surely he has a circle of really reputable acquaintances?'

'Oh, that may be. Even Mademoiselle Blanche may have that. But two years ago Mademoiselle Blanche, on account of a complaint from this same Baroness, was invited by the police to leave the town, and did leave it.'

'How was that?'

'She had appeared here first in the company of an Italian, some sort of prince with a historic name, something like *Barberini* or something of that sort. The man was a mass of rings and diamonds, and not even imitation ones. They went about in a magnificent carriage. Mademoiselle Blanche played *trente et quarante*, at first successfully, but then her luck changed drastically; that is my recollection. I remember that she lost an extremely large sum in one evening. But worst of all, *un beau matin* her prince disappeared, nobody knew where, and the carriage and horses vanished too, everything vanished. The hotel bill was enormous. Mademoiselle Zelma (she had turned suddenly from Barberini into Mademoiselle Zelma) was in the utmost despair. She howled and whined to everybody in the hotel and tore her clothes to shreds in a frenzy. Here in the hotel there was a Polish count (all Polish travellers are counts), and Mademoiselle Zelma, rending her garments and scratching her face like a cat with her beautiful hands steeped in scent, made a certain impression on him. They talked, and by dinner-time she was consoled. In the evening he appeared in the station with her on his arm. Mademoiselle Zelma's laugh was, as usual, very loud, and her manners were a little more unconstrained than before. She had stepped straight into the ranks of those roulette-playing ladies who, when they go up to the tables, will elbow other players aside with all their force, in order to make room for themselves. This is particularly fashionable among such ladies here. You have of course noticed them?'

'Oh yes.'

'They are not worth noticing. To the annoyance of the respectable public they are not expelled here, at least as long as they change thousand-franc notes at the tables every day. As soon, however, as they cease to change notes, they are immediately requested to leave. Mademoiselle Zelma was still continuing to change notes; but her gambling was growing still more unlucky. Note that very frequently these ladies are lucky in their play; they have remarkable control of themselves. My story, however, is finished. One day, exactly like the prince, the count too disappeared.

Mademoiselle Zelma came to the tables in the evening alone; this time nobody had appeared to offer her his arm. In two days she had lost everything. When she had staked her last louis d'or and lost it, she looked round and saw beside her Baron Wurmerhelm, who was watching her attentively and with deep indignation. But Mademoiselle Zelma did not see the indignation and, turning to the Baron with a certain kind of smile, asked him to put ten louis d'or on red for her. In consequence, on a complaint from the Baroness, she received later that day an invitation not to show her face in the station again. If you are surprised that I am acquainted with all these trivial and very unseemly details, it is because I heard them from Mr Feeder, a relative of mine, who took Mademoiselle Zelma with him in his carriage the same evening from Roulettenburg to Spa. Now you must understand that Mademoiselle Blanche wants to become the General's wife, probably so that in future she will not receive any more such invitations from the station police as she did the year before last. She no longer plays now; but that is because, to all appearances, she now has some capital which she lends to gamblers here at interest. That is much more prudent. I even suspect that the unfortunate General is in her debt. So perhaps is de Grieux. Or perhaps de Grieux is her business associate. You must agree that, at least until the wedding, she would not want to attract the Baron and Baroness's notice for any reason at all. In short, in her position a scandal is the worst possible thing for her. But you are connected with their household and your actions might have provoked a scandal, especially as every day she appears arm-in-arm with the General or Miss Polina. Now do you understand?'

'No, I don't,' I shouted, banging my fist on the table so hard that the waiter hurried up in alarm.

'Tell me, Mr Astley,' I repeated in a frenzy, 'if you know all this story and consequently were perfectly well aware what sort of person Mademoiselle Blanche de Cominges is, why didn't you warn me, at least – and the General, and most of all Miss Polina, who has been seen arm-in-arm with Mademoiselle Blanche in public, here in the station? How could you?'

'There was no point in my warning you, because you couldn't do anything,' Mr Astley answered with composure. 'Besides, what was there to give warning about? The General may know even more about Mademoiselle Blanche than I do, and still go on walking with her and Miss Polina. The General is an unfortunate man. Yesterday I saw Miss Blanche riding a beautiful horse, with Monsieur de Grieux and that little Russian prince, and the General galloping along behind them on a chestnut. He had been saying in the morning that his legs ached, but his seat was good. And so at that moment it suddenly came into my head that there went a man who was utterly done for; besides, it is none of my business, and I have only recently had the honour of making Miss Polina's acquaintance. I have already told you, however,' Mr Astley suddenly recollected himself, 'that I can't recognize your right to ask certain questions, although I sincerely like you. . . .'

'That's enough,' I said, getting up; 'it's as clear as daylight to me now that Miss Polina knows all about Mademoiselle Blanche, but she can't part with her Frenchman, and therefore has made up her mind to allow herself to be seen with Mademoiselle Blanche. Believe me, no other reason would have made her be seen in public with Mademoiselle Blanche or beg me in her note not to touch the Baron. This must, in fact, be the influence to which everything is subordinated! And yet, you know, it was she who set me on the Baron! Devil take it, there's no making head nor tail of it!'

'You are forgetting, first that this Mademoiselle de Cominges is the General's fiancée, and secondly that Miss Polina, the General's stepdaughter, has a small brother and sister, the General's own children, whom this madman already utterly neglects and may, I think, have robbed.'

'Yes, yes! that's right! Going away means abandoning the children completely, staying means protecting their interests and perhaps salvaging some small part of the estate. Yes, yes, that's all true! But all the same, all the same! Oh, now I understand why they are all so interested in *grand'maman* now!'

'In whom?' asked Mr Astley.

'That old witch in Moscow who won't die, and they are expecting a telegram to say she is dying.'

'Oh well, yes, of course, everybody's interest is centred on her. The inheritance is everything! when the inheritance is announced, the General will get married; Miss Polina will be free, too, and de Grieux. . . .'

'Well! – and de Grieux?'

'De Grieux will be paid off; that's all he's waiting here for.'

'All! you think that's all he's waiting for?'

'I don't know any more,' – and Mr Astley lapsed into stubborn silence.

'But I do! I know!' I repeated furiously; 'he is waiting for the inheritance too, because Polina will get a dowry, and she will throw herself into his arms the minute she has received the money. Women are all alike. The very proudest of them turn out to be the most abject slaves! Polina is only capable of passionate love, nothing else! That's my opinion of her! Look at her, especially when she is sitting alone and thinking: there is something pre-destined, condemned, fated, there! She is capable of all the horrors of life and passion . . . she . . . she . . . who is that calling to me?' I exclaimed all at once. 'Who is shouting? I heard somebody calling "Alexis Ivanovich!" in Russian. A woman's voice, listen; listen!'

We were by now drawing near to the hotel. A long time earlier we had left the café almost without noticing it.

'I have been hearing a woman calling, but I don't know who to; it's in Russian; now I see where the shouts are coming from,' said Mr Astley, pointing; 'that woman is calling, the one sitting in the big chair there, who has just been carried up the steps by so many footmen. They are bringing luggage behind; that means the train has just got in.'

'But why is she calling me? She is shouting again; look, she's waving to us.'

'I can see she is,' said Mr Astley.

'Alexis Ivanovich! Alexis Ivanovich! Oh Lord, what a block-head!' came despairing cries from the hotel steps.

We almost ran to the entrance. I went up the steps and . . . let my arms fall in consternation, standing rooted to the spot.

CHAPTER NINE

ENTHRONED at the top of the wide flight of steps to the hotel door, in the chair in which she had been carried up them, surrounded by lackeys, maidservants and numerous obsequious menials belonging to the hotel, in the presence of the hotel manager himself, who had come out to greet the distinguished guest arriving with so much bustle and noise, with her own servants and so many portmanteaux and trunks, sat – Grandmamma! Yes, it was herself, the terrible, rich, seventy-five-year-old Antonida Vasilyevna Tarasevichev, landowner and Moscow grand lady, *la grand'-maman*, about whom telegrams had been flying backwards and forwards, who had been dying and was still alive, and who had suddenly descended on us in person out of the blue. She had appeared, although without the use of her legs, and carried about, as she had been for the last five years, in an invalid chair, yet, as usual, brisk, energetic, pleased with herself, sitting up straight, shouting in her loud imperious voice, scolding everybody – in fact, exactly as I had had the honour of seeing her once or twice after I took the post of tutor in the General's house. It was natural that surprise should make me stand there like a dummy. Her lynx eyes had spotted me while I was still a hundred yards away, while she was being carried up the steps in the chair, and she had recognized me and called out my name, which, again as usual, she had learnt once and for all. 'And this is the woman they expected to see in her coffin and buried, leaving them her fortune!' was the thought that flashed through my mind; 'she will outlive all of us and everybody in the hotel! But, my God, what will become of our people now, what will become of the General? She will turn the whole hotel upside down now!'

'Well, what's the matter, young man, why are you standing and staring at me?' Grandmamma went on, still shouting. 'Haven't you been taught to take off your hat and say how d'ye do, eh? Or have you got too proud to do it? Or perhaps you didn't recognize me? Do you hear that, Potapych?' she said, addressing her butler, whom she had brought with her. He was a grey-haired little old man, with a rosy bald patch on the top of his head, wearing a frock-coat and a white tie. 'Do you hear that? – he doesn't know me! They've buried me! They've been sending telegram after telegram: "Is she dead yet or isn't she?" You see I know all about it! Well, now you can see I'm alive, all right.'

'Come now, Antonida Vasilyevna, why should I wish you any harm?' I answered gaily, recovering my wits. 'I was only surprised. . . . How could I help being surprised? it's so unexpected. . . .'

'What is so surprising about it? I got in the train and came. The trains are comfortable, no jolting. Have you been for a walk?'

'Yes, I went as far as the station.'

'It's nice here,' said Grandmamma, looking round. 'It's warm, and there are some fine trees. I like that! Is the family in? The General?'

'Oh, he's sure to be in at this hour, they're all in.'

'They have fixed hours here, then, and observe all the formalities? They set the tone. I'm told they keep a carriage, *les seigneurs russes*! They've got through all their money, so they're off abroad! Is Praskovya with them?'

'Yes, Polina Alexandrovna is here too.'

'And the Frenchman? Well, I shall see them all for myself. Alexis Ivanovich, lead the way, straight to him. And are you comfortable here?'

'Not too bad, Antonida Vasilyevna.'

'You, Potapych, tell that idiot the manager to give me a comfortable suite, a good one, not high up, and take all my things there at once. Why is everybody so anxious to carry me? Why are they all pushing forward? What servility! Who's that with you?' she asked, turning to me again.

'That is Mr Astley,' I answered.

'What Mr Astley?'

'A traveller, a good friend of mine; he knows the General too.'

'An Englishman. Yes, he just stares at me and doesn't open his mouth. However, I like Englishmen. Well, take me upstairs, straight to his rooms; where are they?'

Grandmamma was carried up; I led the way up the broad hotel staircase. Our procession produced a great effect. Everybody we came across stopped and stared. Our hotel is considered the best,

the most expensive and aristocratic in the resort. Everywhere in
the corridors and on the stairs one meets magnificent ladies and
important-looking Englishmen. Many people made inquiries downstairs of the manager, who for his part was deeply impressed. He,
of course, answered all the inquirers that this was a foreign lady
of great importance, *une Russe, une comtesse, grande dame,* and
that she would have the same rooms as those occupied a week ago
by *la grande duchesse de* N. It was Grandmamma's imperious and
commanding appearance that caused the greatest sensation as she
was carried along in her chair. She scanned every new person we
met with inquisitive eyes, and at once questioned me about all of
them in a loud voice. Grandmamma was built on a large scale, and
although she never rose from her chair, one could tell by looking
at her that she was very tall. She kept her spine as straight as a
ramrod and did not lean against the chair-back. Her big grey head,
with its large clear-cut features, was held erect; her glance was
arrogant and even challenging; and it was evident that her looks
and gestures were altogether natural. In spite of her seventy-five
years, her complexion was quite fresh and even her teeth were
fairly good. She wore a black silk dress and a white cap.

'I find her extremely interesting,' Mr Astley whispered as he
walked upstairs beside me.

'She knows about the telegrams,' I thought. 'She knows de
Grieux too, but she doesn't seem to know much about Mademoiselle Blanche yet.' I said as much to Mr Astley at once.

Sinner as I am, I had no sooner got over my first astonishment
than I began to take enormous pleasure in the shock we were
about to give the General. Stimulated by this, I led them cheerfully
on.

Our party was lodged on the second floor; I did not give any
warning, or even knock at the door, but simply flung it wide open,
and Grandmamma was carried in in triumph. They were all
assembled, as if on purpose, in the General's sitting-room. It was
twelve o'clock, and I think they were planning an excursion –
they were going in a body, some in the carriages and some on
horseback; some of their acqaintances had also been invited to join
them. Besides the General, Polina, and the children with their
nurses, there were in the sitting-room de Grieux, Mademoiselle

Blanche, again in her riding-habit, her mother, Madame *veuve*
Cominges, the little prince, and another traveller, some learned
German whom I now saw for the first time. The chair and Grandmamma were set down in the middle of the room, not three paces
from the General. Oh Lord, I shall never forget the effect we produced ! Before our entry the General had been telling people something, with de Grieux setting him right. I must remark that for
two or three days Mademoiselle Blanche and de Grieux had been
dancing attendance on the little prince, for some reason, *à la barbe
du général*, and the mood of the party, although perhaps artificial,
was of the gayest and happiest family intimacy. At the sight of
Grandmamma the General, thunderstruck, gaped and broke off in
the middle of a word. He stared at her with bulging eyes, as though
blasted by the glare of a basilisk. Grandmamma looked at him, also
without saying a word, and without moving – but what a triumphant, challenging and derisive look that was ! They stared at one
another for ten seconds by the clock, while all the rest kept profoundly silent. De Grieux had at first seemed numb, but soon a
shadow of extreme uneasiness flickered over his face. Mademoiselle
Blanche raised her eyebrows, opened her mouth, and stared wildly
at Grandmamma. The prince and the German scholar watched the
scene in profound bewilderment. Polina's look had expressed extreme surprise and perplexity, but suddenly she turned as white
as a sheet; a minute later the blood rushed swiftly into her face
and flooded her cheeks. Yes, this was catastrophic for everybody !
I did nothing but turn my eyes from Grandmamma to the others
round her and back again. Mr Astley, in his usual way, stood
quietly and sedately to one side.

'Well, here I am ! Instead of a telegram !' Grandmamma burst
out at last, breaking the silence. 'What, didn't you expect me ?'

'Antonida Vasilyevna . . . Auntie . . . but how on earth . . .'
muttered the unhappy General. If Grandmamma had kept silence
only a few seconds longer, he might well have had a stroke.

'What do you mean, how ? I got into the train and came. What
is the railway for ? Did you all think I'd turned up my toes and
left you a fortune ? You see, I know all about the telegrams you
have been sending from here. They must have cost you a pretty
penny, I suppose. It's not cheap from here. So I left everything just

as it was, and here I am. Isn't this that Frenchman? Monsieur de Grieux, I think?'

'*Oui, madame,*' de Grieux put in, '*et croyez, je suis si enchanté! ... votre santé ... c'est un miracle ... vous voir ici ... une surprise charmante. ...*'

'*Charmante,* no doubt; I know you, you mountebank, and I don't trust you *that* much !' – and she showed him her little finger. 'Who is this?' she asked, turning and pointing at Mademoiselle Blanche. She was evidently struck by the spectacular French-woman in her riding-habit, with a whip in her hand. 'She lives here, does she?'

'This is Mademoiselle Blanche de Cominges, and this is her mamma, Madame de Cominges; they are staying here in the hotel,' I informed her.

'Is the daughter married?' asked Grandmamma, without ceremony.

'Mademoiselle de Cominges is a single lady,' I answered, as politely as I could, purposely lowering my voice.

'Amusing?'

I hardly understood the question.

'She's not a bore, is she? Does she understand Russian? De Grieux here managed to pick up a few words of the language when he was in Russia.'

I explained that Mademoiselle de Cominges had never been in Russia.

'*Bonjour!*' said Grandmamma, abruptly addressing Mademoiselle Blanche.

'*Bonjour, madame.*' Mademoiselle Blanche swept a ceremonious and graceful curtsey, doing her best, under cover of extraordinary modesty and politeness, to express by the whole aspect of her face and figure her extreme astonishment at such a strange question and such manners.

'Oh, she casts her eyes down, she simpers, she gives herself airs; now I see what she is; she's an actress of some kind. I am staying downstairs here in the hotel,' she went on, turning abruptly to the General; 'I shall be your neighbour; are you pleased or sorry?'

'Oh, Auntie ! Believe me ... my sincere feelings ... my pleasure ...' the General put in quickly. He had already partly recovered his self-possession, and as on occasion he could produce an apt and dignified speech, with some pretensions to effect, he now proceeded to spread himself. 'We were so alarmed and shocked by the news of your indisposition. . . . We have had such despairing telegrams, and now all at once. . . .'

'Oh, lies! lies!' Grandmamma interrupted immediately.

'But how,' the General hastily interrupted in his turn, raising his voice and trying not to notice that word 'lies', '– how did you come to decide on such a journey? You must agree that at your age and with your health . . . at any rate this is all so unexpected that our surprise is understandable. But I am so glad . . . and all of us' (he had begun to wear a sweet and enthusiastic smile) 'will do our utmost to see that you pass the time as pleasantly as possible in your season here. . . .'

'Well, that's enough; empty chatter; you've been talking nonsense, as usual; I know how to spend the time for myself. However, I'm ready to put up with you; I don't nurse grudges. You were asking how I come to be here. But what is surprising about that? It's the simplest thing in the world. Why should everybody be so astonished? Good morning, Praskovya. What do you do here?'

'Good morning, Grandmamma,' said Polina, going up to her; 'did the journey take a long time?'

'Well, now she has asked the most sensible question, otherwise it's been all oh! and ah! Well, you see: I got tired to death of lying in bed and being doctored, so I sent the doctors packing and called in the sexton from St Nicholas. He cured a peasant woman of the same illness with hay-dust. Well, he did me good, too; on the third day I was all in a sweat, and I got up. Then my Germans all came back, put on their spectacles and took charge again: "If you go abroad to a spa," they said, "and take the waters, your constipation will go completely." And I thought, why not? Those fools of Zazhigins made a fuss: "You'll never get there!" they said. Well, you don't say so! I got ready in one day, and on Friday last week I brought a girl, and Potapych, and Fyodor the footman, but I sent Fyodor back from Berlin, because I could see I didn't need him and I could have got here all by myself. . . . I took a special carriage, and there are porters at all the stations, they'll carry you wherever you want for twenty copecks. Well, well, look at the suite you have taken !' she finished, looking round. 'Where did you get the money, my dear? After all, everything you've got is mortgaged. What you must owe this little Frenchman alone ! I know all about everything, you see, all about everything !'

'I . . . I'm surprised, Auntie . . .' began the General quite disconcerted. 'I don't think anyone has the right to dictate to me how . . . and besides, my expenditure doesn't exceed my means, and we are here. . . .'

'Doesn't exceed your means, you say? That must be because you've already robbed your children of the last copeck you held in trust for them !'

'After that, after saying things like that . . .' began the General indignantly, 'I really don't know . . .'

'That's right, you don't know ! I suppose you're never away from the roulette games? Have you thrown everything away yet?'

The General was so shocked that he almost choked with the rush of agitated feeling.

'Roulette ! I? A man of my standing . . . I? Think what you're saying, Auntie; you must still be unwell. . . .'

'Oh, lies, lies ! I don't suppose they can drag you away; you always lie ! I intend to go and see what roulette is like this very day. You, Praskovya, can tell me what there is to look at here and where it is, and Alexis Ivanovich here will show me, and you, Potapych, write down all the places we can go to. What do people go to see here?' she asked turning abruptly back to Polina.

'There are some castle ruins quite near, and then there's the Schlangenberg.'

'What's the Schlangenberg? A wood?'

'No, it's not a wood, it's a mountain; there's a *pointe* . . .'

'What sort of *pointe*?'

'The very highest point of the mountain, it's fenced in. The view from there is magnificent.'

'That means lugging my chair up a mountain? Could it be got up?'

'Oh, we can find porters,' I answered.

At this point Fedosya, the nurse, came up to pay her respects to Grandmamma, and led the General's children up to her as well.

'Well, there's no need to kiss me ! I don't like kissing children;

all children have runny noses. Well, how do you like being here, Fedosya?'

'It's very, very nice here, Antonida Vasilyevna, madam,' answered Fedosya. 'And how have you been, madam dear? We've been worrying ourselves sick about you.'

'I know; you're a good soul. Who have you got here, all visitors, eh?' – she addressed Polina again. 'Who's that shabby-looking little man in glasses?'

'Prince Nilsky, Grandmamma,' Polina whispered.

'Oh, a Russian? and I thought he wouldn't understand! Perhaps he didn't hear! Mr Astley I've seen already. Yes, there he is again,' Grandmamma exclaimed, catching sight of him; 'how d'ye do?' she said to him.

Mr Astley bowed silently.

'Well, what have you got to say to me? Say something! Translate for him, Polina.'

Polina translated it.

'That it is a great pleasure to see you, and I am glad to see you well,' answered Mr Astley solemnly but very readily. This was translated to Grandmamma and evidently pleased her greatly.

'How nicely the English always answer when you speak to them,' she remarked. 'I've always liked Englishmen for some reason, there's no comparison with those nasty Frenchies! You must come and see me,' she said again to Mr Astley. 'I will try not to be too troublesome to you. Translate that to him, and tell him I am downstairs – downstairs – downstairs, do you understand? downstairs,' she went on repeating to Mr Astley and pointing downwards with her stick.

Mr Astley was delighted with the invitation.

Grandmamma examined Polina from head to foot with an attentive and satisfied look.

'I might get fond of you, Praskovya,' she said abruptly; 'you're a fine girl, the best of the bunch, and a will of your own, as well. Well, I've got a will of my own too; turn round, is that a switch you're wearing?'

'No, Grandmamma, it's my own hair.'

'That's right, I don't like these silly modern fashions. You're very pretty. I should fall in love with you if I were a young man.

Why don't you get married? However, it's time I went. And I
want to get some fresh air, it's been nothing but the railway-
carriage all the time. . . . Well, what's the matter, are you still
annoyed?' she asked the General.

'For goodness' sake, Auntie, don't!' the General put in with
renewed cheerfulness. 'I know that at your age . . .'

'*Cette vieille est tombée en enfance,*' de Grieux whispered to me.

'Well, I want to see everything here. You'll let me have Alexis
Ivanovich, won't you?' went on Grandmamma.

'Oh, whenever you like, but I myself . . . and Polina and Monsieur de Grieux . . . we shall all think it a pleasure to go with
you, all of us. . . .'

'*Mais, madame, cela sera un plaisir . . .*' put in de Grieux with
a dazzling smile.

'*Plaisir,* I dare say! I find you ridiculous, young man. However,
I shan't give you any money,' she added abruptly to the General.
'Well, now I'll go to my room; I must look round here and then
we'll go to all the places round about. Well, lift me up.'

Grandmamma was picked up again and we all followed her
chair down the stairs in a body. The General walked like a man
stunned by a blow on the head. De Grieux was pondering over
something. Mademoiselle Blanche had at first meant to stay behind, but had for some reason changed her mind and decided to go
with the rest. Immediately behind her came the prince, and only
the German and Madame *veuve* Cominges were left upstairs in
the General's rooms.

CHAPTER TEN

AT spas – and, I think, all over Europe – hotel-keepers and man-
agers, when they assign rooms to guests, are guided not so much
by the guests' demands and wishes as by their own personal view
of them; and it must be observed that they rarely make mistakes.
But for some cause Grandmamma had been given a suite so luxurious that it was beyond all reason: four magnificently furnished
rooms, a bathroom, servants' rooms, a special room for the lady's-
maid, and so on. A *grande duchesse* really had been occupying the

rooms a week earlier, and of course the new arrivals were immediately informed of this to give an even greater value to the suite. Grandmamma was carried, or rather pushed, round all the rooms and she inspected them with strict attention. The manager, an elderly man, going bald, respectfully escorted her on this first survey.

I don't know what they all took Grandmamma for, but it was apparently for an extremely important and, what mattered most, extremely rich personage. They immediately entered in the register: *Madame la générale princesse de Tarassévitchéva*, although Grandmamma had never been a princess. Her servants, her special railway-carriage, and the enormous numbers of unnecessary portmanteaux, suit-cases and even trunks which had arrived with her, were probably the first causes of her prestige; and her chair, her sharp tone and harsh voice, her eccentric questions, delivered in a most uninhibited fashion and tolerating no objections, in short the whole figure Grandmamma cut – erect, harsh and imperious – completed the awe in which she was held. During her inspection Grandmamma occasionally gave a sudden order for the chair to be stopped, pointed to some item of furniture and addressed unexpected questions to the manager, who was still smiling politely but already beginning to be apprehensive. Grandmamma put her questions in French, which she spoke, however, rather badly, so that I usually translated for her. For the most part the manager's answers were not to her liking and seemed unsatisfactory. And indeed the questions themselves seemed always as it were beside the point, concerned with God knows what. For example, she suddenly stopped in front of a picture, a rather feeble copy of a well-known original, with a mythological subject.

'Whose portrait is that?'

The manager declared that it was probably some countess.

'How is it you don't know? You live here and yet you don't know. Why is it here? Why do the eyes squint?'

The manager was unable to find a satisfactory answer to any of these questions and grew flustered.

'Blockhead!' exclaimed Grandmamma in Russian.

She was carried on. The same story was repeated with a Dresden china statuette, which Grandmamma scrutinized for a long time and then ordered to be removed, I don't know why. Finally, she insisted on knowing what the carpets in the bedroom had cost and where they were made. The manager promised to inquire.

'Donkeys!' grumbled Grandmamma, turning all her attention to the bed.

'That's a very splendid canopy! Turn down the bed.'

They did so.

'More, more, unmake it all. Take off the pillows and pillow-cases, lift up the feather bed.'

They unmade the whole bed. Grandmamma watched closely.

'It's a good thing there are no bugs. Take away all the linen! Put my sheets and pillows on. Only all this is too luxurious; what does an old woman like me want with this kind of suite? It's boring for one person. Alexis Ivanovich, you come to me as often as you can, when the children's lessons are over.'

'I haven't been employed by the General since yesterday,' I answered. 'I am staying in the hotel quite by myself.'

'Why is that?'

'A distinguished German Baron came here from Berlin with the Baroness, his wife, a few days ago. Yesterday when I was out I spoke to him in German and I didn't stick to the Berlin accent.'

'Well, what then?'

'He thought that was impertinent and complained to the General, and the General dismissed me the same day.'

'Why, did you swear at him, this Baron? (Even if you had, it wouldn't matter!)'

'Oh no. On the contrary, the Baron threatened me with his stick.'

'And you allowed your tutor to be treated like that, you little sniveller,' she exclaimed to the General, 'and turned him out of his place into the bargain! You're a feeble lot, I can see, all of you!'

'Don't worry, Auntie,' answered the General, with a touch of haughty familiarity, 'I know how to look after my own affairs. Besides, Alexis Ivanovich has not been quite accurate in his account.'

'And you put up with it?' she asked me.

'I wanted to challenge the Baron to a duel,' I answered as modestly and quietly as possible, 'but the General objected.'

'And why did you object?' Grandmamma turned to the General again. 'And you may go, my man; you can come back when you are called,' she added to the manager; 'there's no need for you to stand there gaping. I can't stand that ugly Nuremburg face of yours!' The manager bowed and went out, of course not understanding Grandmamma's compliments.

'Oh come, Auntie, we can't have duels, can we?' the General answered with a grin.

'Why not? Men are all cocks, so they ought to fight. You're all ninnies, I can see that, you can't stick up for your own country. Well, lift me up. Potapych, arrange to have two porters always ready, hire them, and agree on the payment with them. There's no need for more than two. I only have to be carried up and downstairs, but on the level out of doors I can be pushed, tell them that; and pay them in advance, they'll be more respectful. You must be with me all the time yourself, and you, Alexis Ivanovich, point out this Baron to me in the street: I'd like to have a look at this von-Baron, just to see what he's like. Well, where is this roulette?'

I explained that the roulette tables were in gambling saloons at the railway station. Then followed questions about whether there were many of them, and whether many people played. Did play go on all day? How did one play? I answered at last that it was best to see for oneself; it was rather difficult simply to describe it.

'Well, carry me straight there, then. Lead the way, Alexis Ivanovich!'

'Why, Auntie, aren't you even going to rest after your journey?' asked the General solicitously. He had begun to seem fidgety, and indeed they were all somewhat embarrassed and had begun to exchange glances. Probably they all felt a little awkward and even shamefaced at the idea of accompanying Grandmamma straight to the station, where she might of course do something eccentric, and in public, too; and yet at the same time they all felt called upon to go with her.

'Why should I rest? I'm not tired; I've been sitting still for five days as it is. Afterwards we'll see what kind of springs and

medicinal waters they have here, and where they are. And then
. . . what's that – you told me, Praskovya – *pointe*, was it?'

'Yes, Grandmamma, *pointe*.'

'Well, *pointe* then, if that's what it is. And what else is there
here?'

'There's a lot of things, Grandmamma,' Polina began hesitantly.

'Why, you don't know yourself! Martha, you come with me
too,' she said to her maid.

'But why do you want her, Auntie?' the General began fussily;
'and besides, you can't take her; it's doubtful whether they'll let
even Potapych right into the station rooms.'

'Rubbish! Just because she's a servant, I'm to leave her behind!
She's a human being too, you know; here we've been travelling
on the railways for a week, she wants to see things, too. Who can
she go with, if not me? She wouldn't dare show her nose in the
streets by herself.'

'But Grandmamma . . .'

'Are you ashamed of being with me, eh? Stay at home then,
nobody's asked you to come. A fine general you are! and I'm a
general's widow myself. And anyhow, why should such a long
line of you come trailing along behind me? I can look at everything with Alexis Ivanovich.'

But de Grieux emphatically insisted that everybody must accompany her and launched into the most charming phrases about
the pleasure of escorting her and so on. We all moved off.

'*Elle est tombée en enfance*,' de Grieux repeated to the General;
'*seule elle fera des bêtises. . . .*' I did not hear any more, but he had
evidently formed some sort of plan and perhaps his hopes had
even been renewed.

It was about half a verst to the station. Our way lay along the
chestnut avenue to the square, and round that directly into the
station. The General was a little reassured because our procession,
although odd enough, was nevertheless sedate and respectable.
And besides, there was nothing surprising in the appearance at
the spa of somebody who was weak and ill and could not walk.
But evidently it was the station that the General feared: why
should somebody who was ill and unable to use her legs, and an
old woman into the bargain, go into the gaming rooms? Polina

and Mademoiselle Blanche walked one on each side of the chair as it rolled along. Mademoiselle Blanche smiled, was modestly gay and sometimes even made extremely polite advances to Grandmamma, so that in the end she forced some words of praise from her. Polina, on the other side, was obliged to answer Grandmamma's incessant and innumerable questions, like: 'Who was that who went past? Who's that in the carriage? Is it a big town? Are the gardens big? What sort of trees are those? What are those mountains? Do you see eagles here? What is that funny roof?' Mr Astley, who was walking beside me, whispered that he was expecting a great deal to happen that morning. Potapych and Martha came immediately behind the chair, Potapych in his frockcoat and white tie, but wearing a cap, and Martha, the forty-year-old maid, rosy-cheeked, but already turning grey, in a cap, a cotton-print dress and squeaking goatskin shoes. Grandmamma very frequently turned round and talked to them. De Grieux and the General had fallen a little behind and were conducting an extremely heated conversation. The General was depressed; de Grieux talked with a very positive air. Perhaps he was trying to encourage the General; he was obviously giving him advice. But not long before, Grandmamma had already uttered the fatal words: 'I shan't give you any money.' Perhaps this statement seemed unlikely to de Grieux, but the General knew his Auntie. I noticed that Mademoiselle Blanche and de Grieux continued to signal to one another with their eyes. I could make out the prince and the German traveller at the very end of the avenue: they had lagged behind and were going somewhere else.

We made a triumphal entry into the station. The hall-porter and the footmen showed the same deference as the hotel servants. They looked at us, however, with some curiosity. First of all, Grandmamma had herself carried through all the saloons; some she approved of, some left her completely indifferent; she asked questions about everything. At last we came to the gaming rooms. The footman standing on guard by the closed doors appeared startled and flung them wide open.

Grandmamma's appearance at the roulette table produced an immense effect on the public. Several deep round the roulette tables and at the other end of the room, where there was a table for *trente et quarante*, were clustered perhaps a hundred and fifty or two hundred people. Those who had succeeded in pushing their way through to the table remained there firmly, as usual, and did not yield up their places until they had lost their money; for to stand there simply as spectators, occupying a player's place without playing, is not allowed. Although chairs are placed round the table, few of the players sit down, especially when there is a great concourse of people, because standing they can crowd closer together, thus saving space, and also place their stakes more conveniently. The second and third rows crowded behind the first, waiting and watching for their turn; but sometimes an impatient hand would be thrust through the front row to put down a large sum. Even from the third row some people contrived to push forward their stakes in this way; for this reason ten, or even five, minutes could not pass without the beginning of a 'scene' over disputed stakes at one end or other of the table. The station police are, however, fairly good. It is impossible, of course, to avoid crowding; on the contrary, they are glad that the public should flock there, because it is profitable; but eight croupiers sitting round the table keep a vigilant watch on the stakes: they do the paying out also, and when disputes arise they settle them as well. In extreme cases they call the police and the matter is over in a minute. Plain-clothes policemen are distributed about the room itself, mingling with the spectators so that they cannot be recognized. They keep a special watch for petty thieves and pickpockets, who are especially numerous round the tables because of the unusual facilities for their trade. Everywhere else, indeed, thefts must be carried out by picking pockets or breaking locks and, if unsuccessful, have very troublesome consequences. Here, on the other hand, one need only go up to the table, begin to play, and all at once, openly and publicly, pick up somebody else's winnings and put them in one's pocket; if an argument is started, the thief loudly insists that the stake was his own. If the thing is deftly done and the witnesses hesitate, the thief very often succeeds in getting away with the money, unless, of course, it is a considerable sum. In that case it will probably have been noticed earlier by the croupiers or one of the other players. But if the amount is not very large, the real owner, ashamed of making a fuss, sometimes simply refuses to prolong the dispute and goes away. But if they succeed in detecting a thief, he is publicly disgraced and at once removed.

Grandmamma watched all this with avid curiosity from a distance. She was delighted at the idea of petty thieves being turned out. *Trente et quarante* did not arouse much interest in her; she liked roulette, and seeing the ball roll, better. Finally she expressed a wish to watch the play more closely. I don't understand how it happened, but the footmen and some other officious persons (chiefly Poles who had lost their money and who thrust their services on luckier players and on all foreigners) immediately found and cleared a place for Grandmamma, in spite of all the crowd, right in the middle of the table near the head croupier, and pushed her chair to it. Many visitors who were not themselves gambling but watching the play from one side (chiefly Englishmen with their families) at once crowded closer to the table to stare at Grandmamma from behind the players. A number of lorgnettes were turned in her direction. The croupiers' hopes were aroused: so odd a player really seemed to promise something out of the ordinary. A crippled woman of seventy-five who wanted to play was not, of course, an everyday sight. I also pushed my way to the table and settled myself beside Grandmamma. Potapych and Martha were left far away to the side among the crowd. The General, Polina, de Grieux and Mademoiselle Blanche were also standing to one side among the spectators.

Grandmamma began by scrutinizing the players. She asked me sharp, abrupt questions in a half-whisper: who's that? who is that woman? She particularly liked one very young man at the end of the table, who was playing for very big stakes, putting down thousands at a time, and who, it was being whispered round us, had already won upwards of forty thousand francs, which lay before him in a heap, gold and banknotes piled up together. He was pale; his eyes flashed and his hands shook; he staked in handfuls, without counting, and he went on winning and winning again, raking in more and more money. Footmen were bustling around him, pushing a chair up behind him, clearing a space round him so that he could have more room and not be crowded – all in the expectation of a rich harvest of gratitude. Some players will sometimes tip out of their winnings, also without counting, simply taking handfuls of coins out of their pockets in their joy. Near the young man a Pole had already taken up his position, making a great show of activity, whispering respectfully but incessantly, probably pointing out where to put the stakes, giving advice and trying to direct the play – and of course also expecting a subsequent tip. But the gambler hardly looked at him, staked at random and went on winning. He was evidently losing his head.

Grandmamma watched him for a few minutes.

'Tell him,' she said, nudging me in sudden excitement, 'tell him to stop, tell him to take his money as quickly as possible and leave. He'll lose, he'll lose the lot in a minute!' she cried anxiously, almost breathless with agitation. 'Where's Potapych? Send Potapych to him! Tell him, tell him!' she urged me; 'but where can Potapych be? *Sortez! sortez!*' she began shouting herself to the young man. I stooped towards her and whispered firmly that she must not shout like that here, and that even raising one's voice only a little was not permitted, because it interfered with people's calculations, and we should be turned out in a moment.

'What a pity! The man's done for! Well, it's his own fault. . . . I can't look at him, it makes me feel sick. Stupid fool!' and Grandmamma hurriedly turned to look another way.

There on the left, on the other half of the table, a young woman, by herself except for a dwarf, was conspicuous among the players. Who the dwarf was I don't know: a relative, perhaps, or perhaps she simply brought him with her for effect. I had noticed the young lady before: she appeared at the tables every day at one o'clock in the afternoon, and left at exactly two; every day she played for one hour. They knew her already, and immediately placed a chair for her. She took out of her pocket a little gold and a few thousand-franc notes and began laying her stakes coolly and quietly, with calculation, noting down the numbers on a piece of paper with a pencil and trying to discover the system on which at a given moment the chances grouped themselves. She staked considerable sums of money. Every day she won a thousand or two thousand, or at most three thousand francs, not more, and when she had won, she immediately left. Grandmamma watched her for a long time.

'Well, *she* won't lose! That one there won't lose! Where does she come from? Do you know? Who is she?'

'She must be a Frenchwoman, of a certain class,' I whispered.

'Ah, you can tell the bird by the way it flies. Her claws are sharp, you can see! Now tell me what every turn means and how to stake.'

As well as I could I explained to Grandmamma the meaning of the numerous combinations of *rouge et noir, pair et impair, manque et passe,* and finally the ins and outs of staking on the numbers. Grandmamma listened carefully, remembered, asked questions, and learned bits by heart. It was possible to show an example at once of every method of staking, so that learning and remembering a great deal was both quick and easy. Grandmamma was very pleased.

'And what is *zéro*? That croupier there with curly hair, the head one, called out *zéro* just now. And why did he rake in everything that was anywhere on the table? Such a heap; why did he take it all for himself? What is it?'

'*Zéro* means the bank wins, Grandmamma. If the little ball falls into *zéro*, whatever has been staked goes to the bank. It's true there is one coup that neither wins nor loses, but the bank doesn't pay anything out.'

'Well, well! and I don't get anything?'

'Yes, Grandmamma, if you have staked on *zéro*, you get paid thirty-five times as much when *zéro* comes up.'

'What, thirty-five times, does it often turn up? Why don't they stake on it, the fools?'

'Thirty-six chances against, Grandmamma.'

'Rubbish! Potapych, Potapych! Wait, I have some money with me – here!' She took a tightly stuffed purse out of her pocket and took out a friedrichs d'or. 'Take this and put it on *zéro* at once.'

'Grandmamma, *zéro* has only just turned up,' I said, 'so now it won't turn up again for a long time. You'll lose a lot of stakes; wait a little while.'

'Rubbish, put it down!'

'Very well, but it may not turn up again until evening. You may lose as much as a thousand, it has been known to happen!'

'Oh nonsense, nonsense! Nothing venture, nothing gain. If

people are afraid of wolves they ought to keep out of the forest. Well? has it lost? Stake again!'

The second friedrichs d'or was also lost; we staked a third. Grandmamma could hardly sit still; her blazing eyes were fixed on the little ball skipping over the notches of the spinning wheel. The third coin was lost as well. Grandmamma was beside herself; she could not bear to sit still, she even banged the table with her fist when the croupier announced *trente six* instead of the expected *zéro*.

'Devil take it!' Grandmamma raged; 'isn't that damned little *zéro* turning up soon? As sure as I live, I'll sit here until it does! It's that damned curly-haired croupier that's doing it, it will never turn up for him! Alexis Ivanovich, stake two gold pieces at once! With the amount you're staking, even if *zéro* comes up you won't win anything.'

'Grandmamma!'

'Stake them, stake them! It's not your money.'

I put down two friedrichs d'or. The ball ran along the wheel for a long time, then began bouncing over the partitions. Grandmamma sat rigid, as though turned to stone, clutching my hand, and all at once – plop! 'Zéro,' announced the croupier.

'You see, you see!' Grandmamma turned quickly to me, radiant with delight. 'I told you so, I told you so! And the Lord himself inspired me to stake two gold pieces! Well, how much shall I get now? Why don't they give it to me? Potapych, Martha! where can they be? Where have all the others got to? Potapych, Potapych!'

'Afterwards, Grandmamma,' I whispered. 'Potapych is near the door, they won't let him come here. Look, Grandmamma, they are giving you your money, take it.'

A heavy roll of fifty friedrichs d'or in a sealed blue-paper wrapping was thrust towards Grandmamma, and twenty loose gold pieces counted out after it. I gathered it all up for Grandmamma in a scoop.

'*Faites le jeu, messieurs! Faites le jeu, messieurs! Rien ne va plus!*' the croupier was calling out, inviting the players to place their stakes and preparing to spin the wheel.

'Oh Lord! we're too late! They're going to spin it now! Play,

play !' cried Grandmamma in agitation. 'Don't hang about, be quick !' She was almost beside herself, poking at me with all her strength.

'Where shall I put the stake, Grandmamma?'

'On *zéro*, on *zéro*! put it on *zéro* again! Stake as much as you can! How much have we got altogether? Seventy friedrichs d'or? No need to spare them, put twenty on at a time.'

'Think what you're doing, Grandmamma! It sometimes doesn't come up once in two hundred times! I warn you, you'll lose your whole fortune!'

'Oh rubbish, rubbish! Put it down! You talk too much! I know what I'm doing.' Grandmamma was positively shaking with frenzy.

'The rules say you're not allowed to put more than twelve friedrichs d'or on *zéro*, Grandmamma – well, you see I've staked them.'

'What do you mean, not allowed? You're lying, aren't you? Mossoo, mossoo!' she prodded the croupier, sitting immediately on her left, and preparing to spin the wheel. '*Combien zéro? douze? douze?*'

I hastily rephrased the question in intelligible French.

'*Oui, madame*,' the croupier politely confirmed, 'just as every individual stake must not exceed four thousand florins at one time, according to the rules,' he added in explanation.

'Well, it can't be helped, put down twelve.'

'*Le jeu est fait!*' the croupier called out. The wheel turned, and thirteen came up. We had lost!

'Again, again, again! Stake again!' cried Grandmamma. I raised no more objections but shrugged my shoulders and staked a further twelve friedrichs d'or. The wheel spun for a long time. Grandmamma positively quivered as she followed it with her eyes. 'Can she really believe she will win again on *zéro*?' I wondered, looking at her with astonishment. A definite conviction that she would win shone in her face, an unshakeable expectation that at any moment would come the call of *zéro*. The ball dropped into the compartment.

'*Zéro!*' called the croupier.

'Well!' Grandmamma turned to me with a flourish of triumph.

I was a gambler myself; I realized it at that moment. My arms and legs were trembling and my head throbbed. It was, of course, a rare happening for *zéro* to come up three times out of some ten or so; but there was nothing particularly astonishing about it. I had myself seen *zéro* turn up three times running two days before, and on that occasion one of the players, zealously recording all the coups on a piece of paper, had remarked aloud that no earlier than the previous day that same *zéro* had come out exactly once in twenty-four hours.

Grandmamma, as the winner of a very considerable sum of money, was treated with special consideration and politeness as it was counted out. She received exactly 420 friedrichs d'or, that is 4,000 florins and twenty friedrichs d'or. They gave her the twenty in gold and the 4,000 florins in banknotes.

This time Grandmamma did not try to summon Potapych; she had other things to think about. She was not even quivering or trembling outwardly. If I may so express it, she was trembling inwardly. She was wholly concentrated on one thing, and she simply aimed straight at it.

'Alexis Ivanovich! he did say only four thousand florins can be staked at once, didn't he? Here you are, take this and put all four thousand on red,' Grandmamma decided.

It was useless to argue. The wheel turned.

'*Rouge!*' the croupier announced.

Again a win of 4,000 florins, and consequently a total of 8,000.

'Give four here to me, and put four on red again.' Grandmamma commanded.

I staked 4,000 again.

'*Rouge!*' announced the croupier once more.

'That's twelve thousand altogether; give it all here to me. Pour the gold into my purse, here, and hide the notes.

'That's enough. Home! Push my chair away!'

CHAPTER ELEVEN

THE chair was pushed to the door at the other end of the room. Grandmamma was radiant. The rest of our party at once crowded round her with their congratulations. However eccentric Grandmamma's conduct might be, her triumph had covered up many things and the General no longer feared to compromise himself in public by his family relations with such an odd old woman. With a smile of familiar benignity, he congratulated Grandmamma as though he were humouring a baby. He was evidently impressed, however, as were all the other onlookers. People all round were talking about Grandmamma and pointing her out. Many of them walked past in order to get a closer look at her. Mr Astley was talking about her to two of his English friends a short distance away. A few stately ladies who had been looking on gazed at her with majestic bewilderment, as though at some miracle. De Grieux showered smiles and compliments on her.

'*Quelle victoire!*' he said.

'*Mais, madame, c'était du feu!*' added Mademoiselle Blanche with an ingratiating smile.

'Yes, here I've been and won twelve thousand florins! Twelve? what about the gold? With the gold it will be almost thirteen thousand. How much is that in our money? It will be about six thousand, won't it?'

I informed her that it would be more than 7,000 roubles and at the present rate of exchange might be as much as 8,000.

'Eight thousand, not to be sneezed at! And you ninnies sit here doing nothing. Potapych, Martha, did you see?'

'Oh, madam, how did you do it? Eight thousand roubles!' exclaimed Martha, wriggling.

'Here you are, there's five gold pieces each for you!'

Potapych and Martha hurried to kiss her hand.

'And give the porters a friedrichs d'or each. Give it them in gold, Alexis Ivanovich. Why's that footman bowing and scraping, and the other one, too? They're congratulating me, are they? Give them a friedrichs d'or each as well.'

'*Madame la princesse . . . un pauvre expatrié . . . malheur continuel . . . les princes russes sont si généreux . . .*' – this was a whiskered personage in a threadbare frock-coat and bright-coloured waistcoat, his cap raised high in the air, who was hanging about the chair with an obsequious smile.

'Give him a friedrichs d'or as well. No, give him two; well, that's enough, or there'll be no getting rid of them. Lift me up, take me home! Praskovya,' she turned to Polina Alexandrovna, 'I'll buy you the stuff for a dress tomorrow, and that Mademoiselle . . . what's her name? Mademoiselle Blanche, is it? I'll buy her one as well. Translate that, Praskovya!'

'*Merci, madame,*' Mademoiselle Blanche curtseyed gracefully, her mouth twisted in the wry smile which she was exchanging with de Grieux and the General. The General was somewhat embarrassed and was delighted when we reached the avenue.

'Fedosya, I was just thinking how surprised Fedosya will be now,' said Grandmamma, remembering the General's nurse. 'I must give her enough for a dress, as well. Hey, Alexis Ivanovich, Alexis Ivanovich, give this beggar something!'

A ragged hump-backed wretch was staring at us as he went past.

'Perhaps he's not a beggar at all, but some sort of rogue, Grandmamma.'

'Give him something, I say! Give him a gulden.'

I went up to the man and gave him the gulden. He looked at me with wild astonishment, but took it without a word. He smelt of drink.

'And have you tried your luck yet, Alexis Ivanovich?'

'No, Grandmamma.'

'But your eyes were blazing, I saw them.'

'I shall certainly try later on, Grandmamma.'

'And put your money straight on *zéro*. Then you'll see! How much money have you?'

'Only twenty friedrichs d'or altogether, Grandmamma.'

'Not enough. I'll lend you fifty more, if you like. Take this roll they gave me, but as for you, my fine fellow,' she turned abruptly to the General, 'don't expect me to give you anything, all the same, because I won't!'

He was bitterly disappointed, but he said nothing. De Grieux knitted his brows.

'*Que diable, c'est une terrible vieille!*' he muttered to the General through clenched teeth.

'A beggar, a beggar, there's another beggar!' cried Grandmamma. 'Give that one a gulden as well, Alexis Ivanovich.'

This time we had met a grey-haired man with a wooden leg, wearing some sort of dark-blue long-skirted frock-coat and carrying a long stick. He looked like an old soldier. But when I held out a gulden to him he took a step backwards and stared at me menacingly.

'*Was ist's, der Teufel!*' he shouted, following it with a dozen oaths.

'Well, he's a fool!' cried Grandmamma, with a wave of her hand. 'Get along! I'm starving! We'll have dinner at once, then I'll have a short nap and go back again.'

'Do you want to play again, Grandmamma?' I exclaimed.

'What do you think? That I have to watch you sitting moping here?'

'*Mais, madame,*' urged de Grieux, who had come up to us, '*les chances peuvent tourner, une seule mauvaise chance, et vous perdrez tout ... surtout avec votre jeu ... c'était terrible!*'

'*Vous perdrez absolument,*' twittered Mademoiselle Blanche.

'And what business is it of yours, all of you? It's not your money I'm losing, it's my own! But where is that Mr Astley?' she asked me.

'He stayed in the station, Grandmamma.'

'A pity. He's such a nice man.'

When we reached home Grandmamma, meeting the hotel manager while she was still on the stairs, called to him and bragged about how she had won at roulette; then she summoned Fedosya, gave her three friedrichs d'or and ordered her to serve dinner. Fedosya and Martha never stopped singing her praises all through dinner.

'I was watching you, madam,' chattered Martha, 'and I says to Potapych, what's our madam going to do? And then on the table there was piles and piles of money, why goodness gracious me, I never saw so much money in all my life, and ladies and gentlemen sitting all round, nothing but ladies and gentlemen everywhere. And I said to Potapych, wherever did all those ladies and gentlemen come from, Potapych? I said. I thought, God's blessed mother help her. I was praying for you, madam dear, and I was so frightened my heart nearly stopped, and I was shaking, I was shaking all over. I was thinking, oh, Lord help her! And now you see the Lord has sent you luck. I'm still shaking right up to this minute, madam, I'm all of a shake, look!'

'After dinner, Alexis Ivanovich, get ready about four o'clock and we'll go. And now good-bye for the moment, and don't forget to send for a doctor for me, I must drink the waters as well. Or else you might forget about it.'

I was in a sort of daze when I left Grandmamma. I tried to think what would happen to all the family now, and what course events would take. It was clear to me that none of them (and especially not the General) had yet had time to recover even from the first shock. The fact that Grandmamma had appeared instead of the telegram, expected at any moment, with the news of her death (and consequently of the money she had left), had so shattered their whole framework of plans and intentions that their attitude towards her further exploits at roulette was one of positive bewilderment and a sort of stupor that affected them all alike. And yet this second fact was almost more important than the first, because although Grandmamma had twice repeated that she would not give the General any money, who could tell, after all? – they need not lose hope yet, all the same. De Grieux, who was involved in all the General's business, had not done so. I was sure that Mademoiselle Blanche, also very much involved (and no wonder! the wife of a general, and with a handsome fortune!), would not lose hope and would use all her arts of seduction and coquetry on Grandmamma – in contrast to the proud and stubborn Polina, who did not know how to ingratiate herself with anybody. But now, now that Grandmamma had accomplished such feats at roulette, now that her personality had defined itself so clearly and characteristically (an obstinate, power-loving old woman, *et tombée en enfance*) – now, perhaps, all was lost; she was, after all, childishly delighted at having gratified her greed and, as usually happens, would lightly gamble away everything she had. Heavens! I thought (with, God forgive me, a gloating smile), heavens! every friedrichs d'or Grandmamma staked just now gnawed like

an ulcer at the General's heart, infuriated de Grieux and drove
Mademoiselle de Cominges, who saw the cup being dashed from
her lips, to frenzy. One more fact: even in her triumph and rejoicing, when she was giving away money right and left and
imagined every passer-by was a beggar, even then Grandmamma
had burst out to the General, 'All the same, I won't give you any
money!' That meant she had fastened obstinately and immovably
on that idea, and labelled it in her mind with the word: Danger!
Danger!

All these ideas were passing through my head as I mounted the
great staircase from Grandmamma's rooms to my own small one
on the topmost floor. It all interested me powerfully; although I
had, of course, been able even before this to guess at the thickest
of the threads that had bound together the actors before my
arrival, all the same I had not definitely known all the mysterious
ins and outs of the play. Polina has never trusted me completely.
Even though it is true that at times she has chanced to open her
heart to me, involuntarily, as it were, yet I have noticed that
often, indeed almost always, after such revelations she will either
turn all she has said into a jest or deliberately give it an appearance of falseness and confusion. Oh, she has been hiding many
things! In any case, I felt that the denouement of this whole
tense and mysterious situation was approaching. One more shock,
and everything would be finished and brought to light. I also was
one of those involved in the whole business, but I scarcely gave a
thought to my own fate. I was in a strange mood: I had no more
than twenty friedrichs d'or in my pocket; I was far from home,
in a foreign country, without work or any means of livelihood,
without hope, without plans – and I didn't worry about any of
that! If I had not been thinking of Polina, I should simply have
given myself up completely to the comic interest of the imminent
denouement and roared with laughter. But Polina disturbs me;
her fate hangs in the balance, as I foresaw then, but I am sorry to
say that I am not worrying at all about what will happen to her.
I want to fathom her secrets, I should like her to come to me and
say, 'I love you', and if not, if that is inconceivable madness, then
. . . well, what do I wish for? How am I to know what I want?
I am helpless and hopeless; I only know I must be near her, in

her aura, in her radiance, always, for ever, all my life. I know no more than that! And how can I go away from her?

On the third floor, in their corridor, it was as if something nudged me. I turned round and saw Polina coming out of a door a dozen yards or more away. She seemed to have been waiting and watching for me, and immediately beckoned to me.

'Polina Alexandrovna . . .'

'Hush!' she said warningly.

'Imagine,' I whispered; 'just now I felt as though somebody had nudged me; I looked round – you! Just as if you gave off some kind of electric force!'

'Take this letter,' said Polina with an anxious frown, probably without hearing what I was saying, 'and give it to Mr Astley personally at once. As soon as you can, I beg you. It requires no answer. He will . . .'

She did not finish what she was saying.

'Mr Astley?' I asked in astonishment.

But Polina had already disappeared into the doorway.

'Aha, so they write to one another!' Of course I ran off at once to look for Mr Astley, first to his hotel, where I did not find him, then to the station, where I hurried through all the rooms, and at length, as I was returning home disappointed and almost despairing, I met him quite by chance, on horseback, with a party of English ladies and gentlemen. I beckoned to him, stopped him and gave him the letter. We had not even time to exchange a look. But I suspect that Mr Astley purposely gave his horse its head.

Was it jealousy that tormented me? But I was in a mood of extreme depression. I didn't even want to discover what their correspondence was about. So he is in her confidence! 'Well, he's her friend,' I thought, and it is clear that he is (and also when he managed to become one), but is there love there? Of course not, my reason whispered. But after all, reason alone is not enough in such matters. In any case, I should have to clear this up also. The business was becoming unpleasantly complicated.

I was hardly inside the hotel before the hall-porter, and the manager issuing from his room, informed me that I was being asked for and looked for, that they had sent three times to inquire where I was, and that I was wanted in the General's suite as soon as possible. I was in the worst of humours. In the General's sitting-room I found the General himself, de Grieux, and Mademoiselle Blanche alone, without her mother. The mother was definitely a dummy personage, used only for show; when it came to real *business*, Mademoiselle Blanche handled it by herself. Indeed, it is doubtful whether the lady knew anything about the affairs of her so-called daughter.

The three were conferring earnestly, and they had even closed the sitting-room doors, a thing which never happened. As I approached the doors I could hear loud voices – de Grieux's impudently caustic tones, Mademoiselle Blanche's bold-faced abuse and shrieks of fury, and the pitiful voice of the General, who was plainly trying to make excuses for himself. On my appearance they all seemed to put some constraint on themselves and become calmer. De Grieux smoothed his hair and turned his angry face into a smiling one – but the smile was that nasty, conventionally polite French smile I hate so much. The depressed and browbeaten General put on a dignified air, but somewhat mechanically. Only Mademoiselle Blanche hardly modified the blazing anger of her expression, merely stopped speaking and fixed her impatiently expectant eyes upon me. I may remark that hitherto she had treated me with almost incredible lack of courtesy, not even returning my bows – she had simply ignored me.

'Alexis Ivanovich,' began the General in a gently reproachful manner, 'allow me to remark that it is strange, strange in the highest degree . . . in short, your actions with regard to me and my family . . . in short, it is in the highest degree strange . . .'

'Eh, *ce n'est pas ça*,' interrupted de Grieux with annoyed contempt. (He was definitely in charge!) '*Mon cher monsieur, notre général se trompe* when he takes that tone' (I give the rest of what he said in Russian) 'but he meant to tell you . . . that is, to warn you, or rather to do his very best to persuade you not to ruin him – yes, ruin him! I use that expression precisely . . .'

'But how, how?' I broke in.

'Oh, come, you undertake to act as guide (or what else can I call it?) to this old woman, *cette pauvre terrible vieille*,' de Grieux was himself stumbling, 'but she will lose all her money, you know;

she will gamble away every last farthing! You saw for yourself the way she plays, you were a witness! If she begins to lose, she won't leave the table, out of stubbornness and bad temper, and she'll go on and on playing, and in such circumstances people never recoup themselves, and then . . . then . . .'

'And then,' the General took up, 'then you will have ruined the whole family! I and my family, we are her heirs, she has no closer relatives. I will be open with you: my affairs are in a bad way, a very bad way. You know part of it yourself. . . . If she loses a considerable sum or even perhaps her whole fortune (oh God!) what will become of them, of my children, then?' (the General looked round at de Grieux) 'and of me?' (He glanced at Mademoiselle Blanche, who had disdainfully turned away from him.) 'Save us, Alexis Ivanovich, save us! . . .'

'But how, General, tell me how I can. . . . How do I count in all this?'

'Refuse to do it, refuse, drop her! . . .'

'Then she'll find someone else!' I cried.

'*Ce n'est pas ça, ce n'est pas ça*,' interrupted de Grieux again, '*que diable!* No, don't leave her, but at least make her see reason, persuade her, distract her. . . . Well, at any rate, don't let her lose too much, get her away somehow.'

'But how shall I do that? If you were to undertake that yourself, Monsieur de Grieux,' I added as naïvely as I could.

Here I saw Mademoiselle Blanche throw a rapid, fiery, inquiring glance at de Grieux. Over de Grieux's own face passed a peculiar and revealing expression he could not restrain.

'The thing is, she won't have me now!' cried de Grieux, with a wave of his hand. 'If only! . . . afterwards . . .'

He threw a quick and significant glance at Mademoiselle Blanche.

'*O mon cher monsieur Alexis, soyez si bon*,' Mademoiselle Blanche *herself* advanced upon me with a fascinating smile, seized both my hands and pressed them warmly. Devil take it! That diabolical face of hers could change in an instant. At this moment she showed such a sweet and appealing face, with a childlike and even playful smile; as she finished her sentence she winked roguishly, unseen by the others; was she trying to make a complete conquest of me all in one moment? The result was not bad – only it was crude, dreadfully crude.

The General ran up, positively ran up, behind her.

'Alexis Ivanovich, forgive me for starting off like that with you just now, I didn't mean to say that at all. . . . I beg you, I implore you, I bow down humbly like a true Russian – you alone, only you can save us ! Mademoiselle de Cominges and I implore you – you understand, you do understand, don't you?' he begged, indicating Mademoiselle Blanche with his eyes. He was most pitiful.

At that moment there came three quiet and respectful knocks at the door; it was opened – the floor-waiter had knocked and Potapych was standing a few steps behind him. They were envoys from Grandmamma. They had been required to seek me out and bring me without delay; 'She's cross,' Potapych informed me.

'But it's only half past three, you know !'

'Madam couldn't get to sleep, she tossed about all the time, then all at once she got up and ordered her chair and sent for you. She's waiting at the door already, sir. . . .'

'*Quelle mégère!*' cried de Grieux.

Grandmamma was indeed outside the front door of the hotel, where I found her, rapidly losing patience because I was not there. She had not been able to hold out until four o'clock.

'Well, lift me up !' she cried, and we set off again for the roulette tables.

CHAPTER TWELVE

GRANDMAMMA was in an impatient and fractious mood; she was evidently obsessed with roulette. She was inattentive to everything else, and altogether absent-minded. She did not, for example, ask innumerable questions on the way, as she had done before. Seeing a luxurious carriage bowling swiftly past us, she raised her hand for an instant and asked 'What's that? Whose is it?', but seemed not even to hear my answer; her reflections were constantly disturbed by sharply impatient and fidgety movements. When I pointed out Baron and Baroness Wurmerhelm in the distance as we were getting near the station, she looked at them absently, said 'Oh!' with utter indifference and, turning abruptly on Potapych and Martha, who were walking behind, snapped at them:

'Well, why have you tacked yourselves on? Don't expect to be taken every time! Go home! You're all I want,' she added to me, when they had bowed and hurried away.

They were already expecting Grandmamma at the station. The same place, next to the croupier, was at once cleared for her. It seems to me that the croupiers, always so ceremonious, and presenting the appearance of the most ordinary kind of officials, to whom it is almost completely indifferent whether the bank wins or loses, are really not in the least indifferent to the bank's losses and, it goes without saying, are provided with instructions for attracting people to play and for diligently protecting the interests of the establishment, for which they must certainly receive bonuses and rewards. At any rate, they already regarded Grandmamma as fair game. Then things turned out as had been foreseen.

This is how it happened.

Grandmamma attacked *zéro* straight away, ordering me at once to stake twelve friedrichs d'or at a time. We staked them once, twice, three times – *zéro* did not come up.

'Stake, stake!' Grandmamma nudged me impatiently. I obeyed.

'How many times have we lost our stake?' she asked at last, grinding her teeth with impatience.

'I've staked twelve times already, Grandmamma. We have lost a hundred and forty-four friedrichs d'or. I tell you, Grandmamma, perhaps it will not be till evening that ...'

'Be quiet!' interrupted Grandmamma. 'Stake on *zéro*, and put down a thousand gulden on red at once.'

Red turned up, but *zéro* failed again; they returned a thousand gulden to us.

'You see, you see!' whispered Grandmamma, 'we've got back almost all we lost. Stake again on *zéro*; we'll stake another ten times and then give up.'

But by the fifth time Grandmamma was tired of it.

'To the devil with that filthy *zéro*! Here you are, stake the whole four thousand gulden on red,' she commanded.

'Grandmamma! it's too much; what if red doesn't come up?'
I pleaded; but Grandmamma almost struck me. (She did, indeed,
prod me so hard that she might almost be said to have struck me.)
There was nothing for it, I staked the whole 4,000 gulden we had
so recently won on red. The wheel spun. Grandmamma sat calmly
and proudly upright, never doubting that she was certain to win.

'Zéro,' proclaimed the croupier.

At first Grandmamma did not understand, but when she saw
that the croupier had raked in her 4,000 gulden, together with all
the rest of what was on the table, and realized that zéro, which
had not turned up for so long, and on which we had staked and
lost almost two hundred friedrichs d'or, had come up as if on
purpose at the very time when she had only just cursed it and
abandoned it, she exclaimed aloud and flung up her arms so that
everybody in the room saw it. The people round about even
laughed.

'Well! The confounded thing pops up now!' wailed Grandmamma; 'that damnable, damnable zéro! It's you! It's all you!'
She turned on me furiously, pushing me. 'You talked me out of it.'

'I talked sense to you, Grandmamma, how can I be responsible
for all the chances?'

'I'll give you chances!' she whispered menacingly. 'Get away
from me!'

'Good-bye, Grandmamma' – and I turned to go.

'Alexis Ivanovich, Alexis Ivanovich, stop! Where are you going? Why, what's the matter, what's the matter? Angry, are you?
Fool! Well, stay, stay a bit longer; come, don't be angry, I'm the
fool! Come, tell me what's to be done now!'

'I'm not going to begin telling you what to do, Grandmamma,
because you'll blame me. Do your own playing; you tell me and
I'll stake for you.'

'Well, all right! well, put another four thousand gulden on
red! Here's my pocket-book, take it!' She took it out of her
pocket and handed it to me. 'Well, take it quickly, there's twenty
thousand roubles in cash there.'

'Grandmamma,' I stammered, 'such large sums....'

'As I hope to live, I'll get it all back. Stake!'

We staked and lost.

'Stake, stake! Stake the whole eight!'

'I can't, Grandmamma, the biggest stake is four! . . .'

'Well, stake four!'

This time we won. Grandmamma cheered up.

'You see, you see!' she nudged me; 'stake four again.'

We staked and lost; then we lost a second and a third time.

'Grandmamma, all the twelve thousand is gone,' I announced.

'I can see it's all gone,' she said, with a kind of calm madness, if I may so express it. 'I can see, man, I can see,' she muttered, staring fixedly before her and apparently deliberating something. 'Eh! as I hope to live, stake another four thousand gulden!'

'But there isn't any money, Grandmamma; there are some of our five-per-cent bills here in the pocket-book, and some kind of money orders besides, but no money.'

'And what's in the purse?'

'Some small change, Grandmamma.'

'Are there any *bureaux de change* here? I was told all our bills can be changed,' asked Grandmamma resolutely.

'Oh yes, as much as you like. But what you lose on the exchange that way . . . even a Jew would be horrified!'

'Rubbish! I'll win it all back! Take me there. Call those blockheads!'

I pushed the chair away, the porters appeared, and we rolled out of the station.

'Quick, quick, quick!' Grandmamma commanded. 'Show us the way, Alexis Ivanovich, and take the shortest route . . . is it far?'

'A few steps, Grandmamma.'

But as we turned from the square into the avenue, we were met by all our party: the General, de Grieux, and Mademoiselle Blanche and her mother. Polina Alexandrovna was not with them, neither was Mr Astley.

'Well, well, well! We can't stop,' cried Grandmamma; 'well, what do you want? I've no time for you now!'

I was walking behind; de Grieux hurried up to me.

'She lost all she won before, and then threw away twelve thousand gulden of her own. We are going to change some five-per-cents,' I hurriedly whispered to him.

De Grieux stamped his foot and hurried to tell the General. We went on pushing Grandmamma along.

'Stop her, stop her!' the General whispered frantically.

'You try to stop her,' I whispered back.

'Auntie!' the General said, going up to her, 'Auntie . . . we are just . . . we are just . . .' – his voice trembled and faltered – 'we are hiring horses and going into the country. . . . A marvellous view . . . the *pointe* . . . we were coming to ask you to go with us.'

'Oh, bother you and your *pointe*!' Grandmamma irritably waved him away.

'There's a village . . . we'll have tea there . . .' the General went on, no longer cherishing any hope.

'*Nous boirons du lait, sur l'herbe fraîche*,' added de Grieux, with savage anger.

'*Du lait, de l'herbe fraîche*' is everything that is ideally idyllic for bourgeois Paris; it is well known to be its only conception of '*nature et la vérité*'.

'Oh, bother you and your milk! Swig it yourself, it makes my belly ache. And why do you keep pestering me? I tell you, I've no time to spare!'

'Here we are, Grandmamma,' I called out. 'Here it is!'

We had come to the building where the bank was. I went to change the bills; Grandmamma waited at the door; de Grieux, the General, and Blanche stood to one side, not knowing what to do. Grandmamma looked angrily at them, and they walked away towards the station.

I was offered such dreadful terms that I could not accept them, but went back to Grandmamma to ask for instructions.

'Oh, the robbers!' she cried, flinging up her hands. 'Well! It doesn't matter! Change it!' she exclaimed decisively. 'Wait, send the banker to me.'

'One of the clerks, perhaps, Grandmamma?'

'Well, a clerk, it's the same thing. The robbers!'

The clerk consented to go outside when he heard that an old, invalid countess, unable to walk, was asking him to do so. Grandmamma spent a long time denouncing him loudly and angrily as a swindler and haggling over the rate of exchange in Russian,

French and German, while I helped by translating. The solemn clerk looked earnestly from one to the other of us and silently shook his head. He stared at Grandmamma with an intent curiosity that was positively uncivil; finally he began to smile.

'Well, be off with you!' Grandmamma cried. 'Choke yourself with my money! Change it with him, Alexis Ivanovich; we haven't any time, or else we'd go to somebody else. . . .'

'The clerk says the others give even less.'

I don't remember the exact figures, but they were terrible. I changed upwards of twelve thousand florins into gold and banknotes, took the account, and carried it all outside to Grandmamma.

'Well! Well! Well! No need to count it!' she said, with a wave of her hand. 'Quick, quick, quick!'

'I'll never put a stake on that damned *zéro* again, nor on red either,' she stated as we came up to the station.

This time I tried with all my might to persuade her to stake as little as possible, assuring her that when her luck changed there would always be time to risk higher stakes. But she was so impatient that, although she agreed at first, there was no possibility of restraining her during the actual play. She had hardly begun to win sums of ten or twenty friedrichs d'or, before she was nudging me: 'There you are! There you are! We've won, you see; if that had been four thousand instead of ten on the table, we should have won four thousand, but as it is, what does it amount to? It's all your fault!'

And however vexed I was, watching the way she played, I finally decided to hold my tongue and give her no more advice.

Suddenly de Grieux came hurrying up. All three of them were near by; I had noticed Mademoiselle Blanche standing to one side with her mother and flirting with the little prince. The General was clearly in disgrace, almost banished from her presence. Blanche would not even look at him, although he was exerting every effort to attract her favourable attention. Poor General! He turned pale and red by turns, trembled, and even forgot to follow Grandmamma's play. Finally, Blanche and the little prince went out; the General trotted after them.

'*Madame, madame,*' de Grieux whispered to Grandmamma in a honeyed voice, when he had pushed his way through to her side.

'*Madame*, the stake doesn't go like that . . . no, no, not possible . . .', he went on in mangled Russian, 'no !'

'How, then ? Well, tell me !' Grandmamma said, turning to him.

De Grieux broke into rapid French chatter, giving advice and getting excited, saying one must wait for the lucky moment, beginning to make some calculations or other . . . Grandmamma did not understand a word. He kept asking me to translate for him; rapped the table with his finger, pointing things out; finally seized a pencil and began doing sums on a bit of paper. At last Grandmamma lost patience.

'Oh, be off with you ! You do nothing but talk nonsense ! "*Madame, madame*", but he doesn't know what he's talking about; go away !'

'*Mais, madame*,' twittered de Grieux, and again began urging and explaining. He was beginning to be carried away.

'Well, stake once the way he says,' Grandmamma ordered, 'and we will see : perhaps it really will work.'

De Grieux only wanted to dissuade her from placing big stakes; he suggested she should stake on numbers either singly or in combination. At his direction I staked one friedrichs d'or on all the odd numbers in the first dozen, and five friedrichs d'or each on the two groups from twelve to eighteen and eighteen to twenty-four : we had staked sixteen friedrichs d'or in all.

The wheel turned.

'*Zéro*,' the croupier called.

We had lost everything.

'Blockhead !' cried Grandmamma, turning to de Grieux. 'You nasty little Frenchman ! He'll give you advice, the monster ! Get out, get out ! He knows nothing about it, but he comes poking his nose in !'

Terribly offended, de Grieux shrugged his shoulders, looked contemptuously at Grandmamma and walked away. He felt ashamed now of having interfered, but he had not been able to help it.

An hour later, in spite of all we could do, we had lost everything.

'Home !' cried Grandmamma.

She did not utter another word until we had reached the chestnut avenue. In the avenue and as we approached the hotel, ejaculations began bursting from her lips.

'Fool! great stupid fool! You're an old woman, a great stupid old fool!'

As soon as we got into the suite: 'Bring me some tea!' called Grandmamma, 'and get ready at once. We're going!'

'Where are we going, madam?' Martha was beginning.

'What's that to you? Mind your own business! Potapych, get everything together, all the luggage. We're going back to Moscow! I've gambled away fifteen thousand roubles!'

'Oh madam, fifteen thousand! My God!' exclaimed Potapych, flinging up his hands in a gesture full of feeling, probably supposing he was doing what was required of him.

'Now, now, fool! Snivelling again! Be quiet! Pack! Get me the bill quickly, quickly!'

'The next train leaves at half past nine, Grandmamma,' I informed her, to check her impetuosity.

'What time is it now?'

'Half past seven.'

'What a nuisance! Well, never mind! Alexis Ivanovich, I haven't a copeck. Here are two more notes, hurry to that place and change them, too. Otherwise I shan't have anything for the journey.'

I went. Returning to the hotel half an hour later I found the whole party with Grandmamma. They were apparently still more upset to learn that Grandmamma was going away altogether, to Moscow, than at her losses. Admittedly, going away would save her fortune, but on the other hand, what would become of the General now? Who would pay off de Grieux? Mademoiselle Blanche, of course, would not wait until Grandmamma died, but would probably slip away now with the prince or somebody else. They were all standing in front of her, trying to comfort her and persuade her to stay. Grandmamma was screaming furiously at them.

'Leave me alone, you devils! What business is it of yours? Why do you come pushing your goatee in here?' she shrieked at de Grieux, 'and what do you want, peewit?' she went on to Mademoiselle Blanche. 'What are you making a fuss about?'

'*Diantre !*' whispered Mademoiselle Blanche, her eyes sparkling with fury, but then she laughed suddenly and went out.

'*Elle vivra cent ans !*' she screamed at the General, as she reached the door.

'Ah, so you're counting on my death?' Grandmamma howled at the General; 'get out! Turn them all out, Alexis Ivanovich! What's it got to do with you? It's my own money I've thrown away, not yours!'

The General shrugged his shoulders, bowed and went out. De Grieux followed him.

'Call Praskovya,' Grandmamma ordered Martha.

In five minutes' time Martha returned with Polina. Polina had been sitting in her room with the children all this time, and I think she had deliberately made up her mind not to go out all day. Her face was grave, sad and anxious.

'Praskovya,' began Grandmamma, 'is it true, as I happened to hear a short time since, that that fool of a stepfather of yours wants to marry that silly little French flibbertigibbet? – an actress, isn't she, or something even worse? Tell me, is it true?'

'I don't know for certain, Grandmamma,' answered Polina, 'but from what Mademoiselle Blanche, who doesn't think it necessary to conceal it, says herself, I infer . . .'

'That's enough!' Grandmamma broke in vigorously, 'I understand! I've always thought that was the sort of thing he would do, and I've always considered him the most thoughtless and empty-headed creature. He swaggers and puts on airs because he's a general (but he was really only a colonel, he was promoted on retirement). My dear, I know all about how you kept sending telegram after telegram to Moscow asking whether the old girl would be turning up her toes soon. They were waiting for my money; that low female, what's her name? – de Cominges, isn't it? – wouldn't even have him as a servant without it, and he with false teeth, too! They say she's got plenty herself, she lends money at interest, she's feathered her nest. I don't blame you, Praskovya; it wasn't you that sent the telegrams; and I'm not going to mention what's past. I know you've got a nasty temper – you're a little wasp! When you sting, it raises a lump; but I'm sorry for you, because I loved your poor mother, Katerina. Well, would you like to give all this up and come with me? There's no place for you here, and besides, it's not proper for you to be with them now. Wait!' Grandmamma interrupted Polina, who was beginning to answer, 'I've not finished yet. I'm not asking you for anything. My house in Moscow, you know yourself, is as big as a palace, you can have a whole floor to yourself if you like, and not see me for weeks together, if you don't like my temper. Well, will you do it?'

'Allow me to ask you something first: do you really mean to travel at once?'

'Do you think I'm joking, my dear? I've said it, and I'm going. Today I lost fifteen thousand roubles at your double-damned roulette. Five years ago I promised to rebuild a wooden church on my estate near Moscow in stone, and instead I've thrown the lot away here. Now, my dear, I'm going to build the church.'

'But what about the water, Grandmamma? You came to drink the water, didn't you.'

'Oh, bother you and your water! Don't annoy me, Praskovya; are you doing it on purpose? Tell me, are you coming or aren't you?'

'I am very, very grateful to you, Grandmamma,' Polina began feelingly, 'for the refuge you are offering me. You are partly right about the position I'm in. I am so grateful that I will come to you, believe me, and perhaps very soon, even; but now there are reasons . . . important reasons . . . and I can't make up my mind at once, this instant. If you were staying even a week or two. . . .'

'Do you mean you won't?'

'I mean I can't. And besides, in any case I couldn't leave my brother and sister, and since . . . since . . . since it really might happen that they are abandoned . . . if you will take me with the little ones, Grandmamma, then of course I'll come, and believe me, I'll repay you for it!' she added warmly, 'but without the children I can't, Grandmamma.'

'Well, don't whimper!' (Polina had no intention of doing so, and indeed she never cried); 'there'll be room for the chicks as well; the hen-house is big. Besides, it's time for them to go to school. Well, so you won't come now? Well, Praskovya, look out! I want only your good, but you see I know why you won't come. I know everything, Praskovya! That Frenchman won't bring you any good.'

Polina flushed. I positively jumped. (Everybody knows! So everybody knows except me!)

'Well, well, don't frown. I'm not going to coax you. Only be careful it doesn't turn out badly, understand! You're a clever lass; I shall be sorry for you. Well, that's enough, I wish I'd never seen any of you! Go away, good-bye!'

'I will go with you to the station, Grandmamma,' said Polina.

'No, don't; don't get in the way; besides, I'm tired of all of you.'

Polina kissed Grandmamma's hands, but she drew her hand away and kissed Polina's cheek.

As she passed me, Polina glanced swiftly at me and at once turned away her eyes.

'Well, good-bye to you too, Alexis Ivanovich! It's only an hour to the train-time. And you're tired of being with me, I think. Well, take these fifty gold pieces.'

'I humbly thank you, Grandmamma, but I should be ashamed. . . .'

'Now, now!' cried Grandmamma, with such energy and ferocity that I could not gainsay her, but accepted it.

'When you're running about Moscow out of a job, come to me; I'll give you an introduction somewhere. Well, be off!'

I went into my room and lay down on the bed. I think I lay there for an hour on my back, with my hands behind my head. The catastrophe had come now; there was plenty to think about. I resolved to insist on a talk with Polina the next day. Oh, that Frenchman! So it was true? But what could there be there, all the same? Polina and de Grieux! Good God, what a combination!

It was all simply unbelievable. Suddenly quite beside myself, I leapt up to go and look for Mr Astley immediately, and make him talk at any cost. He knew more about this than I did, of course. Mr Astley? There was another mystery for me!

But suddenly there came a knock at my door. I looked out and saw Potapych.

'Alexis Ivanovich, sir: come to madam, she wants you!'

'What is it? Is she leaving? There's still twenty minutes before the train.'

'Madam's restless, sir, she can't keep still. "Quick, quick!" – that's you, sir; for God's sake make haste.'

I ran downstairs at once. Grandmamma had already been pushed into the corridor. Her pocket-book was in her hand.

'Alexis Ivanovich, lead the way, we're going! . . .'

'Where, Grandmamma?'

'As I hope to live, I'll win it all back! Well, march! No questions! Play goes on till midnight, doesn't it?'

I was dumbfounded, but after a moment's thought I made up my mind.

'Excuse me, Antonida Vasilyevna, I won't go.'

'Why not? What's all this? Have you all gone crazy?'

'Excuse me! I should reproach myself afterwards; I won't do it! I won't either watch it or have anything to do with it; let me off, Antonida Vasilyevna. Here are your fifty friedrichs d'or back; good-bye!' And I laid down the roll of gold pieces on a little table, beside which her chair was standing, and went away.

'What rubbish!' Grandmamma shrieked after me; 'don't come, then, I'll find the way by myself. Potapych, come with me! Well, lift me up, carry me!'

I could not find Mr Astley and went back home. Late that night, after midnight, I heard from Potapych how Grandmamma's day had ended. She had lost everything I had just changed for her, that is ten thousand more roubles of our money. The same little Pole to whom she had not long before given two friedrichs d'or had attached himself to her there and guided her play all the time. To begin with, before the Pole turned up, she was making Potapych place her stakes, but she soon sent him away; the Pole came hurrying up at that point. As luck would have it, he could understand Russian and jabber a mixture of three languages, so that they managed to make one another out. Grandmamma abused him mercilessly all the time, and although he was always 'stretching himself at the noble lady's feet', there was 'no comparison with you, Alexis Ivanovich', Potapych told me. 'She treated you *as if you were a gentleman*, but that man – well, I saw him with my own eyes stealing her money right off the table, may God strike me dead if I didn't! She caught him at it herself a couple of times, and she went for him, and called him everything she could lay her tongue to, sir, and once she even pulled his hair, truly, I wouldn't lie to you, sir, and everybody all round laughed at them. We brought madam back here, she only asked for a little drop of water to drink and she said her prayers and went to bed. Tired out she must have been, because she went straight to sleep. God send her pleasant dreams! Oh, these foreign parts!' Potapych wound up, 'I said it wouldn't come to any good. And the quicker we go back to Moscow the better! There's nothing at all we haven't got in Moscow! There's the garden, flowers like you never see here, scents, the apples are getting ripe, there's lots of room – but no, we had to come abroad! Oh, oh, oh! . . .'

CHAPTER THIRTEEN

ALMOST a month has passed since I touched these notes of mine, begun under the influence of strong, if confused, impressions. The catastrophe, the imminence of which I then foresaw, really did occur, but it was of an infinitely more violent and unlooked-for-kind than I expected. It was all strange, ugly and even tragic, at any rate for me. Certain things happened to me that were almost miraculous; at least that is how I still think of them, although from another point of view, and especially in relation to the dizzy whirl of events in which I was involved at the time, they were no more than a little out of the ordinary. But the most extraordinary thing for me is my own attitude to all those happenings. I still don't understand it to this day! And it all passed like a dream, even my passion, and it really was strong and sincere, but . . . what has become of it now? Indeed, from time to time the thought runs through my mind, 'Surely I must have been out of my mind then? did I spend all that time in a madhouse somewhere, and am I still perhaps there – so that it all only *seemed* to happen, and still only *seems* to have happened? . . .'

I have collected up my pages of notes and read them through. (Who knows, perhaps that was to satisfy myself that I did not write them in a madhouse?) Now I am all alone. Autumn is coming, the leaves are turning yellow. I sit in this melancholy little town (how melancholy small German towns are!), and instead of considering the next step, I live under the influence of the sensations I have only just ceased to feel, the influence of memories still fresh, the influence of all that recent whirl of events that swept me into its vortex and then cast me aside again. At times I still feel as though I were spinning in that vortex, as though that tornado would come sweeping by again at any moment, snatch me up again in its skirts and jolt me out of all sense of order and proportion, and send me spinning, spinning, spinning. . . .

But perhaps I shall somehow settle down and cease to whirl if I give myself, as far as I can, an exact account of all that happened during that month. I feel impelled to take up my pen again; and sometimes there is absolutely nothing to do in the evenings. It is strange, but, in order to have something to occupy me, I take out of the meagre lending-library here the novels of Paul de Kock (in a German translation !), which I can hardly stand, but I read them, wondering at myself : it is as though I were afraid of breaking the spell of the recent past by serious reading or any kind of serious occupation. As though that formless dream and all the impressions it has left behind was so dear to me that I am afraid to let it be touched by anything new, lest it should vanish into thin air ! Is it all so dear to me, then? Yes, of course it is; perhaps I shall remember it even after forty years. . . .

So I settle to my writing. Now, however, I can tell it all only in part and briefly : the effect is quite wrong. . . .

First of all, to finish with Grandmamma. The next day she lost everything she had in the world. It was bound to happen : for anybody of her kind, once started on that path, it is like sliding down a toboggan-run on a sledge, going faster and faster all the time. She played all day, until eight o'clock in the evening; I was not present, and know only what I have been told.

Potapych kept watch beside her at the station all day. The Poles who acted as her guides changed several times in the course of it. She began by driving away the one whose hair she had pulled the day before, and took another, but the second proved to be almost worse than the first. Having dismissed him and returned to the first, who had not gone away, but remained there, pushing and jostling just behind her chair and constantly trying to thrust his head in, during all the time of his banishment, Grandmamma finally fell into utter despair. The second dismissed Pole also refused to leave at any price; one of them stationed himself on her right, the other on her left. They argued and abused each other the whole time over the stakes and the method of placing them, called each other 'worthless loafer' and other endearing Polish names, then made friends again, threw down money at random and made a mess of everything. When they quarrelled, they laid stakes each from his own side, one for example on red and the other at the same time on black. They ended by reducing Grandmamma to utter confusion and bewilderment, so that, almost in tears, she turned at last to the elderly croupier and begged him to protect her and send them packing. They were in fact turned out at once, in spite of their cries and protests: they both shouted at once, trying to prove that Grandmamma owed them money, that she had swindled them somehow and treated them basely and dishonestly. The unhappy Potapych, in tears, told me all this that evening, after it was all over, and complained that they had stuffed their pockets with Grandmamma's money, he had seen them with his own eyes shamelessly robbing her and continually putting her money in their own pockets. For example, one would ask Grandmamma for five friedrichs d'or for his pains, and immediately begin staking with it, next to Grandmamma's stakes. Grandmamma would win, and he would shout that his stake had won and Grandmamma's had lost. When they were turned out, Potapych spoke up and reported that their pockets were full of gold. Grandmamma immediately asked the croupier to deal with the matter, and in spite of all the Poles' outcries (they squawked like two cocks picked up in the hands), the police made their appearance and their pockets were emptied for Grandmamma's benefit. Until she had lost everything, Grandmamma evidently enjoyed full authority that day with the croupiers and all the highest officials of the station. Little by little her fame spread all over the town. All the visitors to the spa, of every country, whether ordinary people or persons of importance, flocked to see 'une vieille comtesse russe, tombée en enfance', who had already lost 'several millions'.

But Grandmamma gained extremely little by being rid of the two Poles. In their place a third, who spoke absolutely pure Russian and was dressed like a gentleman, although he looked like a footman with his huge moustache and his haughty air, put himself at Grandmamma's disposal. He also 'kissed the lady's feet' and 'stretched himself at the lady's feet', but his demeanour to everybody around was overbearing and he gave his orders despotically – in short, he established himself at once as Grandmamma's master rather than her servant. Every moment, at every stage of the play, he turned to Grandmamma and swore with the most terrible oaths that he was 'an honourable Polish gentleman' and that he would not take a copeck of Grandmamma's money. He repeated these oaths so often that she took fright at last. But since the Polish gentleman really seemed to improve her play at first and began to win, Grandmamma found she could not now do without him. An hour later both the other Poles who had been turned out of the station reappeared behind Grandmamma's chair and again offered their services, if only to run errands. Potapych swore that the 'honourable Polish gentleman' exchanged winks with them and even pressed something into their hands. Since Grandmamma did not dine, and hardly left her chair, one of the Poles really was of some use : he slipped into the station dining-room close by and got her a cup of soup, and afterwards some tea. Both of them, however, ran about for her. But towards the end of the day, when it became obvious to everybody that she was running through her last banknote, there were half a dozen Poles, who had not been seen or heard of before, standing behind her chair. Then, when she was losing her last coins, all of them ceased not only to obey but even to notice her, positively climbed over her to the table, snatched the money themselves, made their own decisions and staked it, quarrelled and shouted, and hobnobbed with the 'honourable Polish gentleman'; and the honourable Polish gentleman himself almost forgot Grandmamma's existence. Even when Grandmamma had lost absolutely every penny and was returning to the hotel at eight o'clock, two or three of the Poles still would not leave her but ran along beside her chair, shouting at the top of their voices and gabbling incoherent assertions that Grandmamma had swindled them somehow and ought to pay them back.

They followed her all the way to the hotel, from which they were finally driven away with violence.

According to Potapych's reckoning, Grandmamma had lost altogether something like ninety thousand roubles that day, on top of her losses of the previous day. All her securities – five-per-cent bills, government loans, and all the stocks she had with her, had been changed one after the other. I wondered how she could have endured it for six or seven hours, sitting in her chair and hardly leaving the table, but Potapych told me that two or three times she really began winning considerable sums; and then, carried away by the renewal of hope, she was quite unable to leave. Gamblers know, however, how a man can sit in one place for almost twenty-four hours, playing cards and never turning his eyes to the right or the left.

Meanwhile, decisive events had been happening all that day in the hotel as well. Before eleven o'clock in the morning, while Grandmamma was still at home, the members of our party, I mean the General and de Grieux, had decided on a final move. When they learnt that Grandmamma was not even thinking of leaving, but on the contrary was setting off again for the gambling saloons, they all (except Polina) went to her in a body to discuss the matter for the last time, and even *bluntly*. The trembling General, his heart sinking at the thought of the awful consequences to himself, even overdid it : after half an hour of prayers and entreaties, and even frank and full confessions of all his debts and of his passion for Mademoiselle Blanche (he had quite lost his head), he suddenly adopted a threatening tone and even began shouting and stamping his foot at Grandmamma ; he yelled that she was disgracing their name, had become the scandal of the whole town and, finally . . . finally, 'You are a disgrace to the name of Russia, madam !' cried the General, and added that there were 'police for this kind of thing'. Grandmamma drove him out at last, actually striking him with her stick. The General and de Grieux conferred once or twice more that morning, and what concerned them was precisely the question whether they could not, in fact, somehow or other use the police. Here, they would say, was an unfortunate but respectable old lady who had gone out of her mind and was gambling away the last of her money ; and so on. In short, couldn't they contrive to have her put under some sort of official supervision or prohibition? . . . But de Grieux only shrugged his shoulders and laughed at the General to his face as he, letting his tongue run away with him completely, paced hurriedly up and down his sitting-room. At last de Grieux waved away the whole business with his hand and disappeared somewhere. In the evening it was learnt that he had left the hotel altogether, after some highly crucial preliminary discussion in private with Mademoiselle Blanche. As for Mademoiselle Blanche herself, early in the morning she had taken final measures: she had thrown the General over completely and refused even to allow him in her sight. When the General hurried after her to the station and met her arm-in-arm with the prince, both she and Madame *veuve* Cominges cut him dead. The prince did not bow to him either. All that day Mademoiselle Blanche worked on the prince, using her best endeavours to get him to speak out definitely at last. But, alas, she was cruelly deceived in counting on the prince! It was evening when this little tragedy took place: it transpired suddenly that the prince was as poor as a church mouse and was moreover counting on borrowing money from her in exchange for a note of hand, and using it to play roulette. Blanche indignantly sent him away and shut herself up in her room.

On the morning of that same day I had gone to see Mr Astley, or rather I had spent all morning looking for him but been unable to find him. He was neither at home nor in the station or the park. He did not dine in his hotel on this occasion. Between four and five o'clock I suddenly caught sight of him going straight to the Hotel d'Angleterre from the railway arrival platform. He was in a hurry and very anxious, although it was difficult to discern signs of anxiety or any kind of perturbation in his face. He cordially held out his hand to me, with his usual exclamation, 'Ah!', but then did not pause, continuing on his way at a rather hurried pace. I attached myself to him, but somehow he managed to answer me in such a way that I had no time even to ask questions about anything. I told him about Grandmamma; he listened gravely and attentively and shrugged his shoulders.

'She will lose everything,' I remarked.

'Oh yes,' he replied, 'she had already begun playing, you know, before I left, and so I knew for certain that she would lose every-thing. If there is time, I shall drop in at the station to watch, because it is an interesting thing. . . .'

'Where did you go?' I cried, wondering why I hadn't asked him before.

'I have been in Frankfurt.'

'On business?'

'Yes, on business.'

Well, what further questions could I ask? I continued to walk with him, however, until he turned abruptly into the Hotel des Quatre Saisons, which stood beside the road, nodded and disap-peared. As I returned home I realized little by little that if I talked to him for two hours I should learn absolutely nothing, because . . . I had nothing to ask. Yes, of course that was it! There was absolutely no way I could formulate my question.

All that day Polina either walked in the Park with the children and their nurse or stayed at home. She had been avoiding the General for a long time, and hardly spoke to him, at least on any serious subject. I had noticed it long before. But knowing the General's situation that day, I thought he could not pass her over, that is that there could not fail to be important family discussions between them. When, however, I met Polina and the children as I was returning to the hotel after talking to Mr Astley, her face showed the most unruffled tranquillity, as though she, and only she, had escaped the effects of the family tempest. She nodded in reply to my bow. I reached my room in a very bad temper.

I had, of course, been avoiding all conversation with her, and had hardly spoken to her since the Wurmerhelm episode. Some of this was swagger and posing on my part; but the more time went on, the more my genuine indignation seethed and boiled within me. Even if she had no regard for me at all, she ought not, I thought, to have trampled on my feelings like that or received my declaration of them with such careless contempt. She knew, after all, that I loved her in earnest; she had been willing enough to allow me to talk to her in that way. It is true that the whole thing had begun rather strangely. Some time, in fact as long as two months, earlier, I had begun to notice that she wished to make a friend and confidant of me, and was indeed to some extent trying to do so. But for some reason things never got under way between us at that time; instead, we were left with our present strange relationship; that is why I had begun to speak to her as I did. But if my love was repellant to her, why not flatly forbid me to speak of it?

I was not forbidden; sometimes she even led me on to talk and ... of course, it was done to amuse herself. I know it to be true, I noticed quite definitely, that – she found it agreeable, after listening to me and working me up hurtfully, to disconcert me suddenly by some trick that showed the utmost contempt and lack of consideration. And of course she knew that I could not live without her. Now three days had passed since the episode of the Baron, and I could not endure our *separation* any longer. When I met her near the station, my heart began to beat so heavily that I turned pale. But surely she can't go on living without me, either? She needs me, and – can it really be only as her court buffoon?

She has a secret – that's plain. Her talk with Grandmamma wounded me to the heart. A thousand times I have urged her to be open with me, and she must have known that I really was ready to lay down my life for her. But she has always evaded me, almost contemptuously, or has demanded of me, instead of the proffered sacrifice of my life, some such mad trick as that with the Baron! How could that be anything but shocking? Is that Frenchman really all the world to her? And Mr Astley? But here the question became decidedly incomprehensible, and meanwhile – God, how I tortured myself!

When I reached home, in an access of rage I seized a pen and scribbled the following lines to her:

Polina Alexandrovna, it is clear to me that affairs have reached a climax that will of course affect you too. I repeat for the last time: do you need my life or not? If you need me *for anything at all*, I am at your disposal, and meanwhile I am staying in my room, most of the time at least, and I shall not go away. If it is necessary, write or send for me.

I sealed the note and sent it by the floor-waiter, ordering him to deliver it straight into her hands. I did not expect an answer, but three minutes later the servant returned with the message that 'the lady sends her compliments'.

Between six and seven o'clock I was summoned to the General.

He was in his sitting-room, dressed as if preparing to go out. His hat and stick lay on the sofa. I had the impression as I entered that he was standing in the middle of the room, with legs planted wide apart and drooping head, talking to himself aloud. But as soon as he saw me he rushed towards me almost yelling, so that I involuntarily recoiled and almost hurried away again; but he seized me by both hands and pulled me towards the sofa; he sat down on it himself, placed me in an armchair facing him and, without letting go my hands, began saying in an imploring voice, with trembling lips and tears suddenly glittering on his eyelashes:

'Alexis Ivanovich, save me, save me, have pity!'

For a long time I could not understand; he went on, talking, talking, and incessantly repeating 'Have pity, have pity!' At last I guessed that he was expecting something like advice from me; or rather, abandoned by everybody, in dejection and anxiety, he had remembered me and sent for me just so that he could talk and talk and talk.

He was mad, or at any rate, quite distracted. He was clasping his hands and ready to go down on his knees to me to persuade me (what do you think?) to go to Mademoiselle Blanche and appeal to her, beg her, to return and marry him.

'For goodness' sake, General!' I cried, 'Mademoiselle Blanche has perhaps never even noticed my existence yet! What can I do?'

But it was no use protesting: he did not understand what was said to him. He began talking about Grandmamma as well, but dreadfully incoherently; he still clung to the idea of sending for the police.

'In our country, in our country,' he began, suddenly overflowing with indignation, 'in short, in our country, in a well-organized state, where there is a proper government, guardians would be appointed at once for old women like that! Yes, my dear sir, yes, sir,' he went on, dropping suddenly into a scolding tone, springing up from his place and beginning to wander about the room, 'you did not know that, my dear sir' (he was addressing an imaginary dear sir in the corner) 'so now let me tell you ... yes, sir ... in our country old women like that are kept in their place, in their place, sir, in their place, yes, sir. ... Oh, be damned to it!'

And he flung himself down on the sofa again, but a minute later, almost sobbing, he was breathlessly gabbling that Mademoiselle Blanche would not marry him because Grandmamma had arrived instead of a telegram and that now it was plain that he would not inherit her fortune. He thought that I still knew nothing of all that. I began to talk about de Grieux; he gave a wave of his hand:

'He's gone away! Everything I've got is in pawn to him; I've been stripped naked. The money you brought . . . that money – I don't know how much there is there, I think there's about seven hundred francs left and – need I say more? it's all there is, and beyond that – I don't know, sir, I don't know, sir!'

'Then how will you pay your hotel bills?' I cried in alarm, 'and . . . what will happen afterwards?'

He looked at me thoughtfully, but he did not seem to have understood and perhaps had not even heard anything I said. I tried to talk about Polina Alexandrovna and the children; he hastily answered, 'Yes! yes!' – but immediately began talking about the prince again, and about the fact that Blanche would go away with him now, and then . . . 'and then, what am I to do, Alexis Ivanovich?' he asked, turning suddenly towards me; 'I swear to God I don't know! What am I to do? Tell me, surely that's ingratitude? Surely that's ingratitude?'

At last he dissolved into floods of tears.

Nothing could be done with a man like that; leaving him alone was also dangerous; something might happen to him. I got rid of him somehow, however, but I let Nurse know, so that she would look in as often as she could, and in addition I had a talk with the floor-waiter, a very sensible fellow; he promised me that he also would keep an eye on the General.

I had hardly got away from the General before Potapych appeared with a summons from Grandmamma. It was eight o'clock, and she had only just returned from the station after her last series of losses. I went to her room; the old woman was sitting in an armchair, quite worn out and evidently ill. Martha was giving her a cup of tea, which she almost forced her to drink. Grandmamma's voice and tone were noticeably changed.

'Good evening, Alexis Ivanovich, my dear,' she said, with a slow and dignified inclination of her head, 'excuse me for troubling you again, you must forgive an old woman. I have left everything I had there on the tables, almost a hundred thousand roubles, my friend. You were right not to go with me yesterday. Now I haven't any money, not a farthing. I don't want to delay a single moment, I'm leaving at half past nine. I've sent to your Englishman, Astley, isn't it? and I'm going to ask him to lend me three thousand francs for a week. So you persuade him not to think anything's wrong and refuse me. I'm still fairly rich, my friend. I have three villages and two houses. And besides I can still find some money, I didn't bring it all with me. I'm telling you this so that he won't feel any doubts . . . Oh, but here he is! He's a good man, you can see.'

Mr Astley had hurried over at Grandmamma's first summons. Without stopping to think and without saying more than a few words, he immediately counted out 3,000 francs against a promissory note signed by Grandmamma. As soon as the business was finished he took his leave and hastened away.

'Now you go too, Alexis Ivanovich. There's a little more than an hour left – and I want to lie down, my bones ache. Don't think too hardly of me, I'm an old fool. Now I shan't accuse young people of being heedless any more, and it wouldn't be right for me to blame that unlucky General of yours, either. I shan't give him the money he wants, all the same, because to my mind he's completely and utterly stupid, only I'm no wiser myself, silly old fool that I am. It is true that God visits the sin of pride even on the old. Well, good-bye. Martha, my dear, help me up.'

I, however, wanted to see Grandmamma off. Besides, I was in a state of expectation, I was waiting all the time for something to happen at any moment. I could not sit still in my room. I kept going out into the corridor, and once I even went and strolled in the avenue for a minute or two. My letter to her had been clear and decisive, and the present catastrophe was, of course, final. In the hotel I heard of de Grieux's departure. After all, if she rejected me as a friend, perhaps she wouldn't reject me as a servant. She did need me, if only to run errands, and I would be of use to her, what else?

Towards train-time I hurried down to the station platform and installed Grandmamma in the train. They all took their places in an ordinary carriage. 'Thank you, my friend, for your disinterested sympathy,' she said at parting, 'and tell Praskovya, as I was saying to her yesterday – I shall expect her.'

I went back home. As I passed the General's room I met the children's nurse and inquired about the General. 'Oh, he's all right, sir,' she answered dolefully. I went in, however, but stopped at the sitting-room door in utter amazement. Mademoiselle Blanche and the General were laughing together over something. Madame *veuve* Cominges was sitting there on the sofa. The General was obviously beside himself with joy, babbling all sorts of nonsense and breaking into long nervous peals of laughter, which covered his face with innumerable tiny wrinkles and made his eyes disappear altogether. Afterwards I learnt from Mademoiselle Blanche herself that when, after sending away the prince, she heard of the General's tears, she took it into her head to comfort him and dropped in on him for a few minutes. But the poor General did not know that his fate had already been decided and Blanche had begun to pack in preparation for hurrying away to Paris by the first train the next morning.

I stood for a short time in the doorway of the General's sitting-room, then changed my mind about going in and went away unnoticed. Going up to my room and opening the door, I suddenly saw a figure sitting in the corner near the window. The figure did not rise at my entrance. I hurried up, looked, and – caught my breath in amazement: it was Polina!

CHAPTER FOURTEEN

I POSITIVELY cried out.

'What's the matter? What's the matter?' she asked strangely. She was pale and looked depressed.

'How can you ask? You! here in my room!'

'If I come, I come *all the way*. That is my habit. You shall see that presently; light the candle.'

I lit a candle. She stood up, walked to the table, and laid an open letter before me.

'Read it,' she commanded.

'This – this is de Grieux's writing!' I exclaimed, snatching up the letter. My hands were trembling and the lines danced before my eyes. I forget the exact terms of the letter, but here it is – if not word for word, at any rate idea for idea.

Mademoiselle [wrote de Grieux], unfortunate circumstances oblige me to leave without delay. You will of course have noticed that I have purposely avoided a final explanation with you until such time as all the circumstances had become clear. The arrival of your elderly relative [*de la vieille dame*] and her absurd actions have put an end to my perplexities. The unsettled state of my own affairs forbids me once for all to nurse any longer those voluptuous hopes in which I permitted myself to revel for some time. I regret the past, but I trust that you will find nothing in my conduct unbecoming to a gentleman and an honest man [*gentilhomme et honnéte homme*]. Having lost almost all my money in loans to your stepfather, I find myself under the urgent necessity of availing myself of what remains to me; I have already given my friends in St Petersburg to understand that they are to make immediate arrangements for the disposal of the property mortgaged to me; knowing, however, that your irresponsible stepfather has squandered your personal fortune, I have decided to forgive him fifty thousand francs, and I am returning to him some of the mortgages to the value of that sum, so that you are now in a position to regain possession of all you have lost, by claiming your estate through the courts of law. I hope, *Mademoiselle*, that in the present state of affairs my action will be highly advantageous to you. I hope also that by that action I am completely fulfilling the obligations of a man of honour and good breeding. Be assured that the memory of you is implanted in my heart for ever.

'Well, that is all clear,' I said, turning to Polina; 'you surely didn't expect anything different, did you?' I added indignantly.

'I didn't expect anything,' she answered, with apparent calm, although there was a sort of quiver in her voice; 'I made up my mind long ago; I could read his mind and I knew what he was thinking. He thought I would try . . . that I would insist . . .' (she stopped, without finishing her sentence, bit her lip and was silent). 'I deliberately redoubled my contempt for him,' she began again; 'I was waiting to see what he would do. If the telegram about the legacies had come I would have flung him the money borrowed by that idiot (my stepfather) and sent him packing! I have found him detestable for a long, long time. Oh, he was not the same man before, a thousand times no, but now, now! . . . Oh, with what joy I would have flung that fifty thousand in his nasty face now, and spit at him . . . and ground it in!'

'But the document, the mortgage for fifty thousand he returned, the General has that, hasn't he? Take it and give it back to de Grieux.'

'Oh, that's not the same! It's not the same! . . .'

'Yes, you're right, it's not the same! Besides, what is the General good for now? And what about Grandmamma?' I cried suddenly.

Polina looked at me rather absently and impatiently.

'Why Grandmamma?' said Polina, vexed. 'I can't go to her. And I won't ask anybody's forgiveness,' she added irritably.

'What's to be done, then?' I cried, 'and how on earth could you love de Grieux? Oh, the scoundrel, the scoundrel! Well, if you like I'll kill him in a duel! Where is he now?'

'He's in Frankfurt, and he will be spending three days there.'

'One word from you, and I will go there tomorrow, by the first train!' I said, in a fit of stupid enthusiasm.

She laughed.

'Why, perhaps he will still say: first give me back fifty thousand francs. And besides, why should he fight? . . . what nonsense this is!'

'But then where on earth is one to get those fifty thousand francs?' I repeated, grinding my teeth – just as though it was possible to pick them up all at once off the floor. 'Listen: what about Mr Astley?' I asked, turning to her with the beginning of a strange idea.

Her eyes flashed.

'What, do you yourself really want me to go from you to that Englishman?' she said, looking into my face with piercing eyes and smiling bitterly. She had called me 'thou' for the very first time.

I think she was dizzy with emotion at that moment, and she sat down suddenly, as if exhausted, on the sofa.

I felt as though I had been struck by lightning; I stood there unable to believe my eyes or my ears! What? So she loved me! She had come to me, not to Mr Astley! She, a young girl, had come alone to my room, in a hotel – which meant she had publicly compromised herself – and I could only stand before her uncomprehendingly.

A wild idea flashed into my mind.

'Polina ! Give me only one hour ! Wait here only an hour, and ... I will come back ! It's ... it's essential ! You'll see ! Stay here, stay here !'

And I dashed out of the room without responding to her astonished questioning look; she called out something after me, but I did not go back.

Yes, sometimes the wildest notion, the most apparently impossible idea, takes such a firm hold of the mind that at length it is taken for something realizable. . . . More than that : if the idea coincides with a strong and passionate desire, it may sometimes be accepted as something predestined, inevitable, fore-ordained, something that cannot but exist or happen ! Perhaps there is some reason for this, some combination of presentiments, some extra-ordinary exertion of will-power, some self-intoxication of the imagination, or something else – I don't know : but on that evening (which I shall never forget as long as I live) something miraculous happened to me. Although it is completely capable of mathematical proof, nevertheless to this day it remains for me a miraculous happening. And why, why, was that certainty so strongly and deeply rooted in me, and from such a long time ago? I used, indeed, to think of it, I repeat, not as one event among others that might happen (and consequently might also not happen), but as something that could not possibly fail to happen !

It was a quarter past ten, and I went into the station with a confident hope and at the same time with a wild excitement such as I had never experienced before. There were still quite a few people in the gambling saloons, although only about half as many as in the morning.

After ten o'clock at night those left round the tables are the genuine, desperate gamblers, for whom nothing exists in any health resort but roulette, who have come for nothing else, who hardly notice what is going on around them and take no interest in anything else all the season, only play from morning till night and would perhaps be ready to play all through the night as well, if it were possible. They are always annoyed at having to disperse when the roulette tables close at midnight. And when, about twelve o'clock, before closing the tables, the head croupier announces 'Les trois derniers coups, messieurs!', they are sometimes prepared to stake on those last three turns everything they have in their pockets, and actually do lose the biggest amounts of all at those times. I went to the same table where Grandmamma had sat a little earlier. It was not very crowded, so that I very soon found room to stand, close to the table. Straight in front of me the word 'Passe' was written on the green cloth.

'Passe' means the whole series of numbers from nineteen to thirty-six inclusive. The first series, from one to eighteen inclusive, is call Manque, but what did that matter to me? I did not take into account, I had not heard, what the previous winning number had been, and I began to play without inquiring, as any reasonably prudent gambler would have done. I pulled out all my twenty friedrichs d'or and put them down on the word passe lying before me.

'Vingt deux!' called the croupier.

I had won, and again I staked everything, both the previous stake and my winnings.

'Trente et un!' the croupier announced. Another win! That meant I now had altogether eighty friedrichs d'or! I moved all eighty to the dozen middle numbers (which pays three to one, but the chances are two to one against), the wheel turned, and twenty-four came up. I was paid out with three rolls of fifty friedrichs d'or and ten gold coins; now I had altogether 200 friedrichs d'or, including my first stake.

Feeling as though I were delirious with fever, I moved the whole pile of money to the red – and suddenly came to my senses! For the only time in the course of the whole evening, fear laid its icy finger on me and my arms and legs began to shake. With horror I saw and for an instant fully realized what it would mean to me to lose now! My whole life depended on that stake!

'Rouge!' cried the croupier, and I drew a deep breath, while my whole body tingled with fire. This time I was paid out in banknotes, so that I now had 4,000 florins and eighty friedrichs d'or! (I could still keep count then.)

After that, I remember, I put 2,000 florins on the twelve middle numbers again, and lost; I staked my gold, the eighty friedrichs d'or, and lost. Possessed by frenzy, I seized the 2,000 florins I had left and staked them on the twelve first numbers – haphazard, at random, without stopping to think! There was, however, one instant's expectant pause, perhaps sensation for sensation the same as that experienced by Madame Blanchard in Paris while she was plunging to the ground from the balloon.

'Quatre!' called the croupier. Altogether, with my first stake, I now had 6,000 florins again. I already had the air of a conqueror, I no longer feared anything, whatever it might be, and I flung down 4,000 florins on black. Eight or nine others were quick to follow my example and stake on black also. The croupiers looked at one another and exchanged a few words. People all round were talking and waiting.

Black turned up. After that I remember neither the amount nor the order of my stakes. I only recall, as if it was a dream, that I had already won, I think, about sixteen thousand florins; then I suddenly dropped 12,000 in three unlucky coups; then I pushed my last four thousand on to 'passe' (but by now I hardly felt anything at all; I only waited, almost mechanically, without thinking) – and won again; then I won four more times in succession. I can only remember scooping up money in thousands, and I am beginning to remember also that the middle twelve numbers, to which I had become positively attached, turned up most frequently of all. There was a sort of pattern – they appeared three or four times running, without fail, then disappeared for two turns, then again appeared three or four times in succession. This remarkable regularity occurs sometimes in streaks – and this is what throws out the inveterate gamblers, always doing sums with a pencil in their hands. And what terrible jests fate sometimes plays!

I do not think more than half an hour had passed since my arrival. Suddenly the croupier informed me that I had won 30,000 florins, and as the bank would not be responsible for more than that on one occasion, the game would therefore be closed until the following morning. I picked up all my gold pieces and distributed them among my pockets, then snatched up all the notes and immediately transferred myself to the table in the other room where there was another roulette wheel; the whole crowd streamed after me; a place was cleared for me at once and I began playing again, at random and without even counting. I don't know what saved me!

Now, however, some glimmerings of reason began to appear in my mind. I clung to certain numbers and chances, but soon abandoned them and began staking again almost without knowing what I was doing. I must have been very absent-minded! I remember that the croupiers corrected my play several times. I made gross mistakes. My temples were damp with perspiration and my hands trembled. Various Poles, too, hurried up to offer their services, but I did not listen to anybody. My luck held! All at once there was loud talking and laughter all round. Everybody shouted 'Bravo, bravo!' and some even clapped their hands. Here as well I had broken the bank by winning 30,000 florins, and again the game was closed until the next day!

'Go away, go away,' a voice was whispering from my right. It was a Jew from Frankfurt; he had been standing beside me all the time and had, it appears, sometimes helped me to play.

'For God's sake go away,' whispered another voice close to my left ear. I glanced round. It was a very plainly and respectably dressed lady of about thirty, with an unhealthily pale and weary face, which yet still bore the traces of its former remarkable beauty. At that moment I was stuffing my pockets with carelessly crumpled banknotes and picking up the gold that lay on the table. Taking the last role of fifty friedrichs d'or I managed to thrust it, without being noticed, into the pale lady's hand; I terribly wanted to do this, and her thin slender little fingers, I remember, pressed my hand warmly in sign of the liveliest gratitude. It had all happened in a moment.

When I had picked everything up I hurried over to the *trente et quarante* game. *Trente et quarante* is a game for the aristocratic public. This is not roulette, it is cards. Here the bank will pay out up to 100,000 thaler at once. The highest stake, here also, is 4,000 florins. I was completely ignorant of the game and knew hardly any way of staking except on red and black, which they have there as well. I stuck to these. Everybody in the station crowded round. I don't remember whether the thought of Polina crossed my mind even once during all this time. I felt a kind of irresistible delight in snatching up and raking in the banknotes which grew into a pile in front of me.

It really seemed that it was fate that urged me on. At the time, as luck would have it, something had happened which is, however, fairly frequently repeated in this game. The luck clings, for example, to red, and remains there ten or fifteen times in a row. Two days earlier I had been told that the previous week red had won twenty-two times running; nobody could remember such a thing ever happening in roulette, and people were talking about it with amazement. Of course, in such a case everybody immediately stops staking on red, and after it has come up say ten successive times, hardly anybody at all risks a stake on it. But at such times no experienced player will stake on the opposite colour, black, either. Experienced players know the meaning of such 'freakish chances'. One might suppose, for example, that after red has come up sixteen times, on the seventeenth it will inevitably be black that does so. Novices rush to this conclusion in crowds, double and treble their stakes, and lose heavily.

But I, with strange perversity, deliberately went on staking on red after noticing that it had turned up seven times running. I am sure vanity was half responsible for this; I wanted to astonish the spectators by taking senseless chances and – a strange sensation! – I clearly remember that even without any promptings of vanity I really was suddenly overcome by a terrible craving for risk. Perhaps the soul passing through such a wide range of sensations is not satisfied but only exacerbated by them, and demands more and more of them, growing more and more powerful, until it reaches final exhaustion. And I really am not lying when I say that if the rules of the game had allowed me to stake 50,000 florins at one throw I would certainly have done so. The bystanders exclaimed that this was madness, and that red had already won fourteen times!

'*Monsieur a gagné déjà cent mille florins,*' I heard somebody's voice saying close beside me.

I suddenly came to my senses. What? I had won 100,000 florins that evening! But what use was any more to me? I fell upon the bank notes, crammed them into my pockets without counting, raked together all my loose gold and all the rolls of gold coins and hurried out of the station. Everybody laughed as I went through the rooms, looking at my torn pockets and the staggering gait caused by the weight of the gold. I think there must have been more than twenty pounds of it. A few hands were stretched out towards me; I gave away money in handfuls, just what I happened to snatch up. Near the door I was stopped by two Jews.

'You are a brave man, very brave!' they said, 'but you must leave as early as possible tomorrow morning without fail, or else you will lose everything. . . .'

I did not listen to them. The avenue was so dark that I could not see my hands in front of my face. It was about half a verst to the hotel. I have never been afraid of thieves or robbers, even when I was small; I did not think of them even now. I don't remember, though, what I did think of on the way; it could hardly be called thinking. I only felt a sort of terrible delight in success, victory, power – I don't know how to express it. The image of Polina also passed through my mind; I remembered and fully realized that I was going to her, and that presently I should be with her, telling her, showing her . . . but I hardly remembered what she had said to me not long before, or why I had gone, and all the sensations I had felt only an hour and a half earlier now seemed to be relics of the distant past, ancient and half-obliterated, not to be spoken of again because now everything was starting afresh. I had already almost reached the end of the avenue when sudden terror struck at me: 'What if I am robbed and murdered now?' My panic redoubled at every step. I was almost running. Suddenly the whole hotel, with all its lighted windows, blazed out at the end of the avenue; thank God, I was at home!

I ran up to my own floor and flung the door open. Polina was there, sitting on my sofa with folded arms, the lighted candle in front of her. She gazed at me in astonishment, and of course I must have looked strange enough at that moment. I stopped in front of her and began flinging my money on the table in a great pile.

CHAPTER FIFTEEN

I REMEMBER that she looked very closely at my face, but without moving, or even altering her position.

'I've won two hundred thousand francs!' I cried as I threw down the last roll of gold coins. The enormous heap of notes and gold coins covered the whole table, and I could not take my eyes off it; there were moments when I completely forgot Polina. Now I would begin to tidy those piles of notes, stacking them up neatly, now to move all the gold into a separate pile; then I would abandon everything else and pace rapidly up and down the room, deep in thought, and afterwards go back to the table and begin counting the money again. All at once I seemed to come to myself, rushed to the door, and hastily double-locked it. Then I stopped and brooded in front of my little trunk.

'Shall I put it in the trunk until tomorrow?' I asked, turning to Polina as I suddenly remembered her. She was still sitting in the same place, not moving, but attentively following me with her eyes. The expression of her face seemed somehow strange; I didn't like that look! It would not be wrong to say there was hatred in it.

I went to her quickly.

'Polina, here are twenty-five thousand florins – that's fifty thousand francs or even more. Take it, and throw it in his face tomorrow.'

She did not answer.

'If you like, I'll take it myself, first thing in the morning. All right?'

She laughed suddenly, and went on laughing for a long time.

I watched her in surprise and with a feeling of unhappiness. This laugh was very like those recent frequent bursts of mocking laughter at my expense which had always greeted my most passionate declarations. At last she stopped and frowned, looking at me sternly from under sullen brows.

'I won't take your money,' she said contemptuously.

'What? What's the matter?' I cried. 'Why not, Polina?'

'I won't take money for nothing.'

'I offer it as your friend; I am offering you life.'

She looked at me long and searchingly, as if trying to see right inside me.

'You are giving a high price,' she said with a bitter smile; 'de Grieux's mistress is not worth fifty thousand francs.'

'Oh, Polina, how can you talk to me like that?' I cried reproachfully. 'I'm not de Grieux, am I?'

'I hate you! Yes . . . yes! I don't love you any more than de Grieux,' she cried, her eyes flashing suddenly.

Then all at once she covered her face with her hands and became hysterical. I rushed to her.

I knew something must have happened in my absence. She seemed not to be in her right mind at all.

'Buy me! Would you like to? Would you? For fifty thousand francs, like de Grieux?' she sobbed convulsively. I put my arms round her, kissed her hands and feet, fell on my knees before her.

Her hysterical fit was passing. She laid both hands on my shoulders and scanned my face attentively; she seemed to want to read something there. She listened to me, but evidently did not take in what I was saying. Her face wore a troubled and thoughtful expression. I feared for her; I definitely thought her mind was wandering. Then suddenly she began to draw me gently towards her; a trustful smile played over her face; then all at once she pushed me away and again began gazing at me with a shadowed look.

Suddenly she flung herself into my arms.

'You do love me, don't you?' she said; 'after all, after all . . . you wanted to fight the Baron for my sake!' And she burst out laughing again – as though she had just remembered something amusing and nice. She was laughing and crying both together. Well, what could I do? I felt feverish myself. I remember she began talking to me, but I could hardly understand anything she said. It was a kind of delirious chatter – as though she wanted to tell me something as quickly as possible – interrupted occasionally by peals of cheerful laughter, which was beginning to terrify me. 'No, no, you're nice, you're nice!' she would repeat. 'You are true to me!' – and then she would put her hands on my shoulders again, gazing at me and continuing to repeat, 'You do love me . . . you love me . . . will you love me?' I did not take my eyes off her; I had never before seen her in these fitful moods of tenderness and love; it is true, of course, that this was delirium, but . . . noticing my look of passion she suddenly assumed a sly smile; and all of a sudden she began talking about Mr Astley.

She was, however, constantly beginning to talk about Mr Astley (especially when, just now, she had been making such efforts to tell me something), but I could not fully grasp exactly what she was trying to say; she even seemed to be laughing at him; she repeated again and again that he was waiting . . . and did I know that he was probably standing under the window now? 'Yes, yes, under the window – well, open it and look, look, he's here, he's here!' She pushed me towards the window, but as soon as I made a movement towards it, she would laugh merrily and then I stayed with her and she threw her arms round me.

'We're going away, aren't we? Are we going tomorrow?' was the next thought that flashed into her restless mind, 'Well . . .' (she paused again thoughtfully) 'well, do you think we shall catch up with Grandmamma? I think we'll catch her up in Berlin. What do you think she'll say when we catch her up and she sees us? And what about Mr Astley? . . . Well, he won't jump off the Schlangenberg, do you think?' (She laughed loudly.) 'Oh, listen: do you know where he's going next summer? He wants to go on a scientific expedition to the North Pole, and he's been asking me to go with him, ha, ha, ha! He says we Russians don't know anything and can't do anything without the Europeans. . . . But he's a nice man, too! Do you know, he makes excuses for the General: he says Blanche . . . he says passion – oh, I don't know, I don't know,' she repeated suddenly, as if she was confused and talking at random. 'Poor things, I'm so sorry for them, and for Grandmamma. . . . Oh, listen, listen, how could you kill de Grieux? And did you really think you would kill him, really? Oh, you were silly! Did you really think I would let you fight de Grieux? And you won't even kill the Baron,' she added, laughing again suddenly. 'Oh, how funny you were with the Baron that time; I watched you both from the seat; and how reluctant you were to go when I sent you to him. How I laughed, how I laughed!' she added, with peals of laughter.

Suddenly she was kissing and embracing me again, and tenderly and passionately pressing her face to mine. I no longer thought of anything or heard anything. My head was spinning. . . .

I think it was about seven o'clock in the morning when I came to myself; the sun was shining into the room. Polina was sitting beside me, looking round strangely, as if emerging from some cloudy darkness and trying to collect her thoughts. She also had just waked up, and she was staring at the table and the money. My head was heavy and aching. I tried to take Polina's hand; she pushed me away and sprang up from the sofa. The new day was overcast; it had rained before dawn. She went to the window, opened it, and thrust out her head and shoulders; supporting herself with her arms, her elbows resting against the sides of the window, she remained there about three minutes, without turning towards me or listening to what I was saying. Fear gripped me as I wondered what would happen now and how it would all end. Suddenly she raised herself from the window, walked to the table and, looking at me with an expression of infinite loathing, her lips trembling with fury, said:

'Well, now give me my fifty thousand francs!'

'Polina, again, again!' I was beginning.

'Or have you thought better of it? Ha, ha, ha! Perhaps you are already regretting it?'

The 25,000 florins I had counted out the night before lay on the table, and I took them up and gave them to her.

'It's mine, now, isn't it? That's so, isn't it? Isn't it?' she asked spitefully, holding the money in her hands.

'It always was yours,' I said.

'Well then, here are your fifty thousand francs!' She swung up her arm and threw them at me. The bundle of money gave me a painful blow in the face and scattered over the floor. When she had done it Polina ran out of the room.

I know, of course, that she was out of her mind at the time, although I do not understand this temporary madness. It is true that even now, a month later, she is still ill. But what was the reason of her state, and especially of this extraordinary trick? Wounded pride? Despair because she had been reduced to deciding to come to me? Had I given her the impression that I was gloating over my luck and was in fact, like de Grieux himself, trying to get rid of her by my gift of 50,000 francs? But my conscience tells me that that really was not true. I think her own vanity was partly to blame; it prompted her to distrust and insult me, although the whole thing appeared to her, perhaps, in a very confused light. In that case I of course had to answer for de Grieux, and was held responsible even though my guilt was not very great. It is true this was all the effect of delirium; it is true, too, that I knew she was delirious, and . . . had paid no attention to that fact. Perhaps she could not forgive me for that now? Yes, but that was now; what about then? After all, her fever and delirium had not been so great, had they, that she was completely oblivious of what she was doing when she brought de Grieux's letter to me? She must have known what she was doing.

In haste, I somehow bundled all my notes and my pile of gold hugger-mugger into the bed, covered it up, and went out about ten minutes after Polina. I was certain that she had run back to their suite, and I meant to go there very quietly and in the lobby ask the children's nurse how the young lady was. What was my consternation when I learned from Nurse, whom I met on the stairs, that Polina had not yet returned home and that Nurse was on her way to my room to look for her.

'She left me,' I told her, 'she left me only just now, ten minutes ago; where can she have got to?'

Nurse looked at me reproachfully.

Meanwhile a regular scandal had developed and by now was making its way all over the hotel. In the porter's lodge and the manager's office there were whispers that the *fräulein* had run out of the hotel in the rain at six o'clock in the morning, and gone running towards the Hotel d'Angleterre. From what they said and the hints they gave, I noticed that they already knew she had spent the whole night in my room. There had already been talk, however, about all the General's family: it had become known that the General had gone out of his mind the day before and was weeping all over the hotel. They were saying also that Grand-mamma was his mother, who had come all the way from Russia on purpose to forbid her son's marriage to Mademoiselle de Cominges and disinherit him if he disobeyed, and as he had in fact not obeyed her, the Countess had deliberately lost all her money at roulette before his very eyes, so that he really should get nothing. 'Diese Russen!' the manager indignantly repeated, shaking his head. Others laughed. The manager was making out the bill. It was already known that I had won; Karl, the waiter on my floor, had been the first to congratulate me. But I had no time for them. I hurried to the Hotel d'Angleterre.

It was still early; Mr Astley was not at home to anybody; but when he heard that it was I he came out into the corridor and stopped in front of me, silently fixing me with his pewter-coloured eyes, and waited to hear what I would say. I immediately inquired about Polina.

'She is ill,' answered Mr Astley, as before staring steadily without taking his eyes off me.

'So she really is here with you.'

'Oh yes, she's here.'

'So you ... you intend to keep her with you?'

'Oh yes, I intend to do that.'

'Mr Astley, that will cause a scandal; you can't do it. Besides, she is very ill; perhaps you haven't noticed?'

'Oh yes, I did, and I have already told you she was ill. If she had not been ill, she would not have spent the night in your room.'

'So you know that as well?'

'Yes, I know it. She was coming here yesterday, and I would have taken her to a lady who is a relative of mine, but as she was ill she made a mistake and went to you.'

'Imagine that! Well, I congratulate you, Mr Astley. You have given me an idea, by the way: were you standing under our window all night? All through the night Miss Polina kept making me open the window and look out to see if you were standing there, and she laughed an awful lot.'

'Really? No, I wasn't standing under the window; but I was waiting in the corridor and walking about.'

'But she must be looked after, you know, Mr Astley.'

'Oh yes, I have sent for a doctor, and if she dies you will answer to me for her death.'

I was astounded:

'Excuse me, Mr Astley, what are you trying to say?'

'Is it true that you won two hundred thousand thalers yesterday?'

'It was only a hundred thousand florins.'

'There, you see! So go off to Paris tomorrow.'

'Why?'

'Every Russian who has any money goes to Paris,' explained Mr Astley, in a voice and manner that suggested he had read it in a book.

'What can I do in Paris now, in the summer? I love her, Mr Astley! You know that yourself.'

'Really? I am sure you don't. Besides, if you stay here you will certainly lose everything, and you won't have anything left to get to Paris with. But good-bye; I am quite convinced you will go to Paris today.'

'Very well, good-bye; only I shan't go to Paris. Think a moment about what will happen to us now, Mr Astley. In short, the General . . . and now this adventure of Miss Polina's — it will be all over the town.'

'Yes, it will; but I don't believe the General is thinking of that, and it's nothing to do with him. Besides, Miss Polina has every right to live where she likes. As for the family, you might truthfully say that the family no longer exists.'

As I walked along I laughed to myself at the Englishman's strange certainty that I would go to Paris. 'But he means to kill me in a duel if Mademoiselle Polina dies — that means more trouble!' I was sorry for Polina, I swear, but it was a strange thing — from the moment I touched the roulette table the day before and began raking in piles of money, my love seemed to have retreated into the background. I can say that now; but then I still had not seen it all clearly. Can I really be a gambler, can my love for Polina . . . have really been so strange? No, to this day I still love her, God knows. And at that time, when I had left Mr Astley and was walking home, my suffering and self-accusation were genuine enough. But . . . but at this moment an extremely odd and stupid thing happened to me.

I was hurrying to see the General when suddenly, not far from their rooms, a door opened and somebody called out to me. It was

Madame *veuve* Cominges, and she was calling at Mademoiselle Blanche's behest. I turned into Mademoiselle Blanche's rooms.

They had a small suite of two rooms. I could hear Mademoiselle Blanche laughing and calling out in the bedroom. She was just getting up.

'Ah, *c'est lui! Viens donc, bêtà!* Is it true *que tu as gagné une montagne d'or et d'argent? J'aimerais mieux l'or.*'

'Yes, I did,' I answered, laughing.

'How much?'

'A hundred thousand florins.'

'*Bibi, comme tu es bête.* But come in here, I can't hear you. *Nous ferons bombance, n'est-ce pas?*'

I went into her room. She was lying under a pink satin counterpane, which left uncovered her strong, dark-skinned shoulders, marvellous shoulders – shoulders such as one hardly even dreams of – only partly concealed by a nightgown of fine lawn, trimmed with the whitest lace, which suited her swarthy skin wonderfully.

'*Mon fils, as-tu du cœur?*' she cried when she saw me, and laughed. She always had a merry laugh, and sometimes even a genuine one.

'*Tout autre . . .*', I began, paraphrasing Corneille.

'Now you see, *vois-tu,*' she began chattering away, 'first of all, find my stockings and help me to put them on – and secondly, *si tu n'es pas trop bête, je te prends à Paris.* You know I'm leaving at once.'

'Now?'

'In half an hour.'

Everything had, in fact, been packed. All her trunks and things were standing ready. Her coffee had been served long before.

'*Eh bien!* tu verras Paris, if you want. *Dis donc, qu'est-ce que c'est qu'un outchitel? Tu étais bien bête, quand tu étais outchitel.* But where are my stockings? Well then, put them on for me!'

She thrust out a really exquisite little foot, swarthy-skinned, small, and, unlike almost all those little feet that look so charming in their shoes, not misshapen. I laughed, and began to draw the silk stocking over it. Meanwhile Mademoiselle Blanche sat on the edge of the bed chattering away.

'*Eh bien, que feras-tu, si je te prends avec?* First, *je veux cinquante mille francs.* You can give them to me at Frankfurt. *Nous allons à Paris;* we will live together there *et je te ferai voir des étoiles en plein jour.* You shall see such women as you have never seen before. Listen . . .'

'Wait; so I'm to give you fifty thousand francs, but what will be left for me?'

'*Et cent cinquante mille francs,* you have forgotten, and besides, I am willing to live with you for a month, two months, *que sais-je?* We shall of course get through the whole hundred and fifty thousand francs in two months. You see, *je suis bonne enfant,* and tell you beforehand, *mais tu verras des étoiles.*'

'What, all in two months?'

'Well! It frightens you, does it? Ah, *vil esclave!* But don't you know that one month of that life is better than your whole existence? One month – *et après, le déluge! Mais tu ne peux comprendre, va!* Go away, go away, you're not worthy of it! Ah, *que fais-tu?*'

At that moment I was putting the stocking on her other foot, but I had not been able to help kissing it. She snatched it away and began hitting me in the face with the tip of her toes. Finally she turned me out altogether.

'*Eh bien, mon outchitel, je t'attends, si tu veux;* I'm going in a quarter of an hour!' she called after me.

I returned to my own room with my head in a whirl. Well, I was not to blame if Mademoiselle Polina had flung the whole pile of money in my face and had still preferred Mr Astley to me the day before. A few fallen banknotes still lay on the floor; I picked them up. At that moment the door opened and the manager himself (who had not even looked my way before) appeared to ask me if I would care to move downstairs into an excellent suite in which Count V— had just been staying.

I stood and thought for a moment.

'My bill!' I cried. 'I'm leaving at once, in ten minutes' time.' 'If it's to be Paris, very well, let's go to Paris!' I thought to myself; 'evidently it was written in my stars!'

A quarter of an hour later all three of us, Mademoiselle Blanche and Madame *veuve* Cominges and myself, were sitting together in an unreserved carriage. Mademoiselle Blanche laughed so much as

she looked at me that she became quite hysterical. Madame de
Cominges echoed her; I will not say that I felt very cheerful. My
life had been broken in two, but since yesterday I had got used to
staking everything on a single throw of the dice. It may really have
been true that I could not do with money and had lost my head.
Peut-être, je ne demandais pas mieux. It seemed to me that the
scenery was being changed for a time, but only for a time. 'But in
a month's time I shall be here again, and then . . . then I can still
try conclusions with you, Mr Astley!' No, as I remember now, I
was terribly sad even then, although I vied with that little idiot
Blanche in laughing.

'But what's the matter with you? How silly you are! Oh, how
silly you are!' Blanche would cry, interrupting her laughter and
beginning to scold me in good earnest. 'Well, yes, well, yes, yes,
we'll run through your two hundred thousand francs, but on the
other hand, *mais tu seras heureux, comme un petit roi*; I will tie
your ties for you and introduce you to Hortense. And when we
have spent all our money, you will come back here and break the
bank again. What did the Jews say to you? Courage above all! –
and you have it, and you will bring me back money to Paris more
than once. *Quant à moi, je veux cinquante mille francs de rente
et alors . . .*'

'And what about the General?' I asked her.

'The General, as you know very well, goes out to buy me a
bouquet every day. This time I purposely told him to find me the
rarest kind of flowers. The poor man will return to find the bird
flown. He will fly after us, you'll see. Ha, ha, ha! I shall be very
glad. He'll be useful to me in Paris; Mr Astley will pay his bill
here. . . .'

And so that was how I went to Paris.

CHAPTER SIXTEEN

WHAT can I say about Paris? Of course it was all delirium and
foolishness. I spent only a little more than three weeks altogether
in Paris, and in that time I got right to the end of my 100,000
francs. I speak of only 100,000 francs; the other 100,000 I gave to

Mademoiselle Blanche in cash – 50,000 in Frankfurt and another 50,000 three days later in Paris in the form of a promissory note, for which, however, she got cash from me a week later, '*et les cent mille francs qui nous restent, tu les mangeras avec moi, mon outchitel.*' She always called me *outchitel*. It is difficult to imagine anything on earth more calculating, mean and miserly than the class of beings like Mademoiselle Blanche. But that is in respect of their own money. As for my 100,000 francs, she explained to me later with great frankness that she needed them to set herself up in Paris for the first time, 'as I am now established on a respectable footing and nobody will be able to dislodge me for a long time, or not at least as far as I can ensure it,' she added. I hardly set eyes on that 100,000, however; she kept the money all the time and never more than a hundred francs was allowed to accumulate in my purse, of the state of which she kept herself informed every day; almost always there was less than that in it.

'Well, what do you want with money?' she would sometimes say with the most naïve expression, and I did not argue with her. On the other hand, she furnished her flat very nicely indeed on the money, and later when she took me to her new home she said, as she showed me the rooms: 'You see what can be done, given care and taste, with the scantiest means.' Those scanty means, however, came to exactly my 50,000 francs. With the other 50,000 she acquired a carriage and horses, and in addition we gave two balls, or rather two evening parties, which were attended by Hortense and Lisette and Cleopatra – remarkable women in very many respects, and very far from ugly. At these two parties I was obliged to play the utterly stupid role of host, meeting and entertaining the dullest newly-rich tradespeople, various impossibly ignorant and impudent army lieutenants, and wretched little authors and journalistic gad-flies, who turned up in fashionable tails and yellow gloves, and whose vanity and conceit reached such proportions as would be unthinkable even among us in St Petersburg – and that is saying a lot. They even thought fit to sneer at me, but I got tipsy on champagne and lounged through the time in a back room. I found the whole proceedings nauseating in the extreme. '*C'est un outchitel*,' Blanche told people; '*il a gagné deux cent mille francs*, and without me he wouldn't know how to spend them. Afterwards he will go back to being a tutor again; does anybody know of a post for him? We must do something for him.' I began to have very frequent recourse to champagne, because I was always very sad and bored to death. I was living in the most bourgeois and mercantile surroundings, where every *sou* was counted and doled out. Blanche greatly disliked me for the first two weeks, I noticed; true, she dressed me foppishly and tied my tie with her own hands every morning, but in her heart she genuinely despised me. I paid not the slightest attention to this. Bored and despondent, I began to frequent the Château des Fleurs, where I got drunk regularly every evening, practised the cancan (which is danced very filthily there) and subsequently even achieved celebrity in that line. In the end Blanche learned to know me: earlier she had somehow got the idea that all the time we were living together I should be following her round with a pencil and a piece of paper in my hands, reckoning up how much she had spent, how much she had stolen, how much she was going to spend and how much more she was going to steal, and she was, of course, certain that we should have a battle over every ten-franc piece. She was prepared in advance with retorts in answer to all the attacks she expected from me and when she found I did not attack her, she would at first launch into the retorts of her own accord. Sometimes she began with the utmost vehemence, but seeing that I remained silent – more often than not lying on a couch and staring at the ceiling – she was utterly astounded. To begin with she thought I was simply stupid, '*un outchitel*', and merely broke off her explanations, probably thinking to herself, 'After all, he's stupid; no need to put ideas into his head if he doesn't understand for himself.' She used to go away but then come back again after about ten minutes (this was during the time of her wildest expenditure, expenditure quite out of keeping with our means: for example, she got rid of her horses and spent 16,000 francs on a matched pair instead).

'Well, *bibi*, so you're not angry?' she would ask, coming close to me.

'No-o-o! You bo-o-re me!' I said, pushing her away with my hand, but she found this so intriguing that she immediately sat down beside me.

'You see, if I decided to pay so much, it was because they were a bargain. They can always be sold again for twenty thousand francs.'

'No doubt, no doubt; they are beautiful horses; now you have a splendid turn-out; it will be useful to you; well, that's enough.'

'So you're not angry?'

'Why should I be? You are wise to lay in a stock of a few things that are essential to you. It will all come in useful later on. I quite see that it is really necessary for you to set yourself up in this style; otherwise you'll never make a million. Our hundred thousand francs are only a beginning, a drop in the ocean.'

Talk like this (instead of outcries and reproaches) was the last thing Blanche expected of me, and she was quite bewildered.

'So you . . . so this is what you're like! *Mais tu a l'esprit pour comprendre! Sais-tu, mon garçon*, you may be only a tutor, but you ought to have been born a prince! So it doesn't make you sorry to see our money running out so quickly?'

'Bother the money! The quicker the better!'

'*Mais . . . sais-tu . . . mais dis donc*, you're not rich, are you? *Mais sais-tu*, you're too scornful of money. *Qu'est-ce que tu feras après, dis donc?*'

'*Après*, I shall go to Homburg and win another hundred thousand francs.'

'*Oui, oui, c'est ça, c'est magnifique!* And I know you'll win for certain and bring your winnings here. *Dis donc*, you'll make me really love you! *Eh bien*, because you are the kind of person you are, I will love you all the time you are here and not be unfaithful to you once. You see, all this time, although I didn't love you, *parce que je croyais que tu n'es qu'un outchitel (quelque chose comme un laquais, n'est-ce pas?)*, I was faithful to you all the same, *parce que je suis bonne fille.*'

'Well, that's a lie! What about Albert, that blackavised little officer? Do you think I didn't see you last time?'

'Oh, oh, *mais tu es . . .*'

'Well, it's all lies; do you think it makes me angry? I don't give a damn; *il faut que jeunesse se passe*. You can't be expected to send him away if he was here before me and you love him. Only don't give him money, do you hear?'

'So you're not angry about that, either? *Mais tu es un vrai philosophe, sais-tu? Un vrai philosophe!*' she exclaimed rapturously. '*Eh bien, je t'aimerai, je t'aimerai — tu verras, tu seras content!*'

And from that time on she really did seem to have become attached to me, and even to feel friendly; and in this way our last ten days passed. I did not see the 'stars' she had promised me; but in certain respects she did keep her word. Moreover, she introduced me to Hortense, who was a really remarkable woman in her own way, and was called *Thérèse philosophe* in our circle. . . .

There is, however, no need to enlarge on that; it might all make a separate story, with its own atmosphere, which I don't wish to introduce into this one. The fact is that I longed with all my heart for it to come to an end quickly. But our 100,000 francs, as I have already said, lasted for nearly a month — which genuinely surprised me: Blanche spent at least 80,000 of it on things for herself, and we had no more than 20,000 francs to live on — and yet it lasted. Blanche, who towards the end became almost frank with me (at any rate she didn't lie to me about some things), declared that at least none of the debts she had been obliged to incur would fall upon me: 'I didn't make you sign any bills or promissory notes,' she told me, 'because I was sorry for you; anybody else would certainly have done so and landed you in prison. You see, you see how much I have loved you and how kind I am! That damned wedding alone is going to cost me I don't know how much!'

We really did have a wedding. It happened at the very end of our month, and it must be presumed that the very last dregs of my 100,000 francs were spent on it; that was the end of it all; I mean that it brought our month to an end and after it I formally retired.

It happened like this. A week after our installation in Paris the General arrived. He came straight to Blanche and practically lived with us from the time of his first visit. He had, it is true, his own modest quarters somewhere or other. Blanche greeted him with delighted shrieks and peals of laughter, and even flung her arms round him; the upshot was that she was unwilling to let him go, and he had to be in attendance everywhere, on the boulevards, in her carriage, at the theatre, and when she called on her acquaintances. The General was still fit for these uses; he was quite presentable and looked important – he was almost tall, with dyed whiskers and moustache (he had been in the Cuirassiers), and handsome if rather flabby features. His manners were excellent, and he wore evening dress well. He had begun wearing his Orders in Paris. To walk along the boulevard with such a man was not only possible, it was, if I may so express it, a *recommendation*. The good silly General was immensely pleased with all this; he had not expected anything like it when he called on us on his arrival in Paris. On that occasion he made his appearance almost trembling with fear; he was afraid Blanche would scream and have him turned out; so, when things happened as they did, he was in the seventh heaven and spent all the rest of the month in a state of bemused delight; he was still in it when I left Paris. It was only there that I learned all the details of how, the very morning of our sudden departure from Roulettenburg, he suffered something in the nature of a fit. He fell unconscious, and afterwards for a week he was almost like a lunatic, babbling incoherent nonsense the whole time. The doctors cured him, but then he abandoned everything, got into a train and travelled to Paris. Blanche's welcome proved, of course, to be the best possible medicine for him; but signs of his illness persisted for a long time afterwards, in spite of his happy and joyful state of mind. He was by now completely incapable of reasoning or even of conducting any kind of serious conversation; if there was any, he got himself out of difficulty by saying 'hm!' at every word and nodding his head. He laughed frequently, but with a kind of nervous, sickly laughter, which he seemed unable to control; at other times he would sit for hours together, knitting his heavy eyebrows and looking as black as thunder. He had grown very forgetful; he was shockingly absentminded and had acquired the habit of talking to himself. Only Blanche could revive him; and indeed his attacks of gloom and depression, when he brooded in a corner, signified merely that he had not seen her for some time, or that she had gone away somewhere without taking him or making a fuss of him first. On such occasions he would not say what he wanted and was not conscious of being glum and melancholy. When he had been sitting like this for an hour or two (I noticed this a couple of times when Blanche had gone off for the whole day, probably to see Albert), he would suddenly begin staring round, fidgeting, letting his gaze wander as though he was trying to recall something or wanted to look for somebody; but, not seeing anybody, and unable to remember what he wanted to ask, he would relapse into oblivion until Blanche made her appearance again, gay, high-spirited, showily dressed, with her ringing laugh; she would run to him and begin teasing or even kissing him – although she rarely deigned to do *that*. Once the General was so happy to see her that he even burst into tears – I was positively astounded.

From the first moment of his arrival among us, Blanche immediately began pleading his cause with me. She even became eloquent; she recalled that she had betrayed the General for my sake, that she had been almost openly engaged to him and had given him her word; that for her sake he had deserted his family and that finally I had been in his service and ought to have remembered it, and – wasn't I ashamed of myself? . . . I remained silent, and she went babbling endlessly on. Finally I laughed aloud, and that was the end of it; I mean, she had thought at first I was a fool, but now at last she had arrived at the settled conclusion that I was a very nice and accommodating person. In short, I had the happiness of completely winning the favour of that deserving young woman (Blanche was, in fact, a most good-natured girl, though of course only in her own way; I hadn't appreciated that at first). 'You are good and clever,' she used to say to me towards the end, 'and . . . and . . . the only trouble is you're such a fool! You'll never, never make your fortune!'

'*Un vrai Russe, un calmouk!*' – and she several times sent me to take the General out for a walk, exactly as though he was her whippet and she was putting him in charge of a footman. However, I took him to restaurants and the theatre and the *Bal Mabille*. Blanche even gave me the money for this, although the General had some of his own and liked to bring out his note-case in front of people. Once I was almost obliged to use force to prevent him from buying for 700 francs a brooch which had taken his eye in the Palais Royale and which he had set his heart on giving to Blanche as a present. But what was a 700-franc brooch to her?

Besides, the General didn't possess more than a thousand francs altogether. I never could find out where he had got them from. I suppose it was from Mr Astley, especially as the latter had paid their hotel bill. As far as the General's attitude towards me all this time was concerned, I think he didn't even speculate about my relations with Blanche. Although he had heard in a vague sort of way that I had won a fortune, he probably assumed that I was some kind of private secretary or even servant to Blanche. At all events, he always spoke to me as condescendingly and bossily as ever, and sometimes he even gave me a regular scolding. On one occasion, at our breakfast-table, he gave Blanche and me immense amusement. He was not a particularly touchy person, but now he was suddenly offended with me – why, I don't understand to this day. But of course he didn't understand, either. To cut a long story short, he launched into an endless tirade, *à bâtons rompus*, shouting that I was a young puppy . . . he would soon show me . . . he was going to teach me a lesson . . . and so on. But nobody understood a word he was saying. Blanche laughed till she cried; finally we managed to get him calmed down and sent off for a walk. There were many times, though, when I noticed that he seemed sad, as if he was grieving over somebody or something, or, in spite of Blanche's presence, missing somebody. Once or twice at such times he began talking to me, but seemed unable to make himself clear, rambling on reminiscently about his life in the army, his late wife, his financial affairs and his estate. He would hit on some word or phrase that pleased him and repeat it a hundred times a day, although it did not correspond at all with either his feelings or his ideas. I tried to talk to him about his children, but he would turn it aside with his usual meaningless gabble and change the subject as soon as possible: 'Yes, yes, the children, you're quite right, the children!' Once, and only once, when we were on our way to the theatre, he showed concern for them: 'They are unfortunate children!' he began suddenly; 'yes, sir, yes, they are unf-fortunate children!' And several times during the evening he repeated the phrase, 'unfortunate children!' When I spoke once of Polina, he flew into a positive rage. 'She's an ungrateful woman,' he exclaimed, 'wicked and ungrateful! She has disgraced the family! If there were laws here, I'd bring her to heel! Yes, sir!

yes, sir !' As for de Grieux, he could not bear even to hear his name. 'He's been my ruin,' he said, 'he's a cut-throat and a high-wayman ! He's been a nightmare to me for two whole years ! I dreamt of him for months together ! He's, he, he . . . oh, never mention his name again !'

I could see something was going very smoothly for them, but as usual I said nothing. Blanche was the first to announce the news to me, exactly a week before we parted. '*Il a de la chance*,' she prattled, '*grand'mère* really is ill now, and she is sure to die. Mr Astley has sent us a telegram; you must admit he's her heir, all the same. And even if he isn't, he won't be in the way at all. To begin with, he has his pension, and in the second place, he'll have his own room at the back and be completely happy. I shall be "*madame la générale*". I shall get into a good social circle' (Blanche was always dreaming about this) 'and later I shall be a Russian landowner, *j'aurai un château, des moujiks, et puis j'aurai toujours mon million*.'

'Well, but what if he begins to be jealous and insists on . . . God knows what, you understand?'

'Oh, no, *non, non, non* ! how dare he? I have taken measures, don't worry. I have made him sign several promissory notes of Albert's. The least thing – and he will immediately find himself under arrest; but he won't dare !'

'Well, marry him. . . .'

It was a quiet family wedding, celebrated without any great ceremony. Albert and several other close friends were invited. Hortense, Cleopatra and the rest were resolutely kept away. The bridegroom was extremely concerned about his standing.

Blanche tied his tie and pomaded his hair herself, and in his evening coat with a white waistcoat he looked *très comme il faut*.

'*Il est pourtant très comme il faut*,' Blanche declared as she came out of the General's room, as though the idea of the General's being *très comme il faut* surprised even her. I was so little con-cerned with all the details, taking part as I did only in the capacity of an idle spectator, that I have forgotten a great deal of what happened. I remember only that Blanche turned out not to be de Cominges at all, any more than her mother was *veuve* Cominges, but du Placet. Why they had both been de Cominges up to then I don't know. But the General remained quite satisfied, and indeed even liked du Placet better than de Cominges. On the morning of the wedding, after he was dressed, he walked backwards and forwards up and down the drawing-room, all the time repeating to himself with an extraordinarily solemn and important air 'Mademoiselle Blanche du Placet! Blanche du Placet! du Placet! Miss Blanche du Placet!', and his face shone with some complacency. In the church, at the *mairie* and at home at the wedding-breakfast he was not only pleased and happy, but proud. Something had happened to both of them. Blanche had also begun to wear a look of peculiar dignity.

'I shall have to behave very differently now,' she said to me with extraordinary solemnity, '*mais vois-tu*, I never thought of one dreadful thing: just think, I still haven't learnt how to pronounce my new name: Zagoryansky, Zagoziansky, *madame la générale de Sago – Sago, ces diables de noms russes, enfin, madame la générale à quatorze consonnes! comme c'est agréable, n'est-ce pas?*'

We parted at last, and Blanche, silly Blanche, absolutely shed a tear or two as she said good-bye to me. '*Tu étais bon enfant*,' she said, sniffling. '*Je te croyais bête et tu en avais l'air*, but it suits you.' And then, after she had pressed my hand for the last time, she suddenly exclaimed, '*Attends!*', darted into her boudoir and a minute later brought me out two thousand-franc notes. That was something I never would have believed! 'This will come in useful; you may be a very learned *outchitel*, but you're a terribly stupid man. I wouldn't give you more than two thousand for anything, because – you'd lose it all, just the same. Well, good-bye. *Nous serons toujours bons amis*, and if you win again, be sure to come to me, *et tu seras heureux!*'

I still had about five hundred francs left myself; besides that, I have a magnificent watch worth a thousand francs, diamond cufflinks, and so on, so that I can still hold out for a fairly long time without worrying. I have deliberately settled down in this little town, to collect myself and, above all, to wait for Mr Astley. I have been told for certain that he will pass through here and will stay for twenty-four hours on business. I shall find out about everything . . . and then – then I shall go straight to Homburg. I shan't go to Roulettenburg, except perhaps next year. They say the omens really are always against you if you try your luck twice running at one and the same table, and there is real play in Homburg.

CHAPTER SEVENTEEN

IT is a year and eight months since I looked at these notes, and now I have only read them through by chance, when, in my grief and misery, I took it into my head to amuse myself. So it seems I stopped then at the point where I was going to Homburg. Oh, God! with what a light heart, comparatively speaking, I wrote those last lines! Or rather, not exactly with a light heart, but with what self-confidence and what unshakeable hopes! Had I even the smallest doubt of myself? And now a little more than eighteen months have passed and I am, in my own estimation, far worse than a beggar! And what is beggary? I don't care a rap for beggary! I have simply destroyed myself! There is, however, almost no point in making comparisons, and none at all in drawing morals. Nothing could be more absurd than moral conclusions at a time like this! Oh, self-satisfied people: with what smug vanity the windbags are prepared to mouth their precepts! If only they knew how well I understand the whole loathsomeness of my present situation, they would not have the heart to try to instruct me. Why, what on earth can they tell me that is new or that I don't know already? And is that the point? The point here is this – one turn of the wheel and everything can be different, and those same moralists will be the first (I am sure of it) to congratulate me with friendly facetiousness. And everybody will not turn away from me as they do now. But I don't give a damn for any of them! What am I now. Zero. What may I be tomorrow? Tomorrow I may rise from the dead and begin to live again! I may find a man within myself, before he vanishes for good!

I really did go to Homburg that time, but . . . afterwards I was in Roulettenburg again, and in Spa, and even in Baden, where I went as valet to Councillor Hintze, a scoundrel who had been my master here. Yes, I have even been a servant, for five whole months! It happened immediately after I left prison. (I was held in prison in Roulettenburg for a debt I contracted here. An unknown person bought me out – who was it? Mr Astley? Polina? I don't know, but the debt, 200 thalers in all, was paid and I was set free.) Where could I go? I went to this Hintze. He is young and frivolous, and doesn't like to exert himself, and I can speak and write three languages. I went to him at first as a sort of secretary for thirty gulden a month; but I ended as his real man-servant: it became beyond his means to keep a secretary and he reduced my wages; but I had nowhere to go, I stayed where I was – and so turned myself into a servant. I did not have enough to eat and drink in his service, but on the other hand I saved seventy gulden in five months. One evening in Baden I informed him I wished to leave; the same evening I made my way to the roulette tables. Oh, how my heart thumped! No, it was not money that was dear to me! All I wanted then was for all those Hintzes, all those hotel servants, all those fine Baden ladies to be talking about me the next day, telling my story, admiring and praising me and bowing down before my new winnings. All these were childish dreams and wishes, but . . . who knows, perhaps I should come across Polina too, and tell her everything, and she would see that I was above all these absurd turns of fate. . . . Oh, it was not money that was dear to me. I am convinced that I should have squandered it all on some new Blanche, and driven round Paris for three weeks again behind my own pair of horses worth 16,000 francs. I know for a fact that I am no miser; I even believe I am a spendthrift, and yet with what trepidation and sinking of the heart I hear the croupier's cry of 'trente et un, rouge, impair et passe!' or 'quatre, noir, pair et manque!' With what greedy eyes I look at the table scattered with louis d'or, friedrichs d'or, and thalers, the little piles of gold coins when the croupier's shovel sweeps them into heaps that sparkle like fire, and the two-foot long rolls of silver lying round the wheel. When, on my way to the gaming room, I hear from two rooms away the chink of the coins pouring out of the scoops, I am thrown into a ferment.

Oh, that was another remarkable evening, when I took my seventy gulden into the gambling saloon. I began with ten gulden and once again with passe. I have a prejudice in favour of passe. I

lost. I was left with sixty gulden in silver; I thought for a moment
– and chose *zéro*. I began staking five gulden at a time on *zéro*; on
the third stroke, *zéro* turned up; I almost died of joy when I received 175 gulden; I had not been so pleased to win 100,000
gulden. I immediately staked a hundred gulden on red – and won;
the whole 200 on red – and won; the 400 on black – and won; all
800 on *manque* – and won; including what I had before, that was
1700 gulden – and in less than five minutes ! Yes, in such moments
one forgets all one's previous failures. I had got this, you see, at
the risk of more than life, I had dared to run the risk – and now
I was a man again !

I took a hotel room, locked the door, and sat counting my money
until three o'clock. Next morning I woke up no longer a servant.
I decided to go to Homburg that very day : I had never been a
servant, or in prison, there. Half an hour before the train left I
went to gamble on two further stakes, no more, and lost 15,000
florins. All the same, I did travel to Homburg, and I have been
here for a month now....

I live, of course, in a constant quiver of anxiety, play for the
smallest possible sums, wait for something to happen, make calculations, stand all day near the roulette table and *watch* the play,
even dream of it at night, but with all that it seems to me that I
have grown stiff and numb, as though I was plastered with some
sort of mud. I reach that conclusion from the impression made on
me by meeting Mr Astley. We had not seen each other since the
time I have described, and now we met by accident; it happened
like this : I was walking in the gardens and calculating that I was
now almost without money, but still had fifty gulden – and besides that, I had settled my hotel bill for the cubby-hole I occupy
only two days before. Thus I was left with the possibility of going
back to the tables once more – if I won anything at all, I could
continue to play; if I lost, I should have to become a servant again,
if I could not immediately find a Russian family who were in need
of a tutor. Occupied with these thoughts, I pursued my usual
daily walk through the park and the wood into the next principality. Sometimes I walked like this for as much as four hours,
returning to Homburg tired and hungry. I had only just emerged
from the gardens into the park when I suddenly saw Mr Astley

sitting on a bench. He had noticed me first and called to me. I sat down beside him. Noticing a certain stiffness in him, I at once restrained my delight, otherwise I was overjoyed to see him.

'So you *are* here! I just thought I should meet you,' he said. 'Don't bother to tell me; I know, I know everything; everything about your life for the past year and eight months is known to me.'

'Ha! So you keep track of your old friends like that!' I answered. 'It does you honour that you don't forget them. Wait a minute, though, you've given me an idea : was it you who paid for me to get out of Roulettenburg prison, where I was being kept for a debt of two hundred gulden? It was somebody unknown.'

'No, oh no; I didn't buy you out of Roulettenburg prison where you were kept for a debt of two hundred gulden, but I knew you were imprisoned for a debt of two hundred gulden.'

'Does that mean that you know who did buy me out?'

'Oh no, I can't say that I know who bought you out.'

'That's strange; I am not known to any of our Russians, and it is unlikely that Russians here would buy anybody out, it's at home in Russia that the Orthodox buy out the Orthodox. But I just thought some eccentric Englishman might have been odd enough.'

Mr Astley listened to me with some surprise. I think he had expected to find me crushed and dejected.

'I am very glad, though, to see that you have retained all your independence of spirit and even your cheerfulness,' he declared with a look of some displeasure.

'You mean you are writhing inwardly with annoyance that I am not crushed and depressed,' I said laughing.

It took him some time to understand, but when he did, he smiled.

'I like the things you say. I recognize the same old clever, enthusiastic and yet cynical friend as before in those words; only Russians can find room inside themselves for so many contradictions at the same time. People really do like seeing their best friends humiliated; a great part of friendship is based on humiliation; and this is an old truth known to all intelligent people. But in the present case, I assure you, I am genuinely glad that you are not dejected. Tell me, do you intend to give up gambling?'

'Oh, to hell with gambling! I'd throw it up at once, if only . . .'

'If only you could win back what you've lost now? I thought so; you needn't finish – I know you let that slip out, and consequently you were speaking the truth. Tell me, are you doing anything besides gambling?'

'No, nothing. . . .'

He began cross-questioning me. I was ignorant of everything, I hardly even glanced at the newspapers and I had definitely not opened a single book during all that time.

'You've become insensible,' he remarked. 'You've not only renounced life, your own interests and those of society, your duty as a man and a citizen, your friends (and you did have them, all the same) – you've not only renounced every aim whatever in life, except winning at roulette – you have even renounced your memories. I remember you at a passionate and intense period in your life; but I am sure you have forgotten all the best influences of that time; your dreams, your most urgent present desires, go no further than *pair et impair, rouge, noir,* the middle dozen numbers, and so on, I'm convinced of it !'

'Stop, Mr Astley, please, please don't remind me,' I cried, stung and almost angry; 'let me tell you I've forgotten nothing at all; I've only driven it all out of my head, even my memories, for the time being, until I have radically altered my circumstances; then . . . then, you will see, I shall rise from the dead !'

'You will still be here ten years from now,' he said. 'I am willing to bet I'll remind you of it on this very seat, if I'm still alive.'

'Well, that's enough,' I interrupted impatiently, 'and to show you I'm not so forgetful of the past, allow me to ask where Miss Polina is now. If it wasn't you who bought me out, it must have been her. I've had no news of her from that day to this.'

'No, oh no ! I don't think she bought you out. She is in Switzerland now, and you would be doing me a great favour if you would stop asking about her,' he said firmly and even angrily.

'That means she has already hurt you very much also,' I laughed involuntarily.

'Of all creatures worthy of respect, Miss Polina is most worthy of it, but, I repeat, it would give me great pleasure if you would stop asking me about her. You never knew her, and I consider her name on your lips to be an insult to my sense of moral values.'

'Indeed! However, you're wrong; and besides, what have I got to talk to you about except her? Answer me that. After all, that's what all our memories consist of. Don't worry though, I don't want to know any of your inner secrets. . . . I am only interested in Miss Polina's external situation, so to speak, nothing but her present outward circumstances. That can be told in two words.'

'Very well, so long as the two words are the end of the matter. Miss Polina was ill for a long time, indeed she is still ill; for a time she lived with my mother and sister in the north of England. Six months ago her grandmother – you remember, that mad-woman – died and left her a personal legacy of seven thousand pounds. Now Miss Polina is travelling in Switzerland with my married sister's family. Her little brother and sister are provided for by the grandmother's legacy, and are at school in London. The General, her stepfather, died of a stroke in Paris a month ago. Mademoiselle Blanche treated him well, but she managed to get everything the grandmother left him transferred to herself . . . and that, I think, is all.'

'And de Grieux? Is he travelling in Switzerland too?'

'No, de Grieux is not travelling in Switzerland, and I don't know where he is; moreover, I warn you once and for all to avoid hinting and coupling names in that ungentlemanly manner, otherwise you will certainly have me to deal with.'

'What, in spite of our former friendship?'

'Yes, in spite of our former friendship.'

'I beg your pardon a thousand times, Mr Astley. But excuse me, all the same: there is nothing offensive or ungentlemanly about it; after all, I don't blame Miss Polina in any way. Besides, a Frenchman and a Russian young lady, generally speaking – that is a conjunction that is not for you and me, Mr Astley, to explain or finally understand.'

'If you will not couple the name of de Grieux with another name, I should like to ask you to explain what you mean by the expression "a Frenchman and a Russian young lady". What sort of "conjunction" is that? Why specifically a Frenchman, and why must it be a Russian young lady?'

'You have become interested, you see. But it's a long story, Mr Astley. You need to know a lot of things first. All the same, it is

an important question, however ridiculous the whole thing looks
at first sight. A Frenchman, Mr Astley, is a finished and beautiful
type. You, as a Briton, may not agree; I, as a Russian, don't agree
either – perhaps, if you like, from sheer envy; but our young ladies
may be of a different opinion. You may find Racine affected, distorted and perfumed; you probably won't even bother to read him.
I too find him affected, distorted and perfumed, even from one
point of view ridiculous; but he is charming, Mr Astley, and,
above all, he is a great poet, whether you and I like it or not. The
French national type, I mean the Parisian, had begun to be cast in
an elegant mould while we were still bears. The Revolution was
the heir of the nobility. Now the vulgarest Frenchman may have
manners, modes of behaviour, ways of speech, and even ideas, of a
thoroughly elegant form, without his own initiative, soul, or heart
playing any part in it; he has inherited it all. In themselves they
may be the shallowest of the shallow, the lowest of the low. Well,
Mr Astley, I must tell you now that there is no creature on earth
more frank and trustful than a good, intelligent, not too affected
Russian young lady. A de Grieux, appearing in some character,
wearing a disguise, may conquer her heart with extraordinary
ease; he appears in an elegant shape, Mr Astley, and the young
lady takes that shape for his own soul, the natural form of his soul
and heart, and not for a garment he has inherited. Much to your
displeasure I must own that Englishmen for the most part are
angular and inelegant, and Russians are very sensitive to beauty
and have a taste for it. But in order to distinguish beauty of soul
and originality of character one needs incomparably more independence and freedom than is possessed by our women, and especially our young ladies – and in any case more experience. Miss
Polina, then – forgive me, what's said can't be unsaid – needs a
very, very long time to decide to prefer you to that scoundrel de
Grieux. She will appreciate your worth, become your friend, open
her heart to you, but there will still reign in that heart the odious
scoundrel, the evil and paltry money-grubber, de Grieux. This will
still persist, so to speak, out of sheer obstinacy and vanity, because
this same de Grieux once appeared to her with the glamour of an
elegant marquis, a disenchanted liberal, ruined (allegedly!) by
helping her family and the irresponsible General. All these frauds

were exposed later. But it doesn't matter that they were exposed: give her, all the same, the old de Grieux – that's what she wants! And the more she hates the present de Grieux, the more she hankers after the old one, although the old one only existed in her imagination. You are a sugar-refiner, aren't you, Mr Astley?'

'Yes, I am a member of the well-known sugar firm of Lovell & Co.'

'Well then, you see, Mr Astley. On one side a sugar-refiner and on the other the Belvedere Apollo; somehow they don't seem to have anything in common. And I'm not even a sugar-refiner; I am simply a petty gambler at roulette, and I have even been a servant, a fact which is probably known to Miss Polina, because she seems to have competent investigators.'

'You feel bitter, that is why you are talking all this nonsense,' said Mr Astley coolly and deliberately. 'And besides, there is nothing new in what you say.'

'Agreed! But the horrible thing, my noble friend, is that all these accusations of mine, however antiquated, however trite, however comic, are the truth! You and I have achieved nothing!'

'That's wicked nonsense . . . because, because . . . let me tell you,' declared Mr Astley in a shaking voice and with flashing eyes, 'let me tell you, you ungrateful and unworthy wretch, you miserable little man, that I came to Homburg on her instructions, on purpose to see you and have a long heart-to-heart talk with you and then tell her everything – what you feel, and think, and hope, and . . . remember!'

'Not really? Really?' I cried, and tears poured from my eyes. For, I think, the first time in my life, I could not restrain them.

'Yes, you unhappy man, she loved you, and I can tell you so because you are a lost soul! Moreover, even if I tell you that she loves you to this day, you know you will stay here all the same! Yes, you have destroyed yourself. You had some capabilities, and a lively mind, and you were not a bad chap; you might even have been of some use to your country, which is so short of men, but – you will stay here, and your life is finished. I don't blame you. In my view all Russians are like that, or inclined to be. If it's not roulette, it's something else like it. There are too few exceptions. You are not the first not to understand what work means (I am not speaking about your peasants). Roulette is chiefly a Russian game. Up till now you have been honest and you chose to be a lackey rather than a thief – but I am afraid to think what may happen in the future. That's enough, good-bye! You need money, of course? Here are ten louis d'or for you, I won't give you more, because you will only lose it in any case. Take it and good-bye! Go on, take it!'

'No, Mr Astley, not after everything that has been said now....'

'Ta-ake it!' he roared. 'I am convinced you are still a man of honour, and give it as one true friend to another. If I could be sure that you would drop gambling at once, leave Homburg and go back to your own country, I would be prepared to give you a thousand pounds immediately to start a new career with. But I am giving you not a thousand pounds but only ten louis d'or precisely because at present a thousand pounds or ten louis d'or means the same thing to you; it makes no difference – you will lose it. Take it and good-bye.'

'I will take it if you will allow me to embrace you at parting.'

'Oh, I'll do that with pleasure!'

We embraced warmly, and Mr Astley walked away.

No, he's wrong! If I was harsh and stupid about Polina and de Grieux, he was harsh and stupid about Russians. I am not talking about myself. However ... however, for the time being all that is beside the point: it's all words, words, words, and what we want is deeds! The main thing now is Switzerland! Tomorrow, then – oh, if it were only possible to leave tomorrow! To be restored to life, to rise again. I must show them. . . . Let Polina know that I can still be a man. I need only ... but now it is too late, but tomorrow. . . . Oh, I have a presentiment, and it cannot be otherwise! I have fifteen louis d'or now, and I was beginning with fifteen gulden! If I begin carefully ... and surely I can't, I really can't be such a child! Surely I can understand that I am done for! But why can't I rise again? Yes! I have only to be prudent and patient for once in my life – and that's all! I have only to stand firm once, and I can change the whole course of my destiny in an hour! The chief thing is strength of will. I need only remember the incident of this sort seven months ago at Roulettenburg, before my final ruin.

Oh, it was a remarkable case of determination: I had lost everything then, everything. . . . As I was going out of the station I
looked – and there in my waistcoat-pocket was one surviving
gulden. 'Ah, so I shall be able to have dinner!' I thought, but
when I had walked about a hundred paces I changed my mind and
went back. I staked that gulden on *manque* (that time it was
manque), and there really is something special in the feeling when,
alone, in a strange country, far away from home and friends and
not knowing what you will eat that day, you stake your last
gulden, your very, very last! I won, and twenty minutes later I
left the station with 170 gulden in my pocket. That is a fact! You
see what one's last gulden may sometimes mean! And what if I
had lost courage then, if I had not dared to decide!

Tomorrow, tomorrow it will all come to an end!

Bobok

THE day before yesterday, Simon Ardalyonovich blurted out:

'Are you ever going to be sober, Ivan Ivanovich, for heaven's sake?'

A strange thing to ask. I don't take offence easily, I'm a timid man, but all the same, here I've been made out to be mad. An artist painted a portrait of me, the peculiarities of my appearance: 'You're a literary man, for all that,' he said. I let him do it, and he exhibited the picture. And now I read: 'Go and look at that face, so unhealthy, so close to insanity.'

Well, all right, but really, how can people be so blunt in print? In print everything must be noble, full of ideals, but this! . . .

It might at least have been expressed indirectly, that's what style is for. But no, he didn't want to say it indirectly. Nowadays humour and good style are disappearing and abuse is accepted in place of wit. I'm not offended: I'm not enough of a literary man to go out of my mind. I wrote a story – it was not printed. I wrote an article – it was rejected. I took a lot of these articles round all the magazines, and they were rejected everywhere: there was no salt in them, they said.

'What sort of salt do you want, then?' I asked sarcastically; 'Attic?'

They don't even understand. I do mostly translations from French for the booksellers. I write advertisements for shopkeepers, too: 'A rare opportunity! Finest quality tea from our own plantations! . . .' I got a lot of money for writing a funeral oration on His Excellency the late Peter Matveyevich. I was commissioned by a bookseller to compile *The Art of Pleasing the Ladies*. I have published about six of these little booklets in my life. I should like to make a collection of the witty sayings of Voltaire, but I am afraid it would seem insipid to readers here. What is Voltaire now? – what we want nowadays is a cudgel, not Voltaire! We kick one another's teeth in! Well, that is the sum of my literary activity. I might sometimes send unpaid 'Letters to the Editor' to the magazines as well, signed with my full name. I give warnings and advice, I criticize and point out the right course. Last week I sent my fortieth letter in two years to one editor; that's cost me

four roubles in stamps alone. I've got a nasty character, that's
what it is.

I think that artist painted me not for the sake of literature, but
for the sake of the two symmetrical warts on my forehead; a freak
of nature, he says. They haven't any ideas, so now they exploit
freaks. Well, but how well he painted my warts – just like life!
That's what is called realism.

As for madness, a lot of people have been written down as mad
in the last year. And with what style! 'A most distinctive talent
. . . and now at the very last it transpires . . . a conclusion, however, which should long since have been anticipated. . . .' This is
rather artful; so that it may even be commended from the purely
artistic point of view. Well, but the others have suddenly come
back cleverer than ever. That's where it is: as far as driving people
mad is concerned, we can do that, but we've never made anybody
cleverer.

The cleverest of all, in my opinion, is the man who calls himself a fool at least once a month – nowadays an unheard-of talent.
Formerly, a fool recognized once a year at the very least that he
was a fool, but not now. And they've got things so muddled that
nobody can tell a fool from a wise man. They did that on purpose.

I remember a Spanish witticism at the time the French built
their first mad-house, 250 years ago: 'They have shut up all their
fools in a special building, in order to make us believe they are
wise themselves.' That's right enough: shutting somebody else up
in a lunatic asylum doesn't prove your own sanity. 'K.'s gone mad,
that means we're sane.' No, it doesn't mean that yet.

However, why the devil have I, with all my intellect, let myself
be carried away? I do nothing but grumble. Even the maid is tired
of it. Yesterday a friend called. 'Your style's changing,' he said.
'It's a regular hash. You mince it finer and finer – you have a
parenthesis, and a parenthesis inside that, and then you stick in
something else in brackets, and then you go on mincing it
again. . . .'

My friend is right. Something strange is happening to me. My
character is changing and my head aches. I am beginning to see
and hear some very odd things. Not exactly voices, but as if somebody close to me was going 'bobok, bobok, bobok'!

What *bobok* is that? I must find something to distract me.

Going out in search of distraction, I came across a funeral. A distant relative. But a Collegiate Councillor. A widow and five daughters, all unmarried. What they must cost in slippers alone! Their father had a salary, but now there's only a tiny pension. They'll have to draw their horns in. They have never been very pleased to see me. I wouldn't have gone now, if it hadn't been a very special occasion. I followed the coffin to the cemetery with the others; they kept aloof from me and looked down their noses. My uniform frock-coat really is in a pretty bad way. It must be twenty-five years, I suppose, since I was at the cemetery.

To begin with, the smell. There were about fifteen corpses there already. Palls at various prices; there were even two catafalques: one for a general and one for some fine lady. Many mourners, a lot of pretended mourning, and a lot of open cheerfulness. The clergy can't complain: it's all income. But the unholy odours! I shouldn't like to be in holy orders there.

I glanced cautiously at the dead faces, fearing my own impressionability. There were mild expressions and also unpleasant ones. The smiles generally were not very nice, and some were very much the reverse. I don't like them; they make you dream.

After the Mass I went out of the church into the air; the day was cloudy but dry. It was cold, too; but after all, it's October. I walked about among the graves. There are various classes. The third class costs thirty roubles: decent and not too dear. The first two classes are inside the church and in the porch; well, they'd sting you for those. This time there were about half a dozen third-class burials, among them the general and the lady.

I glanced into the graves – it was horrible: full of water, and what water! Quite green and . . . well, why dwell on it anyhow? The gravedigger kept throwing it out in bucketfuls. I went and loitered outside the gates while the services continued. Close to the gates there's an almshouse, and a little further away a restaurant. It's all right, not a bad restaurant: snacks and everything. Lots of mourners had crowded in there. I saw plenty of cheerfulness and genuine liveliness. I had something to eat and drink.

Then I helped to carry the coffin from the church to the grave.

Why are corpses in their coffins so heavy? They say it's some sort of inertia, the body no longer manages itself, as it were . . . or some such nonsense; it contradicts common sense and the science of mechanics. I don't approve of people with nothing more than a general education thrusting themselves into what ought to be problems for the specialist, and it's done everywhere here. Civilians love to pronounce judgement on military matters, even those that need a field marshal, and people who have been educated as engineers prefer to discuss philosophy and political economy.

I didn't go to the Litany afterwards. I am proud, and if I'm only received on extraordinary occasions, why should I trail along to their dinners, even after a funeral? The only thing I can't understand is why I stayed at the cemetery; I sat down on a tombstone and gave myself up to appropriate reflections.

I began by pondering over the Moscow Exhibition, and finished with the subject of wonder in general. My conclusions on the subject of 'wonder' were these:

'To be astonished at everything is of course stupid, and not to be astonished at anything is much more admirable, and for some reason accepted as good form. But I doubt whether it is so in reality. I think being surprised at nothing is much more stupid than being surprised at everything. More than that: being surprised at nothing is almost the same as respecting nothing. And a stupid man is incapable of respect.'

'What I want, first of all, is to feel respect. I long to feel respect,' an acquaintance of mine once said to me, not so long ago.

He longs to feel respect! Good God, I thought, what would happen to you if you dared print that nowadays?

Here I let my thoughts stray. I don't like reading the inscriptions on graves; they're all alike. On the next stone lay a half-eaten sandwich: stupid and out of place. I threw it on the ground, since it wasn't bread but only a sandwich. However, I don't think it's sinful to throw crumbs on the ground; it's on the floor that it's a sin. I must look it up in Suvorin's Almanac.

I suppose I must have sat there a long time, perhaps too long; or rather, I even lay down, on a long stone like a marble coffin. And how did I happen to begin hearing different voices? I paid no attention at first, but treated it with contempt. But the conversation continued. I listened : the sounds were muffled, as though issuing from mouths covered with pillows, yet in spite of that intelligible and seeming to come from very near. I roused myself, sat up and began to listen attentively.

'Your Excellency, you simply can't do that, sir. You declared hearts, I was your whister, and now suddenly you have seven in diamonds. We ought to have agreed beforehand about diamonds.'

'What, play by rote you mean? Where's the attraction in that?'

'It's impossible, Your Excellency, quite impossible without some safeguards. We absolutely must have a dummy and one hand not turned up.'

'Well, you won't find a dummy here.'

What arrogant talk, though ! It was odd and unexpected. One voice was so weighty and judicious, the other seemed softly honeyed; I should not have believed it if I had not heard it myself. I didn't appear to be at the Litany. But how could they be playing preference here, and what general was this? That the voices came from the graves there was no possible doubt. I stooped down and read the inscription on the stone.

'Here rests the body of Major-General Pervoyedov . . . Chevalier of the Order of This and the Order of That.' Hm. 'He passed away in August of the year . . . fifty-seven . . . Rest, beloved dust, until that joyful morning !'

Hm, damn it, it really was a general ! On the other grave, from which the wheedling voice came, there was no tombstone yet; he must be a newcomer. A Court Councillor by his voice.

'Oh-ho-ho-ho !' came quite a different voice, from a really new grave about a dozen yards away from the General's position – a vulgar masculine voice modified by a touch of sanctimoniousness.

'Oh-ho-ho-ho !'

'Oh, he's hiccuping again !' a fastidious, haughty and irritated voice that apparently belonged to a society lady broke in. 'It's torture to me to be next to that shopkeeper !'

'I wasn't hiccuping, I haven't had anything to eat; it's just my nature. And anyhow your ladyship can't get any peace from your own whims and caprices.'

'Why did you have to lie down here?'

'I was put here, my wife and my little children laid me here, I didn't lie here of my own accord. The mystery of death! Nothing would have induced me to lie beside you at any cost, but I lie according to my fortune, judging by the price. Because that is something we can always do, pay for a third-class grave.'

'Did you make a pile by overcharging people?'

'What chance did we have of overcharging you, when you haven't paid us a copeck since almost as far back as January? There's a nice little bill of yours in the shop.'

'Well, that's stupid, I must say; trying to collect debts here is very stupid, in my opinion! Go upstairs. Ask my niece; she's the heir.'

'There's nowhere to ask now, and nowhere to go to. We've both come to the end, and before God's judgement-seat we are equal in our sins.'

'In our sins!' repeated the deceased lady in scornful mimicry. 'Don't dare speak a word to me!'

'Oh-ho-ho-ho!'

'The shopkeeper obeys the lady, though, Your Excellency.'

'Why shouldn't he?'

'Well, everybody knows why not, Your Excellency, as there's a new order here.'

'What new order?'

'Well, after all, Your Excellency, we are, so to speak, dead.'

'Oh, yes! Well, but still there is *some* order....'

Well, they'd done me a favour; they had consoled me, I must say! If things have gone so far here, why question what goes on upstairs? But what goings-on! I went on listening, however, although it was with unbounded indignation.

'No, I wish I could live a bit longer! No ... you know, I ... I wish I could live a bit longer,' said a new voice suddenly from somewhere between the General and the irritable lady.

'Listen, Your Excellency, our friend is on again about the same old thing. For three days together he never says a word, and then suddenly, "I wish I could live a bit longer; no, I wish I could live a bit longer!" And with such an appetite, you know, he-he!'

'And so thoughtlessly.'

'It takes hold of him, Your Excellency, and, you know, he drops off, he's getting quite sleepy, he's been here since April, you know, and all of a sudden: "I wish I could live a bit longer!"'

'It's rather dull, though,' remarked His Excellency.

'It is rather, Your Excellency; how if we were to tease Avdotya Ignatyevna a little, he-he?'

'No, spare me that, please. I can't endure that screeching female.'

'On the other hand, I can't endure either of you,' the screeching female retorted with disgust. 'You're both extremely boring and can't talk about anything idealistic. Don't try to put on airs, please, Your Excellency – I know a little story about how a servant swept you out with the dust one morning from underneath a married lady's bed.'

'Nasty creature!' muttered the General.

'Avdotya Ignatyevna, madam,' the shopkeeper suddenly piped up again, 'Your Ladyship, don't bear a grudge, but tell me, am I going through my forty days of torment now, or is something else going on? . . .'

'Oh, he's back on the same old thing again; I expected as much, because I can smell the stench from him, and the stench means he's turning over.'

'I'm not turning, madam, and I don't smell so particularly bad either, because while I was still in the flesh I looked after myself properly, but Your Ladyship has gone bad already – because the smell really is unbearable, even for here. It's only politeness that makes me keep quiet about it.'

'Oh, you nasty insulting creature! He positively reeks, and he talks about me.'

'Oh-ho-ho-ho! I only wish my forty-days memorial would come quickly: I shall hear their tearful voices above me, my wife wailing and the children crying quietly! . . .'

'Well, there's a fine thing to cry for: they'll simply gobble up the rice and go away. Oh, if only somebody would wake up!'

'Avdotya Ignatyevna,' said the wheedling civil servant, 'wait just a short time and the new ones will begin talking.'

'Are there any young ones among them?'

'Yes, there are, Avdotya Ignatyevna. Some are not much more than boys, even.'

'Ah, just what we want!'

'Well, haven't they begun yet?' inquired His Excellency.

'Even those from the day before yesterday haven't come round yet, Your Excellency. You know yourself, sir, sometimes they don't say anything for a week. It's a good thing they brought a lot all at once yesterday and the day before, and now today. Otherwise almost everybody within twenty-five yards all round is last year's.'

'Yes, it will be interesting.'

'Now today, Your Excellency, Privy Councillor Tarasevich was buried. I recognized the voices. I know his nephew, he was helping to lower the coffin just now.'

'H'm, where is he now?'

'About four yards away from you to the left, Your Excellency. Almost at your feet, sir. . . . You ought to make his acquaintance, Your Excellency.'

'Hm, no – well . . . why should I make the first move?'

'But he'll do that, Your Excellency. He will even be flattered; leave it to me, Your Excellency, and I'll . . .'

'Oh, oh . . . oh, what on earth is happening to me?' groaned a frightened new voice.

'A newcomer, Your Excellency, a newcomer, thank God, and really, how quick! Another time they'd say nothing for a week.'

'Oh, it sounds like somebody young!' squealed Avdotya Ignatyevna.

'I . . . I . . . I . . . complications, and so suddenly!' babbled the young man again. 'It was only the night before Schultz told me, "You have complications," he said, but I was dead before the morning. Oh! Oh!'

'Well, there's nothing you can do about it, young man,' remarked the General genially, evidently glad of somebody new; 'you must just reconcile yourself to it! Welcome to our Valley of Jehoshaphat, so to speak. We are nice people, you will get to know us and like us. Major-General Vasili Vasilyev Pervoyedov, at your service.'

'Oh, no! No, no, I won't have it! I'm Schultz's patient; I developed complications, you know – at first it was pains in the chest and a cough, then I caught a chill : bronchitis and influenza . . . and here all of a sudden, quite unexpectedly . . . the main thing is, it was so sudden.'

'You say it was pain in the chest first,' the civil servant joined in gently, as though wishing to put heart into the youngster.

'Yes, first in the chest, with phlegm, and then suddenly the phlegm disappeared and I couldn't breathe . . . and you know . . .'

'I know, I know. But if it was your chest, you ought to have gone to Eck at once, not to Schultz.'

'You know, I was meaning to go to Botkin . . . and suddenly . . .'

'Well, Botkin stings you,' remarked the General.

'Oh no, he's not stinging at all, I've heard he's so kind and attentive, and he always tells you everything beforehand.'

'His Excellency's observation referred to his fees,' the civil servant corrected him.

'Oh, come now, he only charges three roubles, and his examination is so . . . and his prescriptions . . . and I didn't want anybody else, because I was told. . . . Well, gentlemen, what should I do, go back to Eck or to Botkin?'

'What? Where?' The General's corpse heaved with friendly laughter. The civil servant's falsetto echoed him.

'Dear boy, dear delightful boy, how I love you!' squealed Avdotya Ignatyevna enthusiastically. 'If only they'd put someone like you next to me!'

No, that I can't tolerate! And so this is the contemporary corpse! However, I must go on listening and not jump to conclusions. This snivelling new arrival – I remembered him in his coffin a short time earlier – with the look of a frightened chicken, an utterly revolting expression! But what next?

Next came such a hullabaloo that my memory couldn't retain it all, for a great many woke up all together: a civil servant, with the rank of Councillor of State, woke up and at once began discussing with the General a project for the setting up of a new departmental sub-committee and the probable transfer of officials in connexion with it – which greatly amused the General. I confess I learnt a good deal that was new myself, so that I marvelled at the channels by which administrative news may sometimes reach one in this capital. Then an engineer half awoke, but for a long time muttered such complete nonsense that our friends didn't badger him but left him to have his sleep out. Finally the great lady buried that morning with a catafalque showed signs of sepulchral animation. Lebezyatnikov (for that proved to be the name of the smooth-tongued civil servant I disliked very much, who lay beside General Pervoyedov) was full of excitement and surprise that everybody had awakened so soon this time. I confess I was surprised, too; several, however, of those who woke up had been buried two days before, like, for example, one very young girl of about sixteen, who giggled all the time . . . with a vile and sadistic giggle.

'Your Excellency, Privy Councillor Tarasevich is waking up,' announced Lebezyatnikov suddenly and hastily.

'Eh? What?' mumbled the suddenly waking Privy Councillor in a finical, lisping voice. There was something arbitrary and despotic in the sound of it. I listened curiously, for I had heard something about this Tarasevich in the last few days – something in the highest degree fascinating and disturbing.

'It's me, Your Excellency, it's only me for the present.'

'What do you want? What can I do for you?'

'Only inform me of Your Excellency's health; at first, not being used to it, everybody feels somewhat cramped, sir. . . . General Pervoyedov would like to have the honour of making Your Excellency's acquaintance and hopes . . .'

'Never heard of him.'

'But surely, Your Excellency, General Pervoyedov, Vasili Vasilyevich . . .'

'Are you General Pervoyedov?'

'No, Your Excellency, I'm only Court Councillor Lebezyatnikov, sir, at your service, and General Pervoyedov . . .'

'Stuff and nonsense! I beg you to leave me in peace.'

'Leave him alone.' With dignity General Pervoyedov finally checked the disgusting haste of his graveyard toady.

'He's not awake yet, Your Excellency, you must bear that in mind; it's because he's not used to it; he will wake up properly and then he will take it differently. . . .'

'Leave him alone,' repeated the General.

'Vasili Vasilyevich! Hi you, Your Excellency!' a quite new voice shouted with reckless loudness from beside Avdotya Ignatyevna. It was an insolent, gentlemanly voice with the fashionable weary tone and impudent intonation. 'I have been watching all of you for two hours; I've been lying here for three days, you see; do you remember me, Vasili Vasilyevich? Klinevich – we met at the Volokonskys', though I don't know why you were admitted there.'

'What, Count Peter Petrovich . . . are you really . . . and so young . . . I am so sorry!'

'I'm sorry myself, only that makes no difference, and I want to get everything I can out of being here. And I'm not a count but a baron, no more than a baron. We're some sort of mangy barons, from a family of flunkeys, and how or why we came to be barons I neither know nor care. I'm only a wastrel belonging to the pseudo-aristocratic world and I'm looked on as a "charming scapegrace". My father is some sort of mingy general, and my mother was once welcome *en haut lieu.* Last year the Jew Siefel and I forged fifty thousand roubles' worth of notes, and then I informed on him, but Julie Charpentier de Lusignan took all the money off with her to Bordeaux. And imagine, I was already engaged to be married – Miss Shchevalevskaya, three months short of sixteen, still at school, and a dowry of about ninety thousand. Avdotya Ignatyevna, do you remember seducing me fifteen years ago, when I was a fourteen-year-old in the *Corps des Pages*?'

'Oh, it's you, you villain; well, God must have sent you, otherwise here . . .'

'You were wrong to suspect your neighbour the merchant of smelling bad . . . I didn't say anything, I only laughed. That was me, you know; I had to be buried in a nailed-up coffin.'

'Oh, you loathsome creature! Only I'm glad all the same; you wouldn't believe, Klinevich, you wouldn't believe what an absence of life and wit there is here.'

'Yes, yes, and I intend to make some original suggestions. Your Excellency – I don't mean you, Pervoyedov – Your Excellency, the other one, Mr Tarasevich, Privy Councillor! Answer me! I'm Klinevich, who used to take you to see Mademoiselle Furie during Lent, can you hear me?'

'I can hear you, Klinevich, and I'm glad to see you, and believe me . . .'

'I don't believe a word, and I don't care. My dear old man, I simply want to kiss you, but I can't, thank God. Do you know what this *grand-père* did? When he died the day before yesterday, or the day before that, imagine, he left behind him a deficit of a full four hundred thousand of government money! It was a fund for widows and orphans, and for some reason he was the sole administrator of it, so that at the end the books weren't inspected for about eight years. I can imagine what long faces they all have now, and what they think of him. It's an enchanting thought, isn't it? All last year I wondered how such a doddering little seventy-year-old, with his gout and his rheumatism, could still keep so much strength for his debaucheries and – and now here's the solution! Those widows and orphans – the mere thought of them must have kindled his ardour! . . . I had known about this for a long time, and I was the only one who knew, it was Charpentier who told me, and as soon as I heard about it I set to work on him like a friend at once, at Easter it was: "Give me twenty-five thousand, or else your books will be inspected tomorrow"; and imagine, he only had thirteen thousand then, so it seems he died just at the right moment. *Grand-père, grand-père*, do you hear me?'

'*Cher* Klinevich, I absolutely agree with you, and there's no point in your . . . going into such detail. There is so much suffering and torment in life, and so little recompense. . . . I wanted to be at rest at last and, as far as I can see, I may hope to extract all I can from here as well. . . .'

'I bet he's got wind of Katish Berestova already!'

'Who? . . . What Katish?' The old man's voice had a predatory quiver.

'Aha, what Katish? Just over here to the left, five paces away from me, and ten from you. She's been here four days already, and if you only knew, *grand-père*, what a wicked little piece she is . . . from a good family, well educated and – a monster, an absolute monster! I didn't show her to anybody up there, I was the only one who knew . . . Katish, answer me!'

'He-he-he!' responded a cracked girlish voice, with a sound in it like the stab of a needle. 'He-he-he!'

'And a nice lit-tle blonde?' babbled *grand-père*, jerking out the syllables.

'He-he-he!'

'I . . . for a long time . . .' panted the old man, 'I have enjoyed dreaming of a nice little blonde . . . about fifteen years old . . . and in those circumstances . . .'

'Oh, monstrous!' exclaimed Advotya Ignatyevna.

'That will do!' Klinevich decided; 'I can see we have some excellent material here. We'll soon have things arranged for the better. The main thing is to spend the rest of the time pleasantly; but what time? Hi you, you from some Ministry, Lebezyatnikov, wasn't it, I heard somebody call you?'

'Lebezyatnikov, Court Councillor, Simon Evseich, at your service, and very, very, very pleased to meet you.'

'I don't give a damn whether you're pleased or not, only you seem to know everything here. First of all, tell me (I've been wondering about it since yesterday), how is it we can talk here? After all, we're dead, and yet we can speak: we feel as if we were moving as well, and yet we are neither talking nor moving. What sort of conjuring trick is that?'

'Well, baron, Platon Nikolayevich could explain that better than me, if you liked to ask him.'

'Who's Platon Nikolayevich? Don't beat about the bush, get to the point.'

'Platon Nikolayevich is our home-grown philosopher, scientist, and M.A. He has published several little books on philosophy, but for three months now he's been dropping off to sleep, so that there's no possibility of rousing him now. Once a week he mutters a few words, quite irrelevant.'

'Get to the point, get to the point! . . .'

'He explains it all by the simplest of facts, namely, that up above, while we were still alive, we were mistaken in supposing that death there was death. The body revives again, as it were, here, the remains of life are concentrated, but only in the mind. It's that – I don't know how to express it – life continues by inertia, as it were, It's all concentrated, or so he thinks, somewhere in the consciousness, and it continues for two or three months . . . sometimes as long as half a year. . . . There is one person here, for example, who's almost completely decomposed, but once every six weeks or so he will suddenly mutter a word or two, quite meaningless, of course, about some little bean : "Bobok, bobok" – but that means that even in him a spark of life still glimmers faintly. . . .'

'That's rather silly. Well then, how is it that here I am without a sense of smell, and yet I'm conscious of a stink?'

'That's . . . he-he. . . . Well, here our philosopher has got himself into a regular fog. What he said about the sense of smell was that the stink we get here is, so to speak, a moral stink – he-he ! A stink, as it were, of the soul, so that in these two or three months we shall be given time to reflect . . . and this is, so to speak, the last mercy. . . . Only I think, Baron, this is all mystical nonsense, quite excusable in his position. . . .'

'That's enough, I'm sure the rest is all rubbish. The main thing is two or three months of life and, at the very end – bobok. I propose that everybody should spend those two months as agreeably as possible and that for this purpose we should arrange everything on a new basis. Ladies and gentlemen ! I suggest we should get rid of all sense of shame !'

'Oh yes, let's, let's not be ashamed of anything !' cried a great many voices, among them, strangely enough, some completely new ones, which means they belonged to people who had meanwhile reawakened. The bass voice of the engineer, now fully awake, thundered out his agreement with special eagerness. The girl Katish tittered delightedly.

'Oh, how much I want to lose all sense of shame !'

'Listen, if even Avdotya Ignatyevna wants to lose her sense of shame . . .'

'No, no, no, Klinevich, I was ashamed, whatever you may think, I was ashamed up there, but here I terribly, terribly want not to be ashamed of anything !'

'I understand, Klinevich,' boomed the engineer, 'that you propose to organize our, so to speak, life here on new and rational principles.'

'Well, as to that I don't care a rap ! Let's wait for Kudeyarov for that; he was brought in yesterday. When he wakes up he'll explain everything to you. He's such a personage, such a gigantic personage ! They'll be bringing in another scientist tomorrow, I think, probably an officer, and a journalist in two or three days, if I'm not mistaken, together with his editor, apparently. Damn them, though, but a little group of us is assembling and everything will organize itself of its own accord. But meanwhile I want us not to lie. That's all I want, because it's the most important thing. It's not possible to live on earth without lying, because life and lies are synonymous; well, here we'll tell the truth for fun. Damn it, the grave means something, you know! We'll all tell the stories of our lives and not be ashamed of anything. I'll be the first to tell about myself. I'm a beast of prey, you know. Everything up there was tied together with rotten ropes. Away with the ropes, and let's spend those two months in unashamed truth! Let's strip ourselves naked!'

'Naked, naked!' The cry was unanimous.

'I terribly, terribly want to be naked!' squealed Avdotya Ignatyevna.

'Oh . . . Oh. . . . Oh, I can see we shall have a good time here; I don't want to go to Eck!'

'No, I want to live a bit longer, no, I want to live a bit longer, you know!'

'He-he-he!' giggled Katish.

'The great thing is that nobody can stop us, and although I can see that Pervoyedov is angry, his arm isn't long enough to reach me, all the same. *Grand-père*, are you agreeable?'

'I'm quite agreeable, quite, and with the greatest pleasure, but on condition that Katish is the first to start her au-to-bi-ography.'

'I protest, I protest as forcefully as I can,' General Pervoyedov announced firmly.

'Your Excellency!' the rascally Lebezyatnikov babbled and coaxed in excited haste, 'Your Excellency, it will be better if we agree. Here, you know, there is this girl . . . and, of course, all these different things. . . .'

'All right, there's the girl, but . . .'

'It will be better, Your Excellency, I swear it will! Well, even if only as an example, well, let us at least try it. . . .'

'We're not left in peace even in the grave!'

'In the first place, General, you play cards in the grave, and in the second place we don't give a damn for you,' said Klinevich with measured deliberation.

'Take care, sir, don't forget yourself.'

'Why? After all, you can't reach me, but I can tease you from here like Julie's pet dog. And to begin with, ladies and gentlemen, what sort of general is he here? He was a general there, but here he's a turd!'

'I'm not a turd ... even here I'm still ...'

'Here you will rot in your grave, and all that's left will be six brass buttons.'

'Bravo, Klinevich, ha-ha-ha!' roared several voices.

'I served my king ... I have a sword ...'

'Your sword is only fit for killing mice, and besides you never even drew it.'

'It makes no difference, sir; I was a part of the whole.'

'There are all kinds of parts in a whole.'

'Bravo, Klinevich, bravo, ha-ha-ha!'

'I have never been able to understand what a sword is,' proclaimed the engineer.

'We shall run away from the Prussians like mice, and they'll harrow us into dust,' shouted a distant voice I had not heard before, positively choking with glee.

'The sword, sir, is honour!' cried the General, but only I heard him. There arose a prolonged and furious outcry, din, and hubbub, and only Avdotya Ignatyevna's hysterically impatient squeals could be distinguished:

'Oh, hurry up, hurry up! Oh, when are we going to begin to be shameless?'

'Oh-ho-ho! Verily my soul is passing through its forty days of torment!' the voice of the common tradesman resounded, and ...

And at this point I sneezed. It happened unexpectedly and unintentionally, but the effect was startling: everything became as silent as the grave, the whole thing vanished like a dream. A real silence of the tomb settled over everything. I don't think my presence had made them ashamed: they had made up their minds not to be ashamed of anything! I waited for about five minutes, but there wasn't another word, not a sound. I can't suppose they were afraid of being reported to the police, for what could the police do? I can't help coming to the conclusion that they must have some secret unknown to mortals, that they are careful to conceal from every mortal.

'Well,' I thought, 'I'll come to call on you again, my dears,' and with that I left the cemetery.

No, that I cannot tolerate; no, really I can't! It isn't bobok that worries me (so that's what bobok turned out to be!).

Debauchery in such a place, the debauching of the last aspirations, depravity in crumbling and decaying corpses – not sparing even the last moments of consciousness! Those moments are granted, bestowed upon them, and . . . But above all, above all, in such a place! No, that I cannot tolerate. . . .

I shall visit other classes of graves, I shall listen everywhere. That's it, one must listen everywhere, not only at one place, in order to form an understanding. Perhaps one may stumble on some consolation as well.

But I shall certainly go back to those ones. They promised to relate their autobiographies and various stories. Ugh! But I shall go, I shall certainly go; it's a matter of conscience!

I shall take this to the *Citizen*: the portrait of one of the editors there has been exhibited too. Perhaps he'll print it.

THIS nasty incident happened just at the time when the renaissance of our beloved country was beginning with such irresistible power, such touchingly naïve impulses, such aspirations on the part of all her valiant sons to new hopes and new destinies. One clear and frosty winter night during that period, some time after eleven o'clock, three extremely respectable gentlemen were sitting in a comfortably, even luxuriously, furnished room in a fine two-storeyed house on the Petersburg Side, conducting a serious and admirable conversation on an interesting topic. The three were all of the rank of general. They were sitting, each in a soft and elegant armchair, round a small table, quietly and comfortably sipping champagne as they talked. The bottle stood on the table in a silver ice-bucket. The fact was that the host, Privy Councillor Stepan Nikiforovich Nikiforov, an old bachelor of about sixty-five, was celebrating his removal into the newly bought house, and incidentally also his birthday, which happened to come at the same time, although he had never celebrated it before. The celebration, however, was nothing out of the way; as we have already seen, he had only two guests, both former colleagues and subordinates of Mr Nikiforov's; they were Actual State Councillor Simon Ivanovich Shipulenko and Ivan Ilyich Pralinsky, also an Actual State Councillor. They had arrived about nine o'clock for tea and then applied themselves to the wine, and they knew that at exactly half past eleven they must leave for home. Their host had liked punctuality all his life. A word about him: he had begun his career as a needy minor official, and pursued the even tenor of his way for some forty-five years, knowing very well the rank to which he would attain; he could not bear trying to reach down the stars from heaven (although he already wore two of them on his breast), and was particularly averse to airing his personal opinions on any subject whatever. He was honest, too, that is to say he had never found himself obliged to do anything particularly dishonest; he was a bachelor because he was an egoist; he was far from stupid, but could not bear to display his intelligence; he particularly disliked slovenliness and enthusiasm (which he regarded as moral slovenliness), and towards the end of his life he

sank completely into a sort of sweetly indolent comfort and deliberate solitude. Although he sometimes visited the best people,
he had never, from his youth onwards, cared for entertaining
guests himself, and recently, if he did not lay out a game of grand
patience, contented himself with the company of his clock, spending whole evenings dozing in his armchair and listening tranquilly
as it ticked away under its glass dome on the mantelpiece. He was
presentable in appearance, clean-shaven, looking younger than his
years, and well preserved, gave promise of living for a long time
yet, and always behaved in a strictly gentlemanly fashion. His post
was fairly comfortable: he sat on some commission and signed
things. In short, he was considered an excellent man. He had only
one passion, or rather one passionate wish: that was to own his
own house, and a house built for the occupation of a gentleman,
not for dividing up and letting off. His wish had been gratified at
last: he had found and bought a house on the Petersburg Side, a
long way away, it is true, but then it had a garden, and was an
elegant house besides. The new master even judged it better to be
rather far away: he did not care for entertaining, and, for going
out or to the office, he had a capital two-seater carriage, painted
chocolate-colour, a coachman, Mikhey, and two small but strong
and handsome horses. All this had been acquired by forty years
of tedious economy, so that it rejoiced his heart. This was why,
when he had got his house and moved into it, Stepan Nikiforovich
felt such contentment in his placid heart that he even invited
guests on his birthday, which before he had carefully concealed
from his closest friends. He even had special designs on one of his
visitors. He himself occupied the upper storey of the house, and
needed a tenant for the ground floor, which was constructed and
arranged on exactly the same plan. Stepan Nikiforovich was counting on Simon Ivanovich Shipulenko and had twice led the conversation in this direction in the course of the evening. But Simon
Ivanovich had nothing to say on the subject. He was another who
had plodded along a narrow beaten track for many years, a man
with black hair and whiskers and a bilious complexion. He was
married, a morose stay-at-home whose household went in fear of
him; he performed his duties with self-confidence and he too knew
very well what he would attain to, and even better what he could

never aspire to achieve; he held a good job from which he had
no intention of being dislodged. He took a somewhat jaundiced
view of the newly introduced reforms, but was not particularly disturbed by them: he was full of self-confidence and listened to Ivan
Ilyich Pralinsky holding forth on the new themes with derisive
malice. All three, however, were slightly fuddled, so that even
Stepan Nikiforovich had condescended to start a slight argument
with Mr Pralinsky on the subject of the new order of things. But
it is time to say a few words about His Excellency Mr Pralinsky,
especially as he is the hero of our story.

Actual State Councillor Ivan Ilyich Pralinsky had been His Excellency for only four months; he was, in short, a very young
general. He was still young in years, too, certainly not more than
about forty-three, but he looked, and liked looking, even younger.
He was tall and handsome, prided himself on his clothes and the
refinement of taste with which he chose them, wore the important
Order round his neck with an air, had been able since he was a
child to assimilate the manners of the great world, and, being a
bachelor, dreamed of a rich and even aristocratic wife. He still
nourished many dreams, although he was far from stupid. There
were times when he liked holding forth and even striking parliamentary attitudes. He came from a good family, was a general's
son who had never had to soil his hands, had worn velvet and lawn
in his tenderest years, and was educated in an aristocratic institu-
tion, and although he did not bring much knowledge away from
it, he had done well in the civil service and reached the rank of
general. His superiors considered him a capable man and even had
great hopes of him. Stepan Nikiforovich, under whose command
he had both begun his service career and continued almost until
he became a general, had never thought him very able or had any
hopes of him at all. But he was pleased to have a subordinate of
good family, possessing a fortune (that is to say a large apartment
house run by a manager), related to fairly prominent people and,
above all, of good presence. Privately, Stepan Nikiforovich cen-
sured him for frivolity and lack of imagination. Ivan Ilyich himself sometimes thought he was too sensitive and indeed touchy.
Strangely enough, at times he had morbid attacks of conscience
and even a feeling of slight remorse for something. Bitterly and

with a secret pang he sometimes admitted to himself that he did not fly as high as he imagined. At such moments he became low-spirited, especially when his haemorrhoids were giving him trouble, called his life *une existence manquée*, and even ceased to believe, of course only in his own heart, in his own parliamentary gifts, calling himself a mere talker, a phrase-monger; but although all this of course did him great credit, it did not prevent him from raising his head again half an hour later and assuring himself all the more obstinately and arrogantly that he still had time to prove himself and become not only an exalted official but even a states-man whom Russia would long remember. Sometimes he even imagined monuments raised to his memory. From all this it will be seen that Ivan Ilyich aimed high, although he kept his uncertain dreams and hopes profoundly and almost apprehensively concealed even from himself. In short, he was a good man and something of a poet at heart. Recently moments of painful disillusionment had begun to visit him more often. He had become particularly irri-table and suspicious and was apt to regard any argument as an insult. But the regeneration of Russia had suddenly given him high hopes. His promotion to general crowned them. He took heart; he raised his head. He began to make long and eloquent speeches on the very newest themes, which he had most unex-pectedly and with extreme rapidity assimilated into a passion of his own. He looked for chances to speak, travelled all over the city, and in many places won the reputation, which he found flattering, of being a desperate liberal. This evening, having drunk about four glasses of champagne, he had really let himself go. He had formed the wish of completely converting Stepan Nikiforo-vich, whom he had not seen for a long time and whom he had hitherto always respected and even obeyed. For some reason he considered him reactionary and had attacked him with unusual warmth. Stepan Nikiforovich made hardly any response, only listened slyly, although the subject interested him. Ivan Ilyich grew excited, and in the heat of the imaginary battle sipped more often than was seemly from his glass. Then Stepan Nikiforovich would take up the bottle and immediately replenish the glass, an action which for some unknown reason suddenly began to seem offensive to Ivan Ilyich, especially as Simon Ivanovich, whom he particularly despised but also feared for his cynicism and malice, sat there cunningly silent and smiled more often than he should. 'They seem to think I'm a mere boy,' was the thought that flashed into Ivan Ilyich's mind.

'No sir, the time is ripe, it was ripe long ago,' he plunged recklessly on. 'We have delayed too long, sir, and in my opinion humanity comes first, humanity towards the underdogs, remembering that they also are men. Humanity will save the day and lead us all . . .'

'He-he-he-he !' Simon Ivanovich tittered audibly.

'But why are you going for us with such fervour, anyhow?' objected Stepan Nikiforovich at length, smiling amiably. 'I confess, Ivan Ilyich, I haven't been able to make head or tail of what you have been explaining up till now. You bring forward humanity. Do you mean philanthropy?'

'Well, philanthropy then, if you like. I . . .'

'Allow me, sir. As far as I can judge, it is not merely a question of that. Philanthropy was always in order. But the reforms are not confined to that. The peasant question has been raised, and questions of the law courts, and agriculture, and the revenues, and morality, and . . . and . . . and there's no end to the questions, and all of them together, all taken at once, may well give rise to great, so to speak, oscillations. That is what we are apprehensive about, not merely humanity . . .'

'Yes sir, it goes deeper,' remarked Simon Ivanovich.

'I quite understand you, sir, and allow me to remark, Simon Ivanovich, that I do not for one moment admit to lagging behind you in the profundity of my understanding of things,' observed Ivan Ilyich caustically and much too sharply, 'but all the same, I will have the temerity to remark to you as well, Stepan Nikiforovich, that you haven't understood me at all, either . . .'

'No, I haven't.'

'And I persist in the idea, and put it forward on every occasion, that humanity, and specifically humanity to inferiors, of the official to the clerk, the clerk to the porter, the porter to the lowest peasant – humanity, I say, may serve, so to speak, as the cornerstone of the coming reforms and generally of our regenerated society Why? Because. Take the syllogism: I am humane, therefore I am loved. I am loved, consequently they feel confidence. They feel confidence, consequently they believe in me; they believe in me, consequently they love me . . . no, what I mean to say is that if they believe in me, they will believe in the reforms as well, they will understand, so to speak, the very essence of the matter, so to speak, they will morally embrace one another and settle the whole thing amicably and fundamentally. What are you laughing at, Simon Ivanovich? Isn't it clear?'

Stepan Nikiforovich was astonished; he silently raised his eyebrows.

'I think I must have drunk a bit too much,' remarked Simon Ivanovich acidly, 'and so I'm hard of understanding. My mind is a little hazy, sir.'

Ivan Ilyich winced.

'We shan't be able to stand it,' Stepan Nikiforovich announced suddenly, after a slightly thoughtful pause.

'How do you mean, we shan't be able to stand it?' asked Ivan Ilyich, astonished at Stepan Nikiforovich's sudden random observation.

'I just mean we shan't be able to stand it.' Stepan Nikiforovich was evidently unwilling to enlarge further.

'You're not talking about new wine in new bottles, are you?' retorted Ivan Ilyich with a touch of irony. 'Well, sir, I don't agree; I can answer for myself.'

At that moment the clock struck half past eleven.

'We ought to be going,' said Simon Ivanovich, preparing to rise from his chair. But Ivan Ilyich anticipated him, got up at once from his place, and took down his sable cap from the mantelpiece. He looked offended.

'Well then, what do you think, Simon Ivanovich?' said Stepan Nikiforovich as he showed his guests out.

'About the flat, sir? I'll think it over, sir, I'll think it over.'

'When you have made up your mind, let me know as soon as you can.'

'Still talking business?' asked Mr Pralinsky with ingratiating amiability, playing with his cap. They seemed to be forgetting him.

Stepan Nikiforovich raised his eyebrows but said nothing, as a sign that he would not detain his guests. Simon Ivanovich hastily made his farewells.

'Oh . . . well . . . after that, just as you please . . . if you don't understand simple politeness,' thought Mr Pralinsky, and he held out his hand to Stepan Nikiforovich with a particularly independent air.

In the hall Ivan Ilyich wrapped himself in his light and expensive fur coat, for some reason trying not to notice Simon Ivanovich's shabby raccoon, and they started down the stairs together.

'The old man seems to have taken offence at something,' said Ivan Ilyich to the silent Simon Ivanovich.

'No, why should he?' the other answered quietly and coldly.

'Slave!' thought Ivan Ilyich to himself.

They came out on the front steps. Simon Ivanovich's sledge with its sorry-looking grey horse was drawn up there.

'What the devil? Where's Trifon put my carriage?' cried Ivan Ilyich, not seeing it.

He looked everywhere, but there was no carriage. Stepan Nikiforovich's man could not understand it. They consulted Varlam, Simon Ivanovich's coachman, and received the answer that he had been standing there all the time, and so had the carriage, but now it wasn't there.

'A nasty business!' commented Mr Shipulenko. 'Would you like me to take you?'

'The common people are scoundrels!' cried Mr Pralinsky furiously. 'The wretch asked me if he could go to a wedding, here on the Petersburg Side, some crony of his was getting married, devil take her. I strictly forbade him to go away from here. Now I bet he's gone there!'

'That's right,' remarked Varlam, 'that's where he's gone, sir; but he promised to come back in a minute, to be here at the right time, I mean.'

'So that's it! I had a feeling he would! I'll give it him!'

'You'd better have him well thrashed at the police-station a time or two, then he'll do as he's told,' said Simon Ivanovich, covering himself up with the rug.

'Please don't trouble yourself, Simon Ivanovich!'

'So you don't want me to take you home?'

'Pleasant journey, *merci*.'

Simon Ivanovich drove away, and Ivan Ilyich set off on foot along the wooden footway, feeling pretty angry.

'No, really, I'll give you what for now, you wretch! I'll go on foot on purpose to bring it home to you, to frighten you! When he gets back he'll hear that his master is walking . . . the miserable scoundrel!'

Ivan Ilyich had never been so abusive before, but he was really furious, and besides his head was buzzing. He was not a drinking man and therefore his five or six goblets of champagne had acted quickly. But it was a wonderful night. It was frosty but unusually calm and still. The sky was clear and starry. The full moon flooded the earth with a sheen of dull silver. It was so fine that by the time he had walked about fifty yards Ivan Ilyich had almost forgotten his misfortune. Somehow he was beginning to feel exceptionally pleased with life. Besides, slightly tipsy people's ideas change rapidly. He was even beginning to like the unattractive little wooden houses in the empty street.

'It's just as well, after all, that I walked,' he thought; 'it's both a lesson to Trifon and a pleasure for me. I really ought to walk more often. What does it amount to? I shall find a cab straight away in the Bolshoi Prospekt. A marvellous night! How small all the houses here are! They must be all little people living round here – minor officials . . . tradesmen, perhaps. . . . That Stepan Nikiforovich! and what reactionaries all those old simpletons are! Simpletons, exactly, *c'est le mot*. All the same, he's an intelligent man; he has that *bon sens*, that sober, practical understanding of things. But still, old men, old men! They haven't that . . . what-you-may-call-it! Well, something is missing. . . . We shan't be able to stand it! – what did he mean by that? He had got quite thoughtful when he said it. He didn't understand me at all, however. And yet how could he fail to understand? It's harder not to understand than to understand. The main thing is that I'm convinced, convinced with all my heart. Humanity . . . love for mankind. Restoring a man to himself . . . reviving his self-respect and then . . . set to work with finished materials. It seems clear enough! Yes, sir! Allow me, Your Excellency, to take the syllogism: we meet, for example, a government clerk, a poor downtrodden government clerk. Well . . . who are you? answer: a government clerk. All right, a clerk; next: what sort of clerk are you? answer: this or that sort of clerk. Are you employed? Yes, I am! Do you want to be happy? Yes. What is necessary for your happiness? This and that. Why? because . . . And the man understands me, you see, at a word: the man is mine, the man is caught, so to speak, in my snare, and I can do anything I want with him, for his own good, I mean. A nasty man, that Simon Ivanovich! and what a nasty face he has! . . . "Have him thrashed at the police-station" – he said that on purpose. Stuff and nonsense! no, thrash him yourself, I'm not going to; I shall wear Trifon down with words, I'll weary him with reproaches, that will make him feel it. As for whipping, hm . . . the question is unsettled, hm. . . . I wonder if I should drop in on Emerans? Pah, what the devil, these damned planks!' he exclaimed aloud, as he stumbled suddenly. 'And they call this a capital! Civilization! You could break your leg. I dislike that Simon Ivanovich intensely; a most repulsive face. He was sniggering at me just now, when I said "morally embrace one another". Well, if they do embrace, what business is it of yours? I certainly shan't embrace you; I'd rather embrace a coarse peasant. . . . If a peasant meets me, I'll talk to him. However, I was drunk, and perhaps I didn't express myself properly. Even now, perhaps, I'm not saying what I mean. . . . Hm. I'm never going to drink again. You talk too much the night before, and in the morning you're sorry for it. Well, after all, I can walk, I'm not staggering. . . . All the same, they're all damned scoundrels!'

So ran Ivan Ilyich's fragmentary and incoherent thoughts, as he continued along the street. The fresh air had affected him and, so to speak, unsettled him. In about five more minutes he would have calmed down and grown sleepy. But suddenly, hardly more than a couple of steps from the Bolshoi Prospekt, he heard music. He looked round. On the other side of the street, in a very ramshackle long low wooden house, a splendid feast was in progress, fiddles squealed, a double-bass croaked and a flute poured out its shrill notes in an extremely merry quadrille-tune. There was an audience standing under the windows, mostly of women in wadded coats with kerchiefs on their heads, all straining to see through the cracks in the shutters. Evidently it was all very gay. The thunderous stamping of the dancers could be heard across the street. Ivan Ilyich noticed a policeman not far away and walked up to him.

'Whose house is that, my lad?' he asked, opening his expensive fur coat just far enough for the policeman to notice the important Order round his neck.

'It belongs to Civil Servant Pseldonimov, the registrator,' answered the policeman, coming smartly to attention as he made out the decoration.

'Pseldonimov, eh? Pseldonimov!... What's he doing? getting married?'

'Yes, Your Honour, he's getting married to Titular Councillor Mlekopitayev's daughter ... he used to be in the municipal offices. The house goes with the bride, sir.'

'So that now the house is Pseldonimov's, not Mlekopitayev's?'

'Yes, your honour. It used to be Mlekopitayev's and now it's Pseldonimov's.'

'Hm. I'm asking you these questions, my good man, because I'm Pseldonimov's chief. I'm a general and the head of the office where he works.'

'Just so, Your Excellency.' The policeman stood even more rigidly to attention, and Ivan Ilyich seemed to be thinking. He stood and pondered....

Yes, Pseldonimov really was from his department, and even from his own office; he remembered that. He was a very minor clerk with a salary of about ten roubles a month. As Mr Pralinsky had taken over his office very recently, he could not be expected to remember all his subordinates in detail, but he did remember Pseldonimov, precisely because of his surname. It had caught his eye the first time he saw it, so that he was curious enough to look closely at its owner. He now remembered a very young man with a long hooked nose and wispy flaxen hair, who looked thin-blooded and under-nourished and was dressed in an impossible uniform coat and positively shocking unmentionables. He remembered entertaining for a moment the idea of giving the poor fellow a New-Year bonus of ten roubles or so to put matters right. But the unfortunate man's face was so glum and his expression so extremely unprepossessing, even repulsive, that the kind thought somehow evaporated of its own accord, and Pseldonimov had gone without the bonus. This had made all the more astounding the same Pseldonimov's request, not more than a week before, for permission to get married. Ivan Ilyich remembered that he had for some reason been unable to spare the time to go thoroughly into the question, so that it was settled hastily and casually. Nevertheless he distinctly remembered that Pseldonimov was to receive with his bride a wooden house and 400 roubles in cash : this circumstance had surprised him at the time; he even remembered being rather witty about the collision of the names Pseldonimov and Mlekopitayev. He remembered it all clearly.

As he went on remembering he became more and more thoughtful. Everybody knows that whole trains of thought can sometimes pass through our heads in the twinkling of an eye, like so many sensations, without being translated into any kind of human, much less literary, language. But we shall try to translate our hero's sensations of that kind and present to our readers at any rate the substance of them, what were, so to speak, their most essential and plausible aspects. Because after all many of our feelings, translated into ordinary language, seem altogether unlikely. That is why they are never brought out into the open, although everybody has them. Ivan Ilyich's feelings and ideas were of course a little incoherent. But you know the reason for that.

'Why !' – the ideas flashed through his mind – 'here we're always talking and talking, but when it comes to action, nothing happens. Here's an example, this Pseldonimov: he's just come back from his wedding, all excitement and hope, and looking forward to the enjoyment of . . . This is one of the happiest days of his life. . . . Now he's busy with his guests, giving a feast – poor and unpretentious, but gay, joyful, whole-hearted. . . . What if he knew that at this very moment I, his superior, his chief, was standing near his house and listening to the music? Yes, indeed, what would happen then? Nay, what would happen if I suddenly took it into my head now to go in? hm. . . . Of course at first he would be terrified, he would be struck dumb with embarrassment. I should disturb him, I should upset them all, perhaps. . . . Yes, that's what would happen if any other general went in; but not me. . . . That's the point, any other, but not me. . . .

'Yes, Stepan Nikiforovich! You didn't understand what I meant just now, but here is a ready-made example for you.

'Yes, sir, we all shout about humanity, but we are incapable of heroism or great deeds.

'What heroism? – this. Consider: Given the present relations between all classes of society, for me, me, to go to the wedding festivities of my subordinate, a registry clerk at ten roubles a month, at one o'clock in the morning, is to cause confusion, turn all ideas topsy-turvy, create a chaos like the last days of Pompeii! Nobody will understand it. Stepan Nikiforovich will die without understanding it. It was he who said we shan't be able to stand it, you know. Yes, but that's you, old men, victims of paralysis and stagnation, but I – will – stand – it! I will turn the last day of Pompeii into my subordinate's happiest day, and a wild gesture into something normal, patriarchal, moral and exalted. How? – like this. Listen carefully....

'Well ... suppose I go in: they are thunderstruck, the dancing stops, they look shy, they back away. Very well, but this is where I show my quality: I go straight to the frightened Pseldonimov and with the sweetest of smiles and in the very simplest words say, after the usual politenesses, "I have been calling on His Excellency Stepan Nikiforovich. I suppose you know him as a neighbour of yours here ..." Well, then I tell about the adventure with Trifon in an easy humorous manner. From Trifon I go on to my setting out on foot ... "Well, I hear music, I am curious, I ask a policeman and I hear, my dear fellow, that you are getting married. Well, I think, let me call on my subordinate and see how my clerks enjoy themselves and ... get married. I don't suppose you'll turn me out, will you?" Turn me out! What a word for an underling. How the devil could he turn me out? I think he will go out of his mind, he'll run his legs off to bring me a chair, he'll tremble with delight, at first he won't even grasp it! ...

'Well, what could be simpler and more graceful than such a question? Why did I go in? That's another question! That is, so to speak, the moral side of the matter. That's where the heart of it lies!

'Hm ... Now what was I thinking about? Oh, yes!

'Well, of course they will put me by the most important guest, some Titular Councillor or a relative, a retired junior captain, with a red nose. . . . Gogol described that kind of eccentric marvellously well. Well, of course I make the bride's acquaintance, I pay her compliments, I put the guests at their ease. I ask them not to mind me, but enjoy themselves and go on dancing, I make jokes, I laugh – in short, I am amiable and charming. I am always amiable and charming when I am pleased with myself. . . . Hm . . . the fact is I am still, I think, a little . . . I don't mean I'm drunk but just . . .

' . . . Of course, as a gentleman I'm on equal terms with them and decidedly don't demand special marks of attention. . . . But morally, morally it's a different matter : they will understand and appreciate it. . . . My gesture will call forth all the nobility in them. . . . Well, I stay for half an hour. Even an hour. I shall leave, of course, before the actual supper, and they will be bustling about, baking and roasting, they will bow very low to me, but I shall only accept one glass, drink a toast, and refuse to stay for supper. I shall say, "Business !" And as soon as I utter the word business everybody's expression will become respectfully stern. By this I shall tactfully remind them that they and I – are two different things. The earth and the sky. It's not that I want to impress it on them, but I must . . . even in a moral sense it is inevitable, whatever you may say. However, I shall smile immediately afterwards, or even laugh, perhaps, and then everybody will cheer up. . . . I shall crack one more joke with the bride; hm . . . perhaps even this : I will hint that I will come back in exactly nine months in the capacity of godfather, he-he ! She'll probably have a baby by about then. They breed like rabbits. Then they'll all laugh, and the bride will blush; I will kiss her feelingly on the forehead, I shall even give her my blessing and . . . and tomorrow my action will be known in the office. Tomorrow I am stern again, tomorrow I am exacting, even inexorable, but now they all know what kind of person I am. They know my heart, they know my essence : "As a boss he's strict, but as a man – he's an angel !" And so I have conquered them; I have caught them with one very small gesture which would never even occur to you; they are mine; I am their father, they are my children. . . . Now then, Your Excellency Stepan Nikiforovich, go and do likewise. . . .

'And do you know, do you understand, that Pseldonimov will

tell his children how the General himself came to his wedding reception and even drank there? And, you know, those children will tell their children, and those again their grandchildren, as a sacred story, that the great official, the elder statesman (I shall be all that by then), did them the honour . . . and so on and so forth. After all, I shall morally raise the humble, I shall restore him to himself. . . . After all, his salary is ten roubles a month ! . . . And you know, if I repeat this five or ten times, or something else of the same kind, I shall win popularity everywhere. My image will be imprinted in every heart, and really the devil only knows what may come of it later, this popularity !'

This or something like it was Ivan Ilyich's chain of thought (a man will say all sorts of things to himself, gentlemen, especially when he is in a slightly abnormal condition). All this reasoning flashed through his head in about half a minute, and of course he might have confined himself to these imaginings and, having mentally shamed Stepan Nikiforovich, gone tranquilly home to bed. Better for him if he had ! But the whole trouble was that this was an abnormal moment.

As if on purpose, the self-satisfied faces of Stepan Nikiforovich and Simon Ivanovich suddenly formed themselves in his heated imagination.

'We shall not be able to stand it !' Stepan Nikiforovich went on repeating, with a superior smile.

'He-he-he !' Simon Ivanovich backed him up, smiling in the most obnoxious manner.

'Well, let us see how we fail to stand it !' said Ivan Ilyich resolutely, with flushed cheeks. He stepped down from the planks of the footway and with firm steps crossed the road straight to the house of his subordinate, the registry clerk Pseldonimov.

His stars led him on. He walked boldly through the open gate, disdainfully pushing away with his foot the hoarse shaggy little dog that launched itself with a wheezy bark under his feet, more for form's sake than because it meant business. Planks laid on the snow led to the little enclosed porch projecting like a sentry-box into the yard, and he went up the three rickety wooden steps into the tiny entrance-passage. Here, although a tallow candle-end or a twist of wick floating in a saucer was burning somewhere in the corner, it did not prevent Ivan Ilyich from putting his left foot, galosh and all, into a dish of galantine which had been put out in the cold to set. Ivan Ilyich stooped down, peering curiously, and saw two more jellied dishes of some kind, and two moulds evidently filled with blancmange, also standing there. The squashed galantine embarrassed him and for one tiny moment he wondered whether he should not slip quietly away at once. But he decided this would be too degrading. Reasoning that nobody had seen and that they could not possibly think of him, he hastily wiped his galosh to hide the traces, groped about until he found a felt-covered door, opened it and found himself in a minute ante-room. One half of it was literally crammed full of greatcoats, overcoats, women's coats, hoods, scarves and galoshes. The other accommodated the musicians, four altogether, two fiddles, a flute and a double bass, all of course brought in from the street. They were sitting at a small unpainted wooden table by the light of a single tallow candle and scraping away at the end of the last figure of a quadrille, loud enough to awaken the dead. Through the open door the dancers could be seen through clouds of dust, tobacco-smoke and fumes from the kitchen. It all looked hilariously gay. There were roars of laughter, shouting, and squeals from the ladies. The gentlemen stamped like a squadron of cavalry. Above the din rose the commands of the caller, an extremely free-and-easy and even unbuttoned fellow: 'Gentlemen advance! ladies' chain! set to partners!' etc., etc. With a thrill of excitement Ivan Ilyich threw off his fur coat, removed his galoshes and stepped into the big room with his cap in his hand.

For the first minute nobody noticed him: they were all too busy finishing the dance. Ivan Ilyich stood like one stunned, unable to make anything out properly in the confusion, while past him whirled ladies' dresses and gentlemen with cigarettes in their mouths. . . . A lady's pale-blue scarf flashed past, hitting him on the nose; after her in wild delight rushed a medical student with his hair flying, cannoning into him as he went. A very junior officer who looked ten feet tall dashed past him. Somebody, stamping in time with the others, cried out in an unnaturally shrill voice as he was swept along, 'Ee-ee-ee, Pseldonimushka!' There was something sticky under Ivan Ilyich's feet: the floor had evidently been waxed. In the room, which was quite large, there were something like thirty guests.

But the quadrille ended a minute later, and almost immediately things began to happen exactly as Ivan Ilyich had imagined while he was day-dreaming out in the street. Among the dancers and the other guests, before they had time to regain their breath and wipe the sweat from their faces, there ran a kind of buzz, an odd sort of whisper. All eyes and all heads were swiftly turned one after the other towards the new arrival. Then they all backed away slightly, making a little room. Those who had not noticed anything were made aware by hands tugging at their garments. They looked round and immediately backed away with the others. Ivan Ilyich still stood in the doorway, not advancing a step, and the open space between him and the guests grew gradually bigger and bigger, exposing a floor strewn with sweet-papers, cigarette-ends and quadrille-tickets. Suddenly a young man with wispy flaxen hair and a hooked nose, wearing the uniform tail-coat of the civil service, stepped timidly into the open space. He advanced, stooping, his eyes on the uninvited guest, with exactly the look of a dog called by his master to be kicked.

'Good evening, Pseldonimov, do you recognize me?' said Ivan Ilyich, and was immediately conscious that he had said it terribly awkwardly; he felt also that he might perhaps now be engaged in a dreadfully silly activity.

'Y-your Ek-ek-excellency!...' mumbled Pseldonimov.

'Well, that's right. I have looked in on you quite by accident, my young friend, as you can probably imagine for yourself....'

But Pseldonimov was obviously unable to imagine anything. He stood there, goggle-eyed and horribly puzzled.

'After all, I don't suppose you'll turn me out.... Like it or not, you must make a guest welcome!...' went on Ivan Ilyich, feeling that he was becoming so flustered as to sound disgracefully feeble, that he could not manage to smile although he wanted to, and that his humorous story about Stepan Nikiforovich and Trifon was growing more and more impossible. But Pseldonimov continued to stand there stunned and idiotically staring, almost as though he was doing it on purpose. Ivan Ilyich felt convulsed with anxiety: one more minute of this and the whole thing would become an unbelievable muddle.

'I . . . have I interrupted something? . . . I will go!' He could hardly speak, and a nerve twitched at the right-hand corner of his mouth. . . .

But Pseldonimov had recovered his wits.

'Your Excellency, please. . . . An honour . . .' he muttered, bowing hurriedly; 'be kind enough to sit down, sir. . . .' Recovering still further, he gestured with both hands towards a sofa, from before which the table had been moved to make room for the dancing. . . .

Relieved, Ivan Ilyich lowered himself to the sofa. Somebody immediately hurried to move the table up to it. He glanced hastily round and saw that he was the only one sitting down; all the others, even the ladies, were standing. A bad sign. But it was not yet time to remind them that this was an occasion for rejoicing. The guests were still hanging back and Pseldonimov, constrained, still uncomprehending and far from smiling, still stood alone in front of him. In short, it was very bad: our hero suffered so acutely in that moment that his Haroun-al-Raschid gesture to an inferior for the sake of principle really might have been accounted a heroic exploit. But another figure suddenly appeared beside Pseldonimov and began bowing to him. To his inexpressible satisfaction, and even delight, Ivan Ilyich immediately recognized the chief clerk of one of the departments in his office, Akim Petrovich Zubikov, whom he knew to be a meek and efficient functionary, although he was not of course personally acquainted with him. He rose at once and held out his hand, his whole hand, not merely two fingers. Akim Petrovich took it in both of his with the most profound respect. The General was triumphant; all was saved.

Now, in fact, Pseldonimov need no longer be thought of, so to speak, in the second person, but only in the third. Ivan Ilyich could address the chief clerk directly with his story, of necessity accepting him as a friend and even an intimate, and meanwhile Pseldonimov could only be silent and tremble with awe. The story must be told; Ivan Ilyich could feel this; he saw that all the guests expected something, and that all the household were crowded round the two doorways, almost scrambling over one another in their efforts to see and hear him. The worst of it was that the chief clerk hadn't had the sense to sit down.

'Why don't you . . .?' said Ivan Ilyich, awkwardly indicating a place beside him on the sofa.

'Excuse me, sir . . . I . . . here, sir . . .' – Akim Petrovich quickly sat down on a chair brought for him almost on the run by Pseldonimov, still obstinately on his feet.

'Imagine,' began Ivan Ilyich, addressing himself exclusively to Akim Petrovich in a slightly unsteady but now fairly confident voice. He was even drawling out and separating his words, overemphasizing syllables, pronouncing the letter *a* almost like *e*; in short he felt, and admitted to himself, that he was being very affected, but he could not help himself; some sort of outside force seemed to be acting on him. He became painfully aware of many things at that moment.

'Imagine, I've just come from Stepan Nikiforovich Nikiforov's, – you've heard of him, perhaps, the Privy Councillor. Well . . . on that commission, you know. . . .'

Akim Petrovich leant forward respectfully, as much as to say, 'How could I fail to have heard of him?'

'He is a neighbour of yours now,' went on Ivan Ilyich, turning for an instant to Pseldonimov for propriety's sake and also to appear at ease, but he turned quickly away again when he saw at once from Pseldonimov's eyes that he didn't care in the least.

'The old man, as you know, has been madly anxious all his life to buy his own house. . . . Well, he's bought it. And it's a splendid house. Yes. . . . And today was his birthday, too, and, you know, he's never kept it before, even tried to hide it and made excuses, out of meanness, he-he! but now he's so pleased with his new house that he invited me and Simon Ivanovich there. You know: Shipulenko.'

Akim Petrovich bowed again. Bowed assiduously! Ivan Ilyich felt a little more comfortable. But then it occurred to him that perhaps the chief clerk guessed that at that moment he supplied His Excellency with an indispensable point of support. That would be worst of all.

'Well, the three of us sat there, and he gave us champagne, and

we talked about business. . . . Well, this and that . . . problems.
. . . We even argued. . . . Ha-ha !'

Akim Petrovich politely raised his eyebrows.

'But that's not the point. Finally I said good-bye to him, he's a
precise old man and goes to bed early, you know, he's getting old.
I went out . . . no Trifon! I was worried and asked everybody,
"Where has my Trifon got to with the carriage?" It turned out
that, counting on my staying for some time, he had gone off to the
wedding of some woman friend, or a sister . . . or goodness only
knows who. Somewhere here on the Petersburg Side. And incidentally taken the carriage with him.' The General again courteously glanced at Pseldonimov. He instantly bent himself double,
but not at all as he ought to have done to a general. 'No sympathy,
no heart,' thought Ivan Ilyich.

'Well I never !' said the profoundly amazed Akim Petrovich. A
quiet murmur of astonishment passed through the whole crowd.

'You can imagine my position . . .' (Ivan Ilyich glanced round
the company.) 'There was no help for it, I walked. I thought if I
got to the Bolshoi Prospekt I'd have every prospect of finding a
cab . . . ha-ha !'

'He-he-he !' politely echoed Akim Petrovich. Another murmur,
but this time of amusement, passed through the crowd. At that
moment the glass of a lamp hanging on the wall burst with a loud
report. Somebody zealously rushed forward to repair the damage.
Pseldonimov started and looked sternly at the lamp, but the General took no notice and everything was quiet again.

'I walked along . . . and the night was so beautiful and quiet.
All of a sudden I heard music and the noise of people dancing. I
inquired of a policeman : "Pseldonimov is getting married." So
you're giving a ball to the whole Petersburg Side, my young
friend ? ha-ha !' – and he turned again to Pseldonimov.

'He-he-he ! yes, sir,' Akim Petrovich chimed in; the guests
stirred again, but the stupidest thing was that although Pseldonimov bowed again, even now he did not smile; he might have been
made of wood. 'What a fool, though !' thought Ivan Ilyich; 'even
a donkey ought to have smiled there, and everything would have
gone swimmingly.' A storm of impatience shook him. 'I thought,
I'll go into my subordinate's house. After all, he won't turn me

out ... like it or not, you must make a guest welcome. Please forgive me, my young friend. If I'm in the way, I'll go. . . . I only
dropped in to have a look at you. . . .'

But little by little a general movement was beginning. Akim
Petrovich had an even sweeter expression than before, as much as
to say, 'Can Your Excellency ever be in the way?' All the guests
stirred and began to show the first signs of relaxation. The ladies
were almost all sitting down by now. A good and favourable sign.
The more daring among them were fanning themselves with their
handkerchiefs. One, wearing a shabby velvet dress, said something
in a purposely loud voice. The officer, whom she had addressed,
was about to reply equally loudly, but as they were the only two
making a noise he shirked it. The men, mostly clerks, with two or
three students, exchanged glances as though urging one another
to be more at ease, coughed and even began to move a step or two.
Nobody was particularly frightened, indeed they were all merely
shy, and nearly all of them looked with hostility in their hearts
at the bigwig who had burst in on them to spoil their enjoyment.
The officer, ashamed of his faint-heartedness, began to edge nearer
to the table.

'Listen, my young friend, will you allow me to ask your name
and patronymic?' Ivan Ilyich asked Pseldonimov.

'Porphyrius Petrovich, Your Excellency,' he answered, goggle-
eyed, as smartly as though on parade.

'Introduce me to your young wife, Porphyrius Petrovich. . . .
Take me to her . . . I . . .'

And he displayed the intention of rising. But Pseldonimov had
rushed at top speed into the drawing-room. The bride, however,
who had been standing there in the doorway, hid herself as soon
as she heard them talking about her. Pseldonimov returned in a
minute with her on his arm. Everybody moved aside to make way
for them. Ivan Ilyich ceremoniously stood up and addressed her
with his most amiable smile.

'I am very, very glad to make your acquaintance,' he said with
a polished inclination, 'especially on a day like this. . . .'

He smiled captivatingly. The ladies were pleasantly agitated.

'*Charmée!*' said the lady in the velvet dress almost aloud.

The bride was worthy of Pseldonimov. She was a thin little

lady, still only about seventeen, with a very small pale face and a pointed little nose. Her small, quick, darting eyes were not at all shy, they were on the contrary intent and perhaps a shade bad-tempered. Pseldonimov evidently took her for a beauty. She was dressed in white muslin lined with pink. She had a thin little neck and a somewhat scrawny body, with projecting bones. She could find nothing to say in answer to the General's greeting.

'She's very pretty indeed,' he continued in a low voice, as though he were speaking for Pseldonimov's ear alone, but he took care that the bride should hear him. But even to this Pseldonimov answered nothing at all, and this time he did not even bow. It even seemed to Ivan Ilyich that he had in his eyes something cold, lurking, even something crafty, peculiar, evil. Nevertheless, at whatever cost, he must arouse his sensibilities. That, after all, was what he had come for.

'But what a pair!' he thought. 'However....'

And he again began talking to the bride, who had sat down beside him on the sofa, but his two or three questions again drew only 'yes' or 'no' for an answer, and to tell the truth, even that he only half heard.

'If she would only show a little shyness!' he continued to himself. 'Then I could begin making jokes. As it is my position is desperate.' Akim Petrovich was also silent, as if on purpose, and although this was only stupidity, all the same it was unforgivable.

'Ladies and gentlemen, I have interfered with your festivities, haven't I?' he said to the whole gathering.

'No, sir.... Don't worry, Your Excellency, we'll begin again presently, but just now ... we're cooling off, sir,' answered the officer. The bride looked at him with approval: the officer was not very old and he wore the uniform of some unimportant regiment. Pseldonimov was still standing in the same place, leaning forward, and his hooked nose seemed to project further than ever. He listened and watched like a footman holding an overcoat in his hands and waiting for the end of his master's farewells. Ivan Ilyich drew this comparison himself; he was getting flustered, he felt uncomfortable, terribly uncomfortable, he felt as if the ground was slipping from under his feet, as if he had got into somewhere he could not get out of, or as if he were groping in the dark.

Suddenly everybody moved aside and there appeared a short sturdy elderly woman, simply dressed, although she had smartened herself up. She had a large shawl round her shoulders, pinned at the throat, and a cap which she was obviously not used to wearing. In her hands was a small round tray on which stood a full, though uncorked, bottle of champagne and two glasses, neither more nor less. The bottle was plainly intended for only two guests.

The elderly woman came straight to the General.

'Please excuse us, Your Excellency,' she said, bowing, 'but since you've been so good as to favour us with coming to my son's wedding, we'll ask you to kindly drink the young couple's health. Don't say no, sir, we'd be much obliged to you.'

Ivan Ilyich clutched at her as if she was his salvation. She was not an old woman – about forty-five or -six, not more. But she had such a kind, round, rosy, open-hearted Russian face, she smiled so good-naturedly and bowed so simply that Ivan Ilyich was almost comforted and began to feel hopeful again.

'So you-ou-ou are the mo-ther of your son?' he said, getting up from the sofa.

'Yes, Your Excellency, my mother,' mumbled Pseldonimov, stretching out his long neck and thrusting forward his nose again.

'Ah! I'm very glad, ve-ry glad to make your acquaintance.'

'Then you won't be too proud, Your Excellency?'

'With the very greatest pleasure!'

The tray was set down and Pseldonimov skipped forward to pour the wine. Ivan Ilyich, still standing, raised his glass.

'I am very, very happy to have this opportunity of being able . . .', he began, 'of being able . . . on this occasion, to testify . . . In short, as your chief . . . I wish you, madam' (he turned to the bride), 'and you, my friend Porphyrius . . . I wish you full, prosperous and lasting happiness.'

And he drained his glass, the seventh that evening, with some feeling. Pseldonimov looked serious and indeed gloomy. The General was growing full of agonizing hatred for him.

'And that daddy-long-legs' (he glanced at the officer) 'is right on the spot. Well, he at least might shout hurrah. Then somebody else would take it up, and somebody else again. . . .'

'And you, Akim Petrovich, drink their health, too,' added the old woman, turning to the chief clerk. 'You are his boss, he is under you. Look after my son, I ask you as his mother. You won't forget us in future, will you, Akim Petrovich? You're a good man.'

'How nice these Russian old women are!' thought Ivan Ilyich. 'She's brightened us all up. I've always loved the common people. . . .'

At that moment another tray was brought to the table. It was carried by a girl in a crackling print dress so new it had never been washed, and with a crinoline. She could hardly stretch her arms round the tray, it was so big. It held an enormous number of small plates of apples, sweets, fruit jellies, candied fruits, walnuts and so on. The tray had until then been standing in the drawing-room for the refreshment of all the guests, especially the ladies. But now it was brought to the General alone.

'Don't despise our humble fare, Your Excellency. You're welcome to all we have,' said the old woman, bowing.

'Delighted . . .' said Ivan Ilyich, and really did feel pleased to take a walnut and crack it between his fingers. He had made up his mind to be popular to the end.

Meanwhile, the bride suddenly giggled.

'What is the joke?' asked Ivan Ilyich with a smile, glad to see signs of life.

'It's Ivan Kostenkinovich here, he's making me laugh,' she answered, looking down.

The General could discern a fair-haired youth, very good-looking, hiding on a chair at the other side of the sofa, who had whispered something to Madame Pseldonimov. The young man got up. He was obviously very shy and very youthful.

'I was telling her about the dream-book, Your Excellency,' he muttered in an apologetic kind of way.

'What dream-book is that?' asked Ivan Ilyich indulgently.

'There's a new one, sir, all about literary figures. I was telling her, sir, to dream of Mr Panayev means you will spill coffee on your dickey, sir.'

'What naïvety!' thought Ivan Ilyich somewhat angrily. The young man, although he had blushed deeply as he spoke, was incredibly pleased to have told the joke about Mr Panayev.

'Hm, yes, yes, I have heard of it. . . .' replied His Excellency.

'No, here's a better one,' said another voice close to Ivan Ilyich himself; 'a new encyclopedic dictionary is coming out, so they say Mr Krayevsky is going to write the articles on Alferaki . . . and *accusative* journalism. . . .'

The speaker was another young man, but this one was not shy, in fact he was rather too free and easy. He wore gloves and a white waistcoat and carried his hat in his hand. He had not been dancing, but had looked on rather superciliously, as a contributor to the satirical journal *The Brand* and a leader of fashion, who only happened to be at the wedding because invited as an honoured guest by Pseldonimov, with whom he was on intimate terms, the two having a year earlier lived together in dire poverty as fellow lodgers in the 'corners' of a German landlady's room. He had, however, been drinking vodka, retiring more than once for that purpose to a snug little back room to which everybody knew the way. He made a very bad impression on the General.

'And the reason that is funny, sir,' gleefully interrupted the fair-haired youth who had told the joke about the dickey and thus incurred the hatred of the white-waistcoated journalist, 'is because the author assumes that Mr Krayevsky doesn't know anything about words and thinks "accusatory" ought to be "accusative". . . .'

But the poor young man was hardly able to finish. He could tell from the look in his eyes that the General had understood this long before, since the General also seemed a little abashed, evidently just because he *had* understood it. The young man was incredibly ashamed of himself. He retreated into the background as soon as he could, and was very depressed for the rest of the evening. In exchange the cocksure contributor to *The Brand* approached still closer, apparently with the intention of sitting down. Such self-assurance seemed to the General to put him in a ticklish position.

'Oh yes! Please tell me, Porphyrius,' he began, for the sake of something to say, 'why – I have always wanted to ask you personally about this – why are you called Pseldonimov and not Pseudonymov? You are probably Pseudonymov really, aren't you?'

'I can't say exactly, Your Excellency,' answered Pseldonimov.

'It was probably that they got his father's name wrong on the forms, when he entered the service, and so he's stayed Pseldonimov to this day,' Akim Petrovich responded. 'These things do happen, sir.'

'Cer-tain-ly,' the General warmed to the topic, 'cer-tain-ly, because you can see for yourself: Pseudonymov, after all, comes from the literary word pseudonym. But Pseldonimov doesn't mean anything.'

'Stupidity, sir,' added Akim Petrovich.

'What is stupidity?'

'The Russian common people, sir; through stupidity they sometimes alter letters, sir, and pronounce things their own way. For example, they say "nevalid" when they ought to say invalid, sir.'

'Yes, yes . . . nevalid, ha-ha-ha . . .'

'They say mumber, too, Your Excellency,' blurted out the tall officer, who had for a long time been itching to distinguish himself in some way.

'What do you mean, mumber?'

'Mumber instead of number, Your Excellency.'

'Oh, yes, mumber . . . instead of number. . . . Yes, yes, yes . . . ha-ha-ha!' Ivan Ilyich felt constrained to produce a laugh for the officer, too.

The officer straightened his tie.

'Another thing they say is chimley,' the *Brand* contributor intervened. But His Excellency tried not to hear. He wasn't going to laugh for every Tom, Dick and Harry.

'*Chimley* instead of *chimney*,' persisted the 'contributor', with evident annoyance.

Ivan Ilyich looked at him sternly.

'Oh, why do you keep on and on?' whispered Pseldonimov.

'What do you mean? I'm making conversation. Can't I even speak now?' the 'contributor' began arguing in a whisper, but then he stopped and went out, concealing his rage.

He went straight through to the inviting little back room where two kinds of vodka, herrings, slices of pressed caviare and a bottle of the strongest sherry in the 'National Wine-Cellar' had been set out for the gentlemen since the beginning of the evening on a little table covered with a linen cloth. With fury in his heart, he was just about to pour himself some vodka when the tousle-haired medical student, who was leader of the dances and cancan expert at Pseldonimov's party, dashed in. With greedy haste he rushed to the decanter.

'They're beginning at once,' he said, hurriedly fortifying himself. 'Come and watch: I'm doing a solo on my head and after supper I'll risk a *fish*. That will be right for a wedding. . . . A friendly hint to Pseldonimov, so to speak. . . . Cleopatra Semyonovna's a good sport, you can risk anything you like with her.'

'He's a reactionary,' answered the contributor gloomily as he emptied his glass.

'Who's a reactionary?'

'Why, he is, that person over there with all the sweets in front of him. He's a reactionary, I tell you!'

'Well, really!' muttered the student, dashing out of the room again as he heard the introductory bars of a quadrille.

The contributor, left alone, poured out another glass to reinforce his courage and independence, drank it, and had something to eat, and never had Actual State Councillor Ivan Ilyich acquired a fiercer enemy or a more implacable seeker of revenge than the despised contributor to *The Brand*, especially after two glasses of vodka. Alas! Ivan Ilyich never suspected anything of the sort. He did not suspect, either, one circumstance of capital importance that influenced the guests' subsequent attitude to His Excellency. The fact was that although he had given a suitable and even minutely detailed explanation of his presence at his subordinate's wedding, the explanation did not really satisfy anybody and the other guests remained shy. But suddenly the whole atmosphere changed as if by magic; everybody was reassured and ready to enjoy himself, laugh, squeal, and dance exactly as though the unexpected guest was not in the room at all. The reason was the rumour, whisper, realization, that began to circulate by some mysterious means, that the guest was apparently . . . somewhat under the influence. And although at first glance this appeared to be a monstrous slander, it began little by little to seem justified, so that all at once the whole thing became clear. What is more, everybody now felt remarkably at ease. And at that very instant the quadrille started, the last before supper, the one the medical student had been in such a hurry to join.

No sooner had Ivan Ilyich decided to turn back to the bride again, this time trying to get past her defences with a pun, than the tall officer skipped up to her and went down on one knee with a flourish. She jumped up at once and flitted away with him to take her place among the quadrille dancers. The officer did not even apologize for taking her away, and she did not so much as glance at the General as she went; she even seemed glad to escape.

'However, she's really within her rights,' thought Ivan Ilyich, 'and besides they have no conception of good manners.'

'Hm . . . you mustn't stand on ceremony with me, Porphyrius, my young friend,' he said to Pseldonimov. 'Perhaps you have something to do . . . some arrangements . . . or something . . . please don't mind me.' 'Why is he keeping watch on me?' he added to himself.

Pseldonimov, with his long neck and the staring eyes fixed immovably on him, was becoming unbearable to him. In short, this was all wrong, altogether wrong, but Ivan Ilyich was far from willing to admit it.

The quadrille began.

'Will you allow me, Your Excellency?' asked Akim Petrovich, who was holding the bottle deferentially in his hands and preparing to fill His Excellency's glass again.

'I . . . I really don't know if . . .'

But Akim Petrovich, his countenance shining with reverence, was already pouring the champagne. When he had filled the glass, he proceeded almost by stealth, almost, indeed, furtively, to pour champagne for himself as well, hesitating and grimacing and with the difference that his own glass was less full by the breadth of a finger, which seemed somehow more respectful. He had been like a woman in labour, sitting there next to his immediate superior. What in heaven's name was he to talk about? And yet since he had the honour of His Excellency's company he was in duty bound to entertain him. The champagne provided a solution, and His Excellency was indeed pleased to have it poured out for him – not for the champagne's own sake, since it was warm and of the most inferior quality, but for moral reasons.

'The old man badly wants a drink himself,' thought Ivan Ilyich, 'and dare not have it without me. So I mustn't stop him. . . . Besides, it looks ridiculous if the bottle stands between us untouched.'

He sipped his wine, and at any rate it seemed better than just sitting there.

'I'm here, you know,' he began, spacing out and emphasizing his words, 'I'm here, you know, by chance, so to speak, and of course many people will find it . . . so to speak . . . im-pro-per for me to be at such a gathering.'

Akim Petrovich listened with timid curiosity and said nothing.

'But I hope you will understand why I am here. . . . I didn't come just to drink wine, you know. Ha-ha !'

Akim Petrovich meant to echo His Excellency's chuckle, but somehow missed fire, and again he could find nothing reassuring to say.

'I am here . . . to encourage, so to speak . . . to show, so to speak, morally, so to speak, the goal,' went on Ivan Ilyich, annoyed with Akim Petrovich's obtuseness, but suddenly he stopped. He had seen poor Akim Petrovich lower his eyes as if he felt somehow guilty. In some confusion the General hurriedly took another sip, and Akim Petrovich, seizing the bottle as though it was his only hope of salvation, topped up the glass.

'Well, you're not very resourceful,' thought Ivan Ilyich, looking severely at the wretched Akim Petrovich. He, feeling the General's stern eyes on him, now made up his mind he would neither speak nor raise his eyes. So they sat facing each other for about two minutes, two very painful minutes for Akim Petrovich.

A word about Akim Petrovich. He was a man of the old stamp, as inoffensive as a sheep, nurtured on servility and yet with a good and even noble nature. He was a St Petersburg Russian, that is to say he, and his father, and his father's father, had been born and brought up and worked in St Petersburg and had never once been away from it. These St Petersburg Russians are a very special type. They have practically no knowledge at all of the rest of Russia, but they don't let that worry them. All their interest is confined to St Petersburg, and principally to their place of employment. All their concern is centred on playing preference for copeck stakes, the shops, and their monthly salaries. They know no Russian customs and not a single Russian song except *The Splinter*, and that only because the street-organs play it. There are, though, two substantial and invariable signs by which a real Russian may be immediately distinguished from a St Petersburg Russian. The first is that all St Petersburg Russians without exception always say *The Academic Gazette*, never *The St Petersburg Gazette*. The second equally important sign is that the St Petersburg Russian never uses the word 'breakfast' but always says 'Frühstück', with great emphasis on the 'Früh'. You can always tell them by these two fundamental distinguishing marks; in short, they are peaceable people who have acquired a definite character in the past thirty-five years. Akim Petrovich was no fool, however. If the General had asked him about any suitable topic, he would have both answered and kept up the conversation, but it was not proper for a subordinate to answer the present questions, although Akim Petrovich was dying of curiosity to know more of His Excellency's real intentions. . . .

Meanwhile Ivan Ilyich plunged deeper and deeper into the contemplation of a kind of vortex of ideas, absent-mindedly sipping from his glass with great frequency, though without noticing it himself. Akim Petrovich kept it assiduously replenished. Neither said anything. Ivan Ilyich began watching the dancing, and soon it was holding his attention. Suddenly one circumstance positively startled him.

The dancing was really cheerful. The dancers, in simplicity of heart, danced in order to feel gay or even reckless. Very few of them had much skill; but the clumsy ones stamped so vigorously that they might have been mistaken for skilled. The officer was the first to distinguish himself : he specially liked the figures where he remained alone to do a kind of solo. Then he bent and swayed in a surprising fashion : holding his body as stiff as a ramrod, he would suddenly lean so far to one side that you would think he was going to fall at any moment; but with the next step he leaned over on the opposite side at the same acute angle to the floor. The expression of his face remained intensely serious and he danced with the full conviction that everybody was marvelling at him. One of the other gentlemen, who had over-fortified himself beforehand, dozed beside his partner from the second figure onwards, so that the lady was obliged to dance by herself. The young registry clerk who danced with the lady in the blue scarf played the same queer trick in every figure, and in all five quadrilles that were danced that evening: dropping a little behind his partner he seized the end of her scarf and, as they changed places with the opposite couple, rapidly imprinted a score of kisses on it. The lady glided along in front of him as if she had not noticed anything. The medical student really did perform his solo standing on his head, calling forth transports of enthusiasm, stamps and squeals of delight. Joy, in short, was unconfined. Ivan Ilyich, on whom the wine had produced its effect, began by smiling, but little by little a bitter doubt crept into his mind: of course he greatly liked naturalness and lack of constraint; he had desired, had even cordially invited, that lack of constraint when they were all backing away from him, but now it seemed to have gone beyond all bounds. One lady, for example, in a shabby fourth-hand gown of dark-blue velvet, pinned her dress up in the sixth figure in such a way that she seemed to be wearing trousers. This was the Cleopatra Semyonovna with whom, to quote her partner, the medical student, you could risk anything you liked. There was nothing to be said about the medical student: he was an absolute Fokine. How had it come about? A short time before they had all hung back and now, so soon, they were completely emancipated! Perhaps it was nothing, but the transition seemed strange; it was a portent. It was as though everybody had entirely forgotten that such a person as Ivan Ilyich existed. He of course was the first to laugh, and he even risked applauding. Akim Petrovich dutifully laughed in unison with him, although with evident pleasure and without the least suspicion that a new worm was beginning to gnaw at His Excellency's heart.

'You dance remarkably well, young man,' Ivan Ilyich was constrained to say to the student as he went past them at the end of the quadrille.

The student turned abruptly towards him, made a grimace and, thrusting his face indecently close to His Excellency's, crowed like a cock at the top of his voice. This was altogether too much. Ivan Ilyich rose to his feet. Nevertheless, there followed a yell of uncontrollable laughter, because the cock's crow had sounded astonishingly real and the grimace had been so unexpected. Ivan Ilyich was still standing, undecided what to do, when Pseldonimov suddenly appeared and with many bows asked him to come to supper. His mother followed him.

'Please, Your Excellency, do us the honour, sir,' she said, bowing, 'don't despise our poverty ...'

'I ... well, really, I don't know ...' Ivan Ilyich began; 'I didn't come here, you know. ... I ... was just going ...'

He was indeed holding his cap in his hand. Moreover, he had just at that very moment promised himself faithfully that he would leave at once, at any cost, without fail, and that nothing should make him stay ... but he stayed. A minute later he led the procession to the supper table. Pseldonimov and his mother went in front and cleared a way for him. They seated him in the place of honour, and again a newly opened bottle of champagne was placed before him. There were herrings and vodka on the table by way of *hors-d'œuvres*. He stretched out his hand, poured himself a large glass of vodka and tossed it off. He had never drunk vodka before. He felt as though he was flying downhill, flying, flying, and that he must stop, catch hold of something, but could not possibly do it.

His position was in fact growing more and more peculiar. More than that: fate seemed to be playing some kind of joke on him. God only knows what had happened to him in the course of something like an hour. When he entered the house he had, so to speak, been stretching out his arms to embrace the whole of humanity and all his underlings; and now before that hour had passed, he felt and knew, with all the pain of which his heart was capable, that he hated Pseldonimov and cursed him, his wife and his wedding. Not only that: he could see from his face and his eyes that Pseldonimov hated him; his eyes, and almost his lips, said 'To hell with you, you damned old man! Foisting yourself on me! ...' He had read it in those eyes a long time ago.

Even now, of course, Ivan Ilyich, sitting down at the table, would sooner have had his hand cut off than honestly admit the true state of affairs even to himself, let alone aloud. The time had not yet quite come, there was still some sort of moral equilibrium. But his heart, his heart . . . it ached! It craved for freedom, fresh air, and rest. Really, Ivan Ilyich was altogether too good-hearted.

He knew, indeed, knew very well, that he ought to have left long before, or rather not so much left as escaped. He knew that everything had suddenly gone wrong, had turned out quite differently from the way he had imagined it out there in the street a short time ago.

'After all, what did I come here for? Surely not to eat and drink here?' he asked himself as he ate a herring. He seemed to have reached an absolutely negative state. At moments irony at his own action awoke in his secret soul. He was even beginning to be unable to understand why he had really come.

'But how could I have left? To leave like that without finishing what I came to do was impossible. What will people say? That I have a taste for low company. It will even prove to be true if I don't finish what I have begun. What, for example, will Stepan Nikiforovich and Simon Ivanovich say tomorrow (for it will certainly get about) in their offices, or at the Shembeleys' or the Shubins'? No, I must leave in a way that makes it clear to everybody why I came, the moral intention must be revealed. . . .' Meanwhile the psychological moment would not come. 'They haven't even any respect for me,' he went on. 'What are they laughing at? they are so much too free, as if they had no feelings. . . . Yes, I have long suspected that all the younger generation are unfeeling! I must stay at all costs! . . . Just now they were dancing, but at table they will all be together. . . . I will talk about the problems of today, the reforms, the greatness of Russia. . . . I shall win them over yet! Yes! perhaps nothing has been lost at all. . . . Perhaps this is how things always happen in real life. Only where shall I begin, so as to gain their interest? What sort of approach shall I adopt? I am getting lost, simply getting lost. . . . And what do they want, what do they need? . . . I can see them laughing among themselves over there. Oh God, surely not at me? And what do I want . . . why am I here, why don't I go, what am I achieving? . . .' So his thoughts ran on, and a feeling of shame, of deep-rooted intolerable shame, rent his heart.

But events kept their course, one thing leading to another.

Exactly two minutes after he sat down, a terrible idea utterly possessed him. He suddenly felt horribly drunk, not tipsy as he had been before, but really drunk. What had caused it was the glass of vodka after all the champagne, whose effects had been immediate. He felt, and sensed with every faculty, that he was becoming helpless. He had of course acquired a good deal of confidence, but his wits had not deserted him, and kept crying to him: 'This is bad, very bad, even quite disgraceful!' His wandering, drunken thoughts could not, of course, be brought to bear on any one point for long; two sides, perceptible even to himself, were suddenly revealed in him. On one side was courage, the desire to conquer and to surmount obstacles, and a desperate confidence that he would yet achieve his aim. The other side made itself known through an agonizing ache in his soul and a kind of gnawing at his heart. 'What will people say? How will it end? What will happen tomorrow, tomorrow, tomorrow? . . .'

Earlier he had felt vague misgivings that there was hostility to him among the guests. 'That's because I was drunk before, I suppose,' he thought, tormented by the uncertainty. What was his horror when he convinced himself now, by unmistakable signs, that he really did have enemies among the guests and that there was no longer any room for doubt!

'What have I done? Why is it?' he thought.

About thirty guests had sat down at the table, a few of them definitely drunk already. The others behaved with a kind of malignant, off-hand independence, shouting, saying everything aloud, proposing toasts prematurely and exchanging a fire of bread-pellets with the ladies. One, an unprepossessing individual in a greasy frock-coat, fell off his chair as soon as he sat down, and remained in that position until the very end of supper. Another insisted on climbing on the table to propose a toast, and only the officer managed to restrain his premature enthusiasm by pulling at his coat-tails. The supper was vulgarly middle-class, although a chef, some general's former serf, had been engaged for it: there was galantine, tongue with potatoes, cutlets and green peas, finally there was a goose and, to end up with, blancmange. The drinks were beer, vodka and sherry. The only bottle of champagne stood before the General, and he was obliged to pour it out for Akim Petrovich as well as himself, because Akim Petrovich would not venture to act on his own initiative at the supper table. The other guests were meant to drink healths in bitters or anything else that was handy. The table consisted of several smaller ones, one of them a card-table, pushed together. It was covered with a number of tablecloths, including one of fine, coloured linen. The guests sat with ladies and gentlemen alternating. Pseldonimov's mother would not sit at the table; she was too busy supervising everything. To make up for it, there appeared a malignant female in a reddish silk dress, with a very high cap and her jaws bound up in a handkerchief, who had not shown herself before. This proved to be the bride's mother, who had at last been persuaded to come out of the back room for supper. She had not emerged before by reason of her implacable hostility to Pseldonimov's mother; but we will speak of that later. This lady glared spitefully and even derisively at the General and was plainly unwilling to be introduced to him. Ivan Ilyich thought her a highly suspicious figure. But besides her there were several other suspicious characters who inspired him with misgiving and anxiety. They even appeared to be hatching some sort of plot among themselves, and it was directed against Ivan Ilyich. At least so it seemed to him, and in the course of supper he became more and more convinced of it. One of the malignants was a bearded gentleman, some sort of free artist; several times he looked at Ivan Ilyich and then whispered something to his neighbour. Another, one of the students, was quite drunk, certainly, but all the same there were certain suspicious indications about him. Little could be hoped from the medical student, either. Even the officer was not altogether to be trusted. But the *Brand* contributor radiated a special and obvious hatred : he lounged so on his chair, had such a proud and arrogant look and snorted with such independence ! And although the other guests paid no particular attention to the journalist (whose contributions to *The Brand* had consisted solely of four lines of verse, in consequence of which he had turned liberal), even plainly disliked him, when a pellet of bread obviously aimed at himself suddenly fell beside Ivan Ilyich he would have staked his life on it that the culprit was none other than the contributor to *The Brand*.

All this had of course a deplorable effect on him.

One further observation was particularly unwelcome. Ivan Ilyich had become convinced that he was beginning to articulate his words slurringly and with difficulty, and that while there were many things he wanted to say, his tongue would not move. Then afterwards he suddenly began to forget himself, snorting without rhyme or reason and beginning to laugh although there was nothing to laugh at. This tendency quickly disappeared after another glass of champagne, which he had not felt like drinking although he had poured it out for himself, but had then inadvertently tossed off. After that he was almost ready to burst into tears. He felt that he was becoming quite abnormally sensitive; he was beginning to love everybody again, even Pseldonimov, even the *Brand* contributor. All at once he wanted to embrace them, all of them, to forgive and forget and make his peace with everybody. More than that: he wanted to tell them everything without concealment, everything, everything; that is to say, what a fine, good man he was and what magnificent abilities he had. How useful he would be to his country, how good he was at amusing the female sex and most of all how progressive he was, how ready he was to condescend humanely to everybody, even the very lowest; and finally, he wanted to declare in conclusion all the motives that had prompted him to appear uninvited at Pseldonimov's house, drink two bottles of his champagne and gladden his heart by his presence.

'Yes, the truth, the sacred truth, and candour, above all! I will win them over with candour. They will believe me, I see it clearly; they look hostile now, but when I reveal all, I shall win them irresistibly. They will fill their glasses and drink my health with acclamation. The officer, I am certain, will smash his glass against his spur. They might even shout hurrah! Even if they took it into their heads to toss me, hussar fashion, I wouldn't object, it would be a very good thing, even. I will kiss the bride on the forehead; she's a nice little thing. Akim Petrovich is a very nice man, too. Pseldonimov, of course, will improve later. He lacks, so to speak,

that worldly polish. . . . And although, of course, none of the new
generation has that delicacy of feeling . . . I shall tell them about
contemporary Russia's destined role among the other European
powers. I shall mention the question of the peasants and
. . . and they will all love me and I shall leave in a blaze of
glory ! . . .'

These dreams were of course very pleasant, but it was unpleasant
for Ivan Ilyich, in the midst of all these rosy hopes, to discover in
himself a completely unexpected aptitude, namely for spitting.
At least, spittle suddenly began flying out of his mouth quite
without his volition. He noticed it from Akim Petrovich, whose
cheek he had sprayed, and who out of deference sat there without
daring to wipe it off at once. Ivan Ilyich took a napkin and himself
wiped it off. But this action immediately seemed so absurd, so far
beyond all good sense, that he fell silent, beginning to wonder at
himself. Although Akim Petrovich had been drinking, he still sat
there like a wet hen. Ivan Ilyich now realized that for very nearly
a quarter of an hour he had been talking to him about some very
interesting subject, but that Akim Petrovich, listening to him,
seemed not only confused but even alarmed. Pseldonimov, sitting
next but one to him, had thrust out his neck and, with his head on
one side and a most disagreeable look, was also listening. He really
seemed to be keeping a watch on him. Glancing round at the
guests, he saw that many of them were looking straight at him
and laughing. But strangest of all was that he was not in the least
disconcerted at this but on the contrary took another sip at his
glass and began to talk loud enough for all to hear.

'Ladies and gentlemen ! As I have already said,' he began at the
top of his voice, 'as I have already said to Akim Petrovich just now,
Russia . . . yes, exactly ! Russia . . . in short, you understand
what I m-mean to s-s-say . . . Russia is experiencing, in my pro-
foundest belief, hu-humanity . . .'

'Hu-humanity !' echoed a voice from the other end of the tab'
'Hu-hu !'
'Mew-mew !'

Ivan Ilyich stopped. Pseldonimov stood up and began
round to see who had shouted. Akim Petrovich stealth
his head, as though appealing to the better feelings of

Ivan Ilyich noticed this distinctly, but it was too painful to hold his tongue.

'Humanity!' he went on obstinately, 'and recently . . . and just a short time ago I was saying to Stepan . . . Niki-ki-forovich . . . yes . . . that . . . that the renewal, so to speak, of things . . .'

'Your Excellency!' a loud voice resounded from the other end of the table.

'Yes, what can I do for you?' answered Ivan Ilyich, trying to see who had interrupted him so loudly.

'Absolutely nothing, Your Excellency, I got carried away, continue! Con-tin-ue!' the same voice said.

Ivan Ilyich winced.

'The renewal, so to speak, of those very things . . .'

'Your Excellency!' cried the voice again.

'What do you want?'

'Good evening!'

This time Ivan Ilyich could not contain himself. He broke off his speech and turned to this violator of good order, his tormentor. He was a schoolboy, very young and very drunk, who had already aroused great suspicions in him. He had been very noisy for a long time, and had even smashed a glass and two plates, asserting that it was the proper thing to do at a wedding. When Ivan Ilyich turned in his direction, the officer had just begun giving the noisy youth a severe tongue-lashing.

'What's the matter with you? What are you yelling for? You ought to be kicked out, that's what!'

'It's not about you, Your Excellency, it's not about you! Continue!' cried the tipsy boy, sprawling on his chair. 'Continue, I am listening and I am very, v-ve-ry, ve-ry pleased with you! Excellent, al-pha plus!'

'The boy's drunk!' whispered Pseldonimov.

'I can see he's drunk, but . . .'

'I've just been telling a good story, Your Excellency,' began the officer, 'about a lieutenant in our battalion, who used to speak to his superior officers just that way; this young man here might be doing an imitation of him! Whenever one of his superiors was talking to him he kept on saying "Alpha plus, al-pha plus". It's ten years since he was discharged from the service for it.'

'Who's this lieutenant you're talking about?'

'In our battalion, Your Excellency. He was out of his mind about "alpha plus". At first they used to treat him leniently, but afterwards he was put under arrest. . . . The colonel talked to him like a father; but all he said was: "Al-pha plus, al-pha plus!" And strangely enough this officer was a manly sort of chap, a six-footer. They were going to put him on trial, but they noticed he was mad.'

'Well . . . so he's a schoolboy. We needn't be too hard on naughty children. . . . For my part I'm ready to forgive. . . .'

'There was medical evidence, Your Excellency.'

'What? Did they ana-to-mize him?'

'Goodness gracious, he was quite alive, sir.'

There was a loud and almost universal shout of laughter from the guests, who had at first behaved very correctly. Ivan Ilyich flew into a rage.

'Ladies and gentlemen!' he shouted, hardly even stuttering for the first few moments, 'I am perfectly capable of understanding that living people don't get anatomized. I assumed that in his madness he was no longer alive. . . . I mean he was dead. . . . I mean, what I want to say is . . . that you don't love me. . . . And yet I love all of you . . . yes, I love Por . . . Porphyrius as well. . . . I am lowering myself by talking like this. . . .'

At this moment a huge mass of saliva flew out of Ivan Ilyich's mouth and splashed on the tablecloth in a most conspicuous place. Pseldonimov rushed to wipe it away with a napkin. This last misfortune utterly overwhelmed him.

'Ladies and gentlemen, this is the last straw!' he cried in despair.

'The man's drunk, Your Excellency,' Pseldonimov whispered again.

'Porphyrius! I see you are . . . everybody . . . yes! I say I hope . . . yes, I challenge you all to say: what is so degrading about what I have done?'

Ivan Ilyich was almost weeping.

'Don't say that, Your Excellency!'

'Porphyrius, I appeal to you. . . . Tell me, if I came here . . . yes . . . yes, to your wedding, I had a reason for it. I wanted to raise . . .

morally . . . I wanted you to feel. I appeal to all of you: have I sunk very low in your eyes?'

Dead silence. That is the point, that there was dead silence, and in answer to such a categorical question. 'Well, what harm would it do them to shout, if only this once, what harm would it do them?': the question sprang into His Excellency's head. But the guests only exchanged glances. Akim Petrovich sat there more dead than alive, and Pseldonimov, dumb with fear, repeated to himself the dreadful question that had occurred to him long before, 'What will happen to me tomorrow for all this?'

Suddenly the contributor to *The Brand*, who was by now very drunk, but who had until this moment been sitting in silent gloom, turned to Ivan Ilyich and with flashing eyes answered for the whole company.

'Yes, sir!' he shouted in a voice of thunder; 'yes, sir, you have sunk very low, yes, sir, you are a reactionary. . . . Re-action-ary!'

'Young man, you forget yourself! Who, so to speak, are you talking to?' Ivan Ilyich shouted furiously, leaping up again from his place.

'I'm talking to you, and besides, I'm not a young man. . . . You came here to put on airs and court popularity.'

'What's this, Pseldonimov?' cried Ivan Ilyich.

But Pseldonimov had jumped up in such a fright that he had no idea what to do, and stood there like a post. The guests had also been struck dumb where they sat, but the artist and the schoolboy applauded and cried, 'Hear, hear!'

The journalist went on shouting in uncontrollable fury, 'Yes, you came here to make a parade of your humanity! You spoiled everybody's pleasure. You drank champagne without stopping to think that it's too expensive for a clerk with a salary of ten roubles a month, and I have a strong suspicion you are one of those bosses who have a soft spot for their subordinates' young wives! What's more, I'm quite certain you support the spirits concessions. . . . Yes, yes, yes!'

'Pseldonimov, Pseldonimov!' cried Ivan Ilyich, stretching out his hands to him. He felt that every word of the journalist's was a dagger in his heart.

'At once, Your Excellency! please don't worry,' Pseldonimov

cried energetically, as he rushed at the journalist, seized him by the scruff of the neck and dragged him away from the table. Nobody could have suspected a weakling like Pseldonimov of so much physical strength. But the journalist was extremely drunk and Pseldonimov quite sober. Then he gave him a few thumps on the back and pushed him out of the door.

'You're all scoundrels,' shouted the journalist, 'and I'll pillory the lot of you in *The Brand* tomorrow ! ...'

They were all on their feet now.

'Your Excellency, Your Excellency !' exclaimed Pseldonimov, his mother and some of the guests, crowding round the General, 'Your Excellency, be calm !'

'No, no !' cried the General, 'I'm ruined ... I came here ... I wanted, so to speak, to bless. ... And this is what I get for it, this is what I get ! ...'

He sank down on his chair as though losing consciousness, put both arms on the table and let his head droop on them and straight into a plate of blancmange. There is no need to describe the general horror. A minute later he got up with the evident intention of going away, lurched, tripped over a chair-leg, fell flat on the ground and began to snore. ...

This sometimes happens with non-drinkers when they chance to get drunk. They retain consciousness up to the very last moment and then go crashing down as though they had been felled. Ivan Ilyich lay on the floor completely unconscious. Pseldonimov clutched his hair and remained as though frozen in that posture. The guests hastily began to disperse, each putting his own construction on what had happened. It was now three o'clock in the morning.

The fact was that Pseldonimov's circumstances were much worse than might have been imagined even from all the unpleasantness of his present situation. And while Ivan Ilyich lies on the floor and Pseldonimov stands over him tearing his hair in desperation we will interrupt the flow of our narrative and say a few explanatory words about Porphyrius Petrovich.

No more than a month before his marriage he was on the brink of irretrievable disaster. He came from the provinces, where his

father had held a post in the civil service and where he died while
awaiting trial for some offence. When, about five months before
the wedding, Pseldonimov obtained his post at ten roubles a month,
after starving for a whole year in St Petersburg, he was like a new
man in mind and body, but soon nearly succumbed again to circumstances. There were only two Pseldonimovs left in the world,
himself and his mother, who had left the province on her husband's
death. Mother and son ate dubious food and almost perished of the
cold. There were days when Pseldonimov took a mug to the Fon-
tanka canal for water to quench his thirst. When he got his post,
he somehow contrived to set up house with his mother in the
corner of a room. She went out washing and he scrimped and saved
for four months to get himself boots and an overcoat. And how
many calamities he endured in the office! His superiors used to
go up and ask him when he last went to the baths. The rumour
went round that he had nests of bugs under the collar of his uniform. But Pseldonimov had a strong character. He was mild and
quiet in appearance; he had had very little education and was almost never heard to say anything. I cannot say positively whether
he ever thought, constructed plans and schemes or indulged in
dreams. But instead an instinctive, indestructible, unconscious
determination to find a way out of his evil circumstances was growing up within him. He had the tenacity of an ant; destroy an ants'
nest and they will immediately begin to rebuild it, destroy it again
and they will begin rebuilding again, and so on indefatigably. He
was an orderly and thrifty creature. It was written on his forehead
that he would make his way, build his nest and perhaps even lay
something in store for the future. He had nobody in the world to
love him except his mother, and she loved him devotedly. She was
a strong, tireless, hard-working woman, and good-hearted as well.
So they might perhaps have gone on living in their corner for five
or six years longer, until their circumstances changed, if they had
not come across Titular Councillor (retired) Mlekopitayev, a former
cashier, once employed in their province, who had recently settled
in St Petersburg with his family. He knew Pseldonimov and had
been under some sort of obligation to his father. He had acquired
a little money, not of course very much, but some; how much it
really was nobody knew, neither his wife nor his elder daughter

nor any of his relatives. He had two daughters, and since he was
a pig-headed despot, a drunkard, a domestic tyrant and moreover
a sick man, he took it into his head that he would give the hand
of one of his daughters to Pseldonimov: 'I know him,' he said,
'his father was a good man and the son will be a good man too.'
Whatever Mlekopitayev wanted to do, he did; if he said something, it was as good as done. He was a strange, obstinate old fool.
He spent most of his time sitting in an armchair, having been deprived of the use of his legs by some illness, which did not, however, prevent his drinking vodka. He would sit drinking and
swearing for days together. He was an evil man; somebody he
could torment unfailingly and ceaselessly was necessary to him.
For this purpose he kept several distant female relatives with him:
his peevish invalid sister, his wife's two sisters, also bad-tempered
and long-tongued, and his old aunt, who by some mischance had
broken a rib. He also had living in the house another woman, a
Russianized German, whom he kept because of her gift for telling
stories from the Arabian Nights. His only pleasure was bullying
all his unfortunate female dependants and swearing at them constantly on the slightest pretext, while they, not excluding even
his wife, who had been born with chronic toothache, did not dare
utter a sound in his presence. He set them at one another's throats,
invented and introduced all sorts of scandals and quarrels among
them, and then laughed with pleasure to see them almost coming to
blows. It rejoiced his heart when his elder daughter, a widow who
had lived in poverty with her officer-husband for some ten years,
returned to his house with her three sickly little children. He
could not bear the children, but since their appearance increased
the number of subjects on whom he could practise his daily experi-
ments, the old man was very pleased to have them. All this huddle
of malicious women and ailing children were crammed into the
wooden house on the Petersburg Side; they were underfed because
the old man was stingy and doled out money in copecks, although
he did not grudge himself vodka; they got insufficient sleep because the old man suffered from insomnia and demanded to be
amused. In short, they lived in poverty and cursed their fate. It
was at that time that Mlekopitayev singled out Pseldonimov. He
had been struck by his long nose and submissive air. His sickly

and ill-favoured daughter had just turned seventeen. Although she had at one time been at some German *Schule*, she had brought practically nothing away with her except a knowledge of the alphabet. Afterwards she had grown up scrofulous and anaemic, dominated by her crippled and drunken father's crutch, in the hubbub of domestic tittle-tattle, tale-bearing and scandal-mongering. She had never had any girl friends, nor any brains. She had long wanted to get married. In company she was silent, but at home with her mamma and the other women she was sly and as sharp as a needle. She was particularly fond of pinching and slapping her sister's children and sneaking on them for stealing sugar and bread, all of which was the cause of endless embittered quarreling with her sister. The old man offered her to Pseldonimov as a wife. Poor though Pseldonimov was, he asked for time to consider. He and his mother thought it over for a long time. But the house was being put in the bride's name, and although it was wooden and had only one storey and was altogether very nasty, it was still worth something. Besides, 400 roubles went with her – and when could one amass as much for oneself? 'Do you know why I'm taking a man into the house?' the drunken old despot shouted. 'First it's because you're all women, and I'm sick of nothing but womenfolk round me. I want Pseldonimov to dance to my piping as well, because I'm his benefactor. Secondly, it's because none of you wants it and you're all annoyed. So I shall do it to spite you. I've said it and I will do it. And you, Porphyrius, beat her, when she's your wife; she's had seven devils inside her ever since she was born. You drive them out and I'll get a crutch ready for you. . . .'

Pseldonimov said nothing, but his mind was made up. His mother and he were taken into the house before the wedding, washed and dressed and shod and given money for the preparations. The old man gave them his protection, perhaps because his household bore them ill-will. He even took such a liking to Mrs Pseldonimov that he restrained himself and did not try to bully her. He made Pseldonimov himself, however, dance a *kazachok* for him. 'Well, that's enough, I just wanted to see you didn't forget your position,' he said at the end of the dance. He handed over only just enough money for the wedding preparations, and invited all his own relations and friends. On Pseldonimov's side there

were only the *Brand* contributor and Akim Petrovich, the guest of
honour. Pseldonimov knew very well that his bride loathed him
and very much wanted to marry the officer instead of him. But he
bore with everything, as he had agreed with his mother to do. All
through the wedding-day itself and throughout the evening the
old man sat drinking himself drunk and swearing blasphemously.
On account of the wedding the whole family took refuge in the
back rooms, where they were packed to suffocation. The front
rooms were set aside for the supper and for dancing. Finally, when
the old man, completely drunk, fell asleep at about eleven o'clock,
the bride's mother, who had been particularly bad-tempered with
Pseldonimov's mother all day, decided to change her angry mood
for a gracious one and come out to the dance and supper. The
appearance of Ivan Ilyich upset everything. Mrs Mlekopitayev
was flustered and offended, and began abusing them for not telling
her beforehand that they had invited the General himself. They
assured her that he had come of his own accord, without being
asked, but she was too stupid to believe it. Champagne was required. Pseldonimov's mother had only one rouble and Pseldonimov himself hadn't a copeck. They had to abase themselves to the
angry old woman and beg her for the money just for one bottle
and then for a second. They urged Pseldonimov's career and future
relationships within the service, and tried to appeal to her better
nature. In the end she gave them some of her own money, but she
made Pseldonimov drink such a cup of wormwood and gall that
more than once he ran into the little room where the bridal couch
was prepared, silently clutched his hair and flung himself head
first on the bed intended for the delights of Paradise, trembling all
over with impotent rage. Yes, Ivan Ilyich little knew the cost of
the two bottles of champagne he drank that evening! What then
was Pseldonimov's horror, anguish and indeed despair when the
business ended in such an unexpected fashion! He was again
faced with the prospect of trouble, and perhaps a whole night of
screams and tears from the capricious bride and reproaches from
her stupid family. Already his head ached and his eyes were dim
with fumes and darkness. And now Ivan Ilyich had to be helped,
a doctor must be found at three o'clock in the morning, or else a
carriage to take him home, and it must be a carriage, because it

was impossible to send such a person home in a cab in such a state. And where was he to find the money for a carriage? Mrs Mlekopitayev, enraged by the fact that the General had not said two words to her or even looked in her direction all through supper, declared that she hadn't a copeck. Perhaps she really had not. Where could he get some money? What was he to do? Yes, he had reason to tear his hair.

Meanwhile Ivan Ilyich was lifted for the time being to a small, leather-covered sofa which stood there in the dining-room. While the tables were being cleared and moved back to their places, Pseldonimov went rushing round everywhere trying to borrow some money, even from the servant, but nobody had any. He even risked asking Akim Petrovich, who had stayed longer than the others. But he, kind-hearted as he was, was so perplexed and even frightened at the mention of money that he talked the most unexpected nonsense.

'Another time I should be delighted,' he mumbled, 'but just now ... really you must excuse me. ...'

And he took up his cap and ran out of the house as quickly as he could. Only the good-hearted youth who had talked about the dream-book was any help, and that not entirely appropriate. He had also remained behind, taking a sympathetic interest in Pseldonimov's misfortunes. In the end Pseldonimov, his mother and the young man decided by common consent not to fetch a doctor, but rather to send for a carriage and take the sick man home, and meanwhile, until it arrived, to try some homely remedies, such as wetting his temples and head with cold water, applying ice to his head, and so on. Pseldonimov's mother set about this. The youth raced off to look for a carriage. As there was not even a cab to be found on the Petersburg Side at that hour, he had to go a considerable distance looking for a hiring establishment, where he woke up the coachmen. They began to haggle about the price, stating that even five roubles was too little at that time in the morning. They finally, however, agreed to take three. But when, just before four o'clock, the young man returned to Pseldonimov's with the hired carriage, they had long since changed their minds. It appeared that Ivan Ilyich, who was still unconscious, had grown so much worse and was groaning and tossing about so much that moving him or taking him home in that state had become completely impossible, even dangerous. 'What will happen next?' said the utterly disheartened Pseldonimov. What could be done? A new problem arose: if the sick man was to be kept in the house, where was he to be moved and where could he be laid down? In the whole house there were only two beds: one enormous double bed in which old Mlekopitayev and his wife slept and a newly bought one, also double, in imitation walnut, intended for the young couple. All the other inhabitants of the house slept on the floor in a row, mostly on feather-beds, which were in rather poor condition and smelt bad, that is, were highly unsuitable, and of these there were only just enough for the household, indeed hardly even that. Where could they put the sick man? A feather-bed might perhaps be found – at a pinch it was possible to pull one out from under somebody, but where could it be put down, and what on? It seemed it would have to be made up in the drawing-room, as that room was the furthest removed from the bosom of the family and had its own special exit. But what could it be made up on? Surely not chairs? It is well known that beds are made up on chairs only for high-school boys when they come home for the weekend, and for somebody like Ivan Ilyich it would be very disrespectful. What would he say the next morning, when he found himself sleeping on chairs? Pseldonimov would not even hear of it. There remained only one thing: to carry him to the bridal couch. This, as we have already said, had been set up in a little room next to the dining-room. On the bed was a double mattress, newly purchased and never used, clean linen, four pink calico pillows with frilled white muslin cases, and a pink satin coverlet with a quilted pattern. Muslin curtains hung from a gilt ring above the bed. In short, it was all just as it should be, and the appointments had been highly praised by the guests, nearly all of whom had visited the bedroom. The bride, although she could not bear Pseldonimov, had slipped stealthily into the room several times in the course of the evening to look at it. What then was her indignation and fury when she learnt that it was intended to put a sick man who was suffering from something in the nature of diarrhoea in her bridal bed! The bride's mamma took her side, scolding and threatening to tell her husband in the morning; but Pseldonimov showed what he was made of, and insisted: Ivan Ilyich was carried in and a bed was made up on chairs in the drawing-room. The bride whimpered and was ready to pinch, but she dared not disobey: her papa had a crutch with which she was well acquainted, and she knew that in the morning he would demand a detailed accounting of certain matters. To pacify her the pink satin quilt and the muslin-covered pillows were carried into the drawing-room. At this moment the youth arrived with the carriage; when he learnt that it was no longer required he was terribly frightened. He had to pay for it himself, and he had never possessed as much as ten copecks in his life. Pseldonimov declared his utter bankruptcy. They tried to talk the driver over. But he began making a row and even banging on the shutters. How it all ended I don't know exactly. I think the youth went off as the driver's prisoner in the carriage all the way to Fourth Christmas Street in Peski, where he hoped to wake up a student who was spending the night there with some friends of his, to see if he had some money. It was five o'clock in the morning when the young couple were left shut up in the drawing-room together. Pseldonimov's mother stayed by the sick man's bed all night. She lay down on a rug on the floor and covered herself with her old fur coat, but she got no sleep, as she was always having to get up: Ivan Ilyich had terrible diarrhoea. That generous and courageous woman, Mrs Pseldonimov, undressed him completely and looked after him as if he was her own son, carrying the necessary vessel across the corridor from the bedroom and back into it again all night. But the misfortunes of the night were by no means over yet.

The young couple had not been shut up in the drawing-room alone for more than ten minutes before there came a heart-rending shriek, a cry not of joy but of outrage. It was followed by a resounding crash and what seemed to be the falling of chairs, and an instant later a crowd of frightened and noisy women, in all stages of undress, burst into the still darkened room. They were the bride's mother, her elder sister, who had for the moment abandoned her ailing children, and her three aunts, including the one with a broken rib. Even the cook was there, and the German story-teller who had been forcibly deprived of her feather-bed, the best in the house and her sole possession, for the young couple. All these respectable and sagacious ladies had made their way out of the kitchen and across the corridor on tiptoe a full quarter of an hour earlier and had been eavesdropping in the lobby with devouring, if quite inexplicable, curiosity. Now somebody hastily lit a candle and an unexpected spectacle was revealed. The chairs, which had supported the wide feather-bed only at the sides, had been unable to take the double weight and slid apart, letting it fall to the floor between them. The bride was whimpering with rage; this time she was offended to the very soul. The utterly dejected Pseldonimov stood there like a criminal caught in the act. He didn't even attempt to justify himself. There was a chorus of excited exclamations. The noise brought Pseldonimov's mother running as well, but this time the bride's mamma definitely had the upper hand. She heaped Pseldonimov with strange and for the most part unwarranted reproaches, all variations on the same theme: 'What sort of a husband do you call yourself now, sir? What good are you for anything after a disgrace like this?' and so on; finally she seized her daughter by the hand and took her away from her husband into her own room, personally undertaking the responsibility for answering the stern father's demands for an explanation the next morning. The rest, still exclaiming and shaking their heads, followed her out of the room. Only his mother was left behind to try to console Pseldonimov. But he drove her away immediately.

He had no use for consolation. He made his way to the sofa and sat down as he was, barefooted and wearing only the essential minimum of underclothes, in a mood of the blackest melancholy. Thoughts crossed and re-crossed each other in his head in utter confusion. From time to time he glanced almost mechanically round the room, where the riotous dancing had gone on so very recently, and cigarette smoke still hung in the air. Cigarette-ends and sweet-wrappings littered the bespattered and dirty floor. The ruins of the bridal couch and the overturned chairs bore witness to the frailty of even the best and truest earthly hopes and dreams. He sat for nearly an hour in this state. Nothing but gloomy thoughts came into his head; for example, what lay before him now in the office? He was painfully aware that he must at all costs change his place of employment; to remain in his present office was impossible because of everything that had happened that night. It occurred to him that Mlekopitayev might make him dance a *kazachok* again tomorrow to test his meekness. He imagined also that although every copek of the fifty roubles Mlekopitayev gave them for the wedding had gone, the old man would not dream of giving him the dowry of 400 roubles yet; it had not even been mentioned again. Indeed, the house itself had not yet been formally transferred to him. He thought about his wife, too, who had abandoned him at the most critical moment of his life, and of the tall officer going down on one knee to her. He had had time to notice that; and he thought now of the seven devils living inside his wife, according to her father's testimony, and of the crutch made ready to drive them out. . . . He felt, of course, strong enough to stand a great deal, but fate had got in so many surprises lately that in the end it was possible for him to doubt his own strength.

So Pseldonimov sat moping, while the candle-end burnt out. Its flickering light, falling directly on Pseldonimov's profile, cast his enormous shadow on the wall, with his long neck, hooked nose and two tufts of hair sticking out over his forehead and at the back of his head. At last, when the chilly dawn wind arose, he got up, frozen in body and numb in mind, made his way to the feather-bed lying among the overturned chairs and without straightening it or extinguishing the candle, or even laying a pillow under his head, crept on all fours on to the bed and fell asleep with the dead, leaden sleep that must visit those who are condemned to public execution on the morrow.

On the other hand, what could be compared with the night of torment spent by Ivan Ilyich Pralinsky on the unhappy Pseldonimov's bridal couch? For some time headache, vomiting and other unpleasant paroxysms did not leave him a moment's peace. It was like the tortures of the damned. The as yet only momentary flickerings of consciousness revealed such endless terrors, such repellantly gloomy pictures, that it would have been better to remain unconscious. His mind, however, was still one chaotic confusion. He recognized Pseldonimov's mother, for example, and heard her mild appeals to 'Be patient, dear, be patient, my dear; what can't be cured must be endured' – recognized her and yet could not account to himself logically for her presence by his side. Loathsome visions appeared before him: the most frequent was of Simon Ivanovich, but when he looked closer he saw it was not Simon Ivanovich at all but Pseldonimov's nose. He caught momentary glimpses of the artist, and the officer, and the old woman with her face tied up. But what worried him most was the gilt ring, with curtains looped through it, hanging above his head. He could distinguish it clearly by the dim glow of the candle that lighted the room, and he kept trying to understand what it was used for, why it was there, and what it signified; he asked the old woman about it several times, but evidently he could not say what he meant, and she plainly did not understand, however hard he tried to explain. At last, towards morning, the attacks ceased and he fell asleep and slept soundly, without dreaming. He slept for about an hour and woke up almost fully conscious, with a head that ached unbearably and a foul taste in his mouth, in which his tongue felt like a piece of flannel. He sat up in bed, looked round and tried to think. The pale light of dawn, striking through the cracks of the shutters in a narrow band, trembled on the wall. It was about seven o'clock in the morning. But when Ivan Ilyich suddenly realized and remembered all that had happened to him since the previous evening; when he remembered all the incidents at supper, the failure of his heroic exploit, his speech at the table; when he realized all at once with terrifying clarity everything that might now result from it all, and everything that would be said and thought about him; when, finally, he looked round and saw to what a sorry and scandalous state he had reduced his subordinate's peaceful marriage bed – oh, then his heart was invaded by such anguish and such deadly shame that he shrieked, covered his face with his hands, and flung himself back on his pillows in despair. A minute later he leapt out of bed, saw his clothes on a chair close by, laid out neatly and already brushed, seized them and hastily began to pull them on, as quickly as he could, glancing round and terribly afraid of something or other. There on another chair lay his fur coat and his cap, with his yellow gloves inside it. He wanted to slip away quietly. But suddenly the door opened and old Mrs Pseldonimov came in with an earthenware jug and basin. A towel hung over her shoulder. She put down the basin and declared without more ado that he absolutely must wash.

'Come along, dear, get washed, you can't go out without washing....'

And at that moment Ivan Ilyich became aware that if there was one creature in the whole world with whom he might now feel unafraid and unashamed, it was precisely this old woman. He got washed. And long afterwards, in the difficult moments of his life, he remembered, among other weights on his conscience, all the circumstances of this awakening, the earthenware jug and faience basin full of cold water with bits of ice still floating on it, the fifteen-copeck oval cake of soap with raised letters on it, wrapped in pink paper, evidently bought for the newly married pair but now perforce sacrificed to Ivan Ilyich, and the old woman with a damask linen towel over her left shoulder. The cold water refreshed him; he dried himself and without a word, without even thanking his sister of mercy, seized his cap, slung the fur coat held out to him by Mrs Pseldonimov over his shoulder, ran across the corridor, through the kitchen where the cat was already mewing and the cook, raising herself from her bed of straw, gazed after him with eager curiosity, out into the yard and the street, and threw himself into a passing cab. The morning was frosty; a frozen yellow fog still hung over the houses and everything around. Ivan Ilyich turned up his collar. He thought everybody was looking at him, everybody knew him, they would all come to know....

For eight days he never left the house nor appeared at his office. He was ill, painfully ill, but more morally than physically. In those eight days he lived through all the torments of hell, and they will probably be reckoned to his credit in the next world. There were times, there really were, when he thought of turning monk. His fancy even began to stray very frequently in that direction. He imagined the peaceful subterranean chanting, the open coffin, the existence in a solitary cell, the forests and caves; but when he roused himself, he almost immediately admitted that all this was the most utter rubbish and exaggeration, and was ashamed of it. Then he began to have attacks of conscience over his *existence manquée*. Then shame flared up again in his heart, overwhelming it, searing and destroying everything. He shuddered as he imagined various scenes. What would they say about him, what would they think, how could he show his face in the office, what whispers would follow him for a whole year, ten years, his entire life? The story would be handed down to posterity. At times he even became craven enough to be ready to go at once to Simon Ivanovich and ask for his forgiveness and friendship. He did not even try to find excuses for himself, he blamed himself entirely: he could find no justification for his action and was ashamed to look for one.

He also thought of resigning immediately and dedicating himself, in simplicity and solitude, to the happiness of mankind. In any case he absolutely must drop all his acquaintances, and even do it in such a way as to eradicate all recollections of him. Then the thought would come to him that this too was nonsense and that he could set matters straight again by increased severity to his subordinates. Then he began to hope and pluck up his courage. Finally, after eight days of doubt and agony, he felt that he could no longer bear the uncertainty, and *un beau matin* he decided to go to the office.

Earlier, while he still sat at home in anguish, he had imagined a thousand times how he would enter his office. He told himself with horror that he would hear ambiguous whispers behind him, see ambiguous faces and reap a harvest of malignant smiles. What then was his surprise when nothing of the sort happened in fact! He was greeted respectfully, with low bows, and everybody was serious, everybody was busy. Gladness welled up in his heart when he reached his own room.

He immediately and very seriously set to work, heard several reports and explanations and made decisions. He felt that he had never before reasoned and judged so wisely and efficiently as that morning. He saw that people were satisfied, esteemed him, and treated him with deference. The most susceptible feelings could not have noticed anything. Things were going magnificently.

At last Akim Petrovich appeared with some papers. At his

appearance something seemed to pierce Ivan Ilyich's inmost heart, but only for an instant. He attended to Akim Petrovich, uttered solemn comments, pointed out how he should proceed, and explained what he meant. He noticed only that he seemed to avoid looking at Akim Petrovich for too long, or rather that Akim Petrovich seemed to be afraid of looking at him. But now Akim Petrovich finished his business and began collecting up his papers.

'I have one more request,' he began in the dryest possible manner, 'from the clerk Pseldonimov for transfer to another department. His Excellency Simon Ivanovich Shipulenko has promised him a post. He requests your kind assistance, Your Excellency.'

'Oh, so he is being transferred,' said Ivan Ilyich, feeling that an enormous weight had been lifted from his heart. He looked at Akim Petrovich and at that moment their glances met.

'Well, for my part . . . I will use my . . .' answered Ivan Ilyich, 'I am ready to help him.'

Akim Petrovich evidently wished to slip away as quickly as possible. But suddenly, in a burst of nobility, Ivan Ilyich made up his mind to speak out, once and for all. He was evidently inspired again.

'Tell him,' he began, bending a serene look, full of the most profound meaning, on Akim Petrovich, 'tell Pseldonimov that I wish him no harm, no, I wish him no harm ! . . . On the contrary, I am ready to forget all that has happened, to forget everything, everything . . .'

But Ivan Ilyich stopped short, staring in amazement at the strange conduct of Akim Petrovich who had unaccountably changed from a reasonable person to the most terrible fool. Instead of listening, and listening to the end, he suddenly blushed to an utterly stupid extent, began bowing himself out in an almost indecent hurry, with a series of little bobs, and at the same time retreated to the door. His whole look expressed the desire to sink through the earth, or rather to get back to his desk as soon as possible. Ivan Ilyich, left alone, rose from his chair in dismay. He looked in the mirror without noticing what he saw there.

'No; severity, severity, nothing but severity !' he almost unconsciously whispered to himself, and suddenly his face was suffused with bright red. He felt ashamed and oppressed as he had never

READ MORE IN PENGUIN

In every corner of the world, on every subject under the sun, Penguin represents quality and variety – the very best in publishing today.

For complete information about books available from Penguin – including Puffins, Penguin Classics and Arkana – and how to order them, write to us at the appropriate address below. Please note that for copyright reasons the selection of books varies from country to country.

In the United Kingdom: Please write to *Dept. JC, Penguin Books Ltd, FREEPOST, West Drayton, Middlesex UB7 OBR*

If you have any difficulty in obtaining a title, please send your order with the correct money, plus ten per cent for postage and packaging, to *PO Box No. 11, West Drayton, Middlesex UB7 OBR*

In the United States: Please write to *Penguin USA Inc., 375 Hudson Street, New York, NY 10014*

In Canada: Please write to *Penguin Books Canada Ltd, 10 Alcorn Avenue, Suite 300, Toronto, Ontario M4V 3B2*

In Australia: Please write to *Penguin Books Australia Ltd, 487 Maroondah Highway, Ringwood, Victoria 3134*

In New Zealand: Please write to *Penguin Books (NZ) Ltd, 182–190 Wairau Road, Private Bag, Takapuna, Auckland 9*

In India: Please write to *Penguin Books India Pvt Ltd, 706 Eros Apartments, 56 Nehru Place, New Delhi 110 019*

In the Netherlands: Please write to *Penguin Books Netherlands B.V., Keizersgracht 231 NL–1016 DV Amsterdam*

In Germany: Please write to *Penguin Books Deutschland GmbH, Friedrichstrasse 10–12, W–6000 Frankfurt/Main 1*

In Spain: Please write to *Penguin Books S. A., C. San Bernardo 117–6° E–28015 Madrid*

In Italy: Please write to *Penguin Italia s.r.l., Via Felice Casati 20, I–20124 Milano*

In France: Please write to *Penguin France S. A., 17 rue Lejeune, F–31000 Toulouse*

In Japan: Please write to *Penguin Books Japan, Ishikiribashi Building, 2–5–4, Suido, Tokyo 112*

In Greece: Please write to *Penguin Hellas Ltd, Dimocritou 3, GR–106 71 Athens*

In South Africa: Please write to *Longman Penguin Southern Africa (Pty) Ltd, Private Bag X08, Bertsham 2013*

READ MORE IN PENGUIN